Christopher Pressler was born in Belfast. He writes in a variety of fields and this is his second novel.

www.christopherpressler.com

For Amy, Dan, Ben & Joe,

with love

Chris

(hope you all get to read it
one day)

94 Degrees in the Shade

A Diary of Lies

CHRISTOPHER PRESSLER

94 Degrees in the Shade

A Diary of Lies

Vanguard Press

A CIP catalogue record for this title is
available from the British Library.

ISBN 9781784650780

*Vanguard Press is an imprint of
Pegasus Elliot Mackenzie Publishers Ltd.*
www.pegasuspublishers.com

First Published in 2016

**Vanguard Press
Sheraton House Castle Park
Cambridge England**

Printed & Bound in Great Britain

For Brett. For always being true. For being the act of remembering.

Acknowledgements

Special thanks to:

Professor Andrew Hodges – for Turing

Miranda Carter – for Blunt

Andrew Lownie and Dr Geoff Andrews – for Burgess

Dr Claire Donovan – for Dartington

Thanks are also due to:

Colin & Gail Stanley, John Spiers, Adrian Woodhouse, the estates of Louis MacNeice and Julian Bell, the mathematical Wikipedians, The Master and Fellows of Trinity College, Cambridge, the Provost and Fellows of King's College, Cambridge

'It is this we learn after so many failures,
The building of castles in sand, of queens in snow,
That we cannot make any corner in life or in life's
beauty,

That no river is a river which does not flow.'
'I wonder now whether anything is worth
The eyelid opening and the mind recalling.'

Louis MacNeice

'Even if we need a religion, how can we find it in the turbid rubbish of the red bookshop? It is hard for an educated, decent, intelligent son of Western Europe to find his ideals here, unless he has first suffered some strange and horrid process of conversion which has changed all his values.'

—*John Maynard Keynes*

'I do not believe in perpetual peace; not only do I not believe in it but I find it depressing and a negation of all the fundamental virtues of a man.'

—*Benito Mussolini*

'That tower founded King Nimrod that was king of that country; and he was the first king of the world.'

—*Sir John Mandeville, 1371*

Contents

Embryo
Michaelmas

One – The Horses' Echo

As I lay in the warm grass I could sense the future. I closed my eyes and listened to the summer sing. In the next field I heard horses beginning to gallop and then felt an echo in the soil coming up through my chest. I could feel their weight, hitting the ground and entering me. I felt their strength transmit into my body, pushing vigour through me, giving me speed. It went on and on.

I opened my eyes.

The corner of the field, my field, was green near the dividing hedgerow. I had come to this place many times alone to read and to listen. I was preparing to go up to Cambridge to read mathematics. It was the 1930s, I was eighteen and full of belief in my ability to make a go of life, to gallop. I did not know where the coming year would take me, but I had a certainty that I knew what I was doing. I was sure of myself.

The rest of the field was golden. Hay bales stood wide beneath the strong sun. Drying slowly and releasing a faint odour of dying earth, of nutrients pulled through the roots to seep back from the dead bundles into the soil and circle again next year. The net I had been using to catch butterflies lay beside me, empty and worn. I was dressed in white to repel some of the heat. I was glad I had found some shade. I pulled my hat down my forehead and closed my eyes.

Above me, I could hear seagulls coming to follow the ploughs in the fallow fields. Everything was being prepared. All was ready.

*

'Dr Cyprian?' said a soft voice. 'Dr Cyprian, it's time to come down for dinner. We're having lamb chops with your favourite: mint sauce.'

'I don't really feel like coming down this evening, Sister.'

'Nonsense, Daniel, honestly a man never changes. Over ninety and still stubborn. Come on, let's lift you into this chair.'

*

The first time I saw my college I believed I was seeing heaven cast in stone. Trinity rose around its court in ageless symmetry. I sensed all my predecessors beside me as I walked through the Great Gate into the court, under monarchs standing caught, in a place beyond time. This place was what I had waited for. These were the people I was destined to watch.

I don't remember being nervous when going up, as I had been brought to Cambridge many times by my parents. Father, a local clergyman, adored the strictness of college dinners and Mother: well, she was an unconventional woman for the time. She was an academic, a renowned educationalist, then in her early forties and known to many as one of the sharpest minds of her generation. She expected me to go to Trinity, of course: in fact, I think she also expected me to become an Apostle. On arriving at the Great Gate that first day I had no idea I would spend the rest of my life in this ancient place. I also could not have predicted that I would become the friend of traitors.

'Take the steps up to the second floor of the South Range building after crossing the Great Court, but walk around the grass,' said the Porter as he handed me a key. 'Your rooms will be shared this year; now let me see who you're with... Cyprian and... Burgess. We don't usually room first and second years together, but there's been a mistake, so you'll just have to make the best of it.'

Chance and fate, the shadows of the unwary, have been my constant companions.

I walked around the court, not quad of course, as in Oxford, and took the steps up to my rooms. Much of Trinity is fifteenth-century and many of its steps are worn in the middle by centuries of undergraduate life – running late to supervisions, chasing after victory on the river, silently returning from a night spent climbing over the moonlit rooftops of the city.

When I reached room four hundred I was just about to place the key in the lock when a quite short but astonishingly handsome man opened the door. Burgess left me in his wake even before I could introduce myself that first time.

'Come on... Daniel Cyprian isn't it? Far too good a day to waste in here... the Cam is calling.'

He grabbed my bags and flung them into our rooms, then pulled me down the steps and I ran, trying to keep up with him down to the river. I still wonder to this day why I followed him but I did. It all started that afternoon, lying back letting him punt. Listening.

Punting is almost completely silent. The pole is thin enough to make only a small indentation in the water and so you are moved by the smoothest of power. It is also not an exertion and so the person standing, pushing, lifting, pushing is rarely out of breath. Burgess was expert at this. He talked as though we had known each other for years, mainly about the surroundings. Each bridge elicited a short speech about the history of the Backs: the lawns of colleges which run to the river. As we passed St John's his conversation turned to that evening.

'How exciting it will be, Cyprian, to dress for dinner for the first time as an undergraduate! I remember it well myself.'

'Yes,' I said, 'although I must confess to being a little nervous.'

'What is there to be nervous about?' he laughed. 'I mean, it's perfectly normal, isn't it?'

'Yes,' I said, 'perfectly normal.'

We moved on through the water in silence for a while. At one point a swan and her family drifted past us, emitting almost imperceptible noises to one another. I held my fingers in the river and let a small wake form behind them. A willow tree brushed its subtle branches over the boat as we pushed under it, ruffling my hair. My mind wandered. I looked up at Burgess and relaxed. Stretching my legs into the length of the punt I felt calm, in a way detached from the world. Cambridge powdered us with its legacy and advantage.

'Don't you think, Cyprian, that at some point all of this must change?'

'What do you mean?' I said.

'This,' he said, sweeping his hand in the direction of the lawns, 'these buildings, those intellects, this privilege.'

'Don't you mean our privilege?' I said.

'It's not mine,' he said quickly. 'I don't want it. Come on, it's time to go and change.'

We pulled into the bank and rested the punt along the side. Then, with no sense at all that I had just had one of the most important conversations of my life, I followed Burgess back to college.

In our rooms he said, 'Drink?'

'Yes, sweet sherry please.'

'Now, Cyprian, let's get one thing straight: if we're going to get along you'll have to change to dry. No one seriously drinks sweet sherry; well, unless it's the only thing left, and as it isn't…'

'All right then,' I said, 'dry it is.'

'Good man,' he said, and turned to pass me a small glass full to its limit.

'Another?' he said, holding his empty glass. Mine hadn't even touched my lips.

The light was changing in the room. Our furniture was emblematic of a college that was known as moneyed. We moved to two opposing wing-backed chairs of soft green leather, either side of a large fireplace. They in turn stood on a faded but intricate red-threaded rug, probably originating from the East via one of the cheaper shops in London. There was no fire as the late summer had warmed the room during the day.

I brushed the leaves of an aspidistra away as it reached across the arm of my chair and watched Burgess cross his legs. His eyes flitted round the room. There was no doubting his intelligence. He moved quickly but accurately, placing his glass on the side-table in a fascinating way by dropping the glass through his fingers and catching it at the top. Given the delicacy of the glass and the importance of its contents to him I found this to be a miniature act of bravery.

He turned his face towards me. 'Who is your father?'

'Jacob Cyprian,' I said.

'The vicar?' he said.

'Yes, do you know him?' I asked, surprised.

'He's at St Edwards, isn't he? That dreadful little dark church overlooking G. David's bookshop?'

'Yes,' I said, 'but how do you know him?'

'Oh, I wouldn't say I *know* him,' said Burgess with a smile, 'just know the church. Superior pulpit.'

'Yes,' I said, 'it's rather famous.'

Burgess picked up a book. He had fine hands. His nails were immaculate, and a faint path of hair ran from his wrists to the beginning of his little finger. Strong hands though. His fingers leafed through the pages as though running down a piano keyboard, a strange quick action making it far too fast for him to be reading.

'Do you like Forster?' he said. 'This one's quite the hidden gem. Lots of messages in here.'

'What is it?' I asked.

'*A Room with a View*,' said Burgess, 'starts in Italy, and by the end everyone is…'

'I've read it,' I interrupted.

'Well, what did you think?' he said. 'What did you really *think* about it?'

I looked him in the eyes, and taking a sip of sherry said, 'I liked the bathing scene.'

He lifted an eyebrow and said, 'The bathing scene. Did you indeed? And why was that?'

'I thought it to be the most honest part of the whole book,' I said firmly.

'Really', he said. 'So you like honesty. This is going to be an interesting year.'

Burgess moved in his chair, as if to stand. On the mantelpiece a gentle ticking emanated from a fairly ugly clock. I recall at that moment feeling happy. I remember noticing that it was a quarter to seven in the evening. We had been talking for longer than I'd realised. There must have been silences.

He stood up and said, 'Well, I shall dress for dinner. Have you got a gown or would you like to borrow one of mine?'

'I've brought my own, thank you,' I said. In fact, my father had bought it for me a couple of years previously as he had begun by then to bring me to his college, King's, for the occasional dinner. He'd said to me as he handed me the robe, 'Daniel, you need to own one of these. One day you'll go up of course, but you might as well have this now.'

'Fine. Well, see you in a few minutes then.' Burgess quickly poured and downed another sherry and went into his bedroom.

I thought nothing of it then, that he left the door wide open while he changed.

*

I intend to record my memories of Cambridge, of those times before my own name is recorded beyond me. I probably do not have long, but that does not make me uncomfortable, quite the reverse, in fact. I suspect it is the only way I can see the one I admired.

The smell of mint rose like hypnosis.

I remember my father from those times. He was an endearing man, large in the waist and slightly arrogant, but very gregarious. Most people thought of him as substantial and enjoyed his company. As a vicar, he did possess a firm conviction, but not to the detriment of his ability to enjoy himself. King's suited him well, with its vaulted voices and unpredictable wines. He was a Cambridge man to his collar: quick, effervescent but with informed parochial warmth. It was no surprise to me that once he had found the city he never again intended to leave it.

Mother, of course, was completely different. She was considerably cleverer and more difficult. Her view of the world was that of a prodigious child: demanding, honest and energetic. She had become one of the first women professors of education and although the title meant nothing to her, she knew her personal achievement was noteworthy.

'Sister?' I asked.

'Yes, Daniel,' she said.

'I'm finished, thank you, can you take me back to my rooms?'

'You mean room, Daniel,' she said with a small laugh.

'Oh yes, of course,' I said, 'my apologies.'

*

I remember thinking that some music would be good before dinner. I went to Burgess's collection of records and chose something I thought wouldn't make me look a fool but also not too heavy for the early evening: Beethoven Piano Trios. It is music I have always found hard to grasp. Strong though they are, in comparison with his other works it wouldn't really matter if they had not been written. Ever since that first evening at Trinity, I have always thought of Burgess when I listen to them. It might have been better if he'd never existed either.

He had a slightly wicked attitude to nudity in that he had no reservations about it. I could see him, through the door, at his bathroom mirror. He was running his fingers through his hair. His body was well formed and white. Pure white.

I closed my eyes.

I had become an observer.

I opened my eyes.

I went to change, and closed my bedroom door.

"Fancy a quick one before we go down?' he said coyly, holding my empty sherry glass up to the light.

'Yes, why not,' I said.

I had seen him drink at least four sherries, and those were the ones I had been aware of.

'Now, this is your first college dinner, isn't it, Cyprian?'

'Well, not quite,' I said. 'My father was a Kingsman and he took me there a couple of times.'

'Well, this is not King's,' he said quickly, 'although there are worse colleges in which to take dinner.'

We stood in the room, smiling. We looked either side of one another. He knew what I had seen. We caught one another's eyes every few seconds. He never made me nervous. He made me feel part of something private to him.

*

Cambridge evenings are the constant in my life. I have grown old here but only during the day. The first sign of the sun resting is when the Cam drifts from bright green to silver and orange; a reflection of ending afternoons turning to sherry and talk and to friends.

It is the early evening when the always-striking city is at its most beautiful. I find it difficult now, but the finest way to begin an evening in this place is to walk alone for a while through the history of its streets. There are many who have done so before, and I am certain a number of those still stand unseen in doorways and gatehouses, or sit staring on the banks of the river, forever waiting for laughter. I hope Burgess is here amongst them. Russia never suited him.

It was his privacy that always attracted me to him, mainly because he tried so hard to give the impression of not having any part of himself hidden. Of course, this was a double bluff to the mirror, as much as it was to others. I could always see though, that hand-in-hand with his idealism was the loneliness only possessed by the very gregarious. Drink and conversation genuinely helped him, but I suspect that nothing ever quite sustained his personal battle against fear.

*

'Right,' he said, 'let's go across for dinner.'

We walked around the court to Hall, our short, dark blue gowns dragging in the air behind us. It was a warm evening and I must confess that I did feel nervous. I think it was almost a sense of hope, of something new opening before me. I also had a peculiar feeling that in some way I would be found out. I knew even then that I belonged in Cambridge, but perhaps the intensity of those first few hours with Burgess had unbalanced my confidence, making me question for a moment my previous belief and vocation.

Burgess sensed this too. 'Come on,' he said with his disarming smile, 'you're going to enjoy this far more than you think.'

I turned to him and stopped in the middle of the path. 'Look, Burgess, this is fine, it really is. I'm just hungry and all that sherry is taking effect.'

'Yes, of course,' he said dryly, 'it's nothing to do with the fact that you are about to meet the most remarkable men in Cambridge.' We began walking towards Hall again.

'Am I indeed?' I said.

'Oh yes, and I think they are going to be rather interested in you too,' he said.

'Isn't it a little presumptuous to assume I will be interested in them?' I asked, a slightly defensive tone in my voice.

'Now, now,' said Burgess, 'there's no need to take that attitude. Some encounters are inevitable and you meeting me is only the start. Come on, let's go in,' he said, and ushered me through the great wooden door into the candlelight.

Within the hall was the boisterous sound of a college preparing for dinner, which was to offer so much resonance throughout my life. One might almost refer to that sound as home.

Two long tables ran in parallel down the length of the room and at its end, on a slightly raised area, High Table perched horizontal to the others. The smell was of wood, linen, wine, balm, cigarettes, meat, fire smoke and of lilies standing in vases every four feet along the tables. White at the undergraduate seats. Orange for the Fellows.

Candles were held hot and still in enclosed cases, their light resting on silver cutlery and crystal. Opened red wine bottles had been placed in the centre of the tables. A fire crackled behind its huge grate. I stood and took this in. Trinity. Still and ordered, even in the noise.

I closed my eyes.

Inside my head the smells intensified, and I was able to distinguish clearly between them, carefully, as if searching for only one. I could hear the fire too, and the indigenous, perfectly toned accents of most of my peers. A Scottish discord? I listened. The sounds of the kitchen occasionally reached above the hall. Metal on metal. A shout of instruction. Water pouring.

I opened my eyes.

'This is Cyprian,' said Burgess, and a tall man brought his hand forward to meet mine. 'Extraordinary thing, isn't he?' Burgess said.

'Hello,' his friend said, 'I'm Maclean. Why were your eyes closed?'

I thought for a second and then said, 'It helps me to see, well, to concentrate.'

'I told you they'd find you interesting, didn't I,' Burgess said. 'What do you think Maclean?'

'He's quite something, isn't he?' Maclean said, pulling slightly away from me to look me up and down.

'Maclean here is joining us for dinner tonight, although he's at a tired little college called Trinity Hall,' said Burgess, with a wink.

'Tired it may be,' said Maclean, 'but we have a finer chapel.'

'You most certainly do not, and you know it,' said Burgess, and the two friends wandered away from me, into the hall, still arguing.

*

I know now, of course, that life has a habit of launching you into situations you would not have chosen personally. That evening I looked around the room, with its Tudor elegance, its affectation and did not realise that this was one of those situations. If I had known, if I had been sharper, I would have done the unthinkable: gone down and restarted my studies the following year at Oxford.

Or would I? I do not live now – indeed, I have never lived – with regret. I have always lived in the present. It is a failing perhaps in the eyes of some but for me it is simply a way of seeing.

*

'Come on, Cyprian,' called Burgess from across the room, 'I've got a seat here for you.'

I edged my way along the lines of undergraduates, talking and clinking wine glasses, and sat next to him. He put his hand firmly on my knee and said, 'Welcome to Trinity, Cyprian, here's to us,' and raised a glass filled to the brim with wine. We toasted and waited for grace by the senior fellow. It came as it has always come:

Benedic, Domine, nos et dona tua,
quae de largitate tua sumus sumpturi;
et concede, ut illis salubriter nutriti,
tibi debitum obsequium praestare valeamus,
per Christum Dominum nostrum.

Food has continuously been an interest of mine. I have no personal skill in the kitchen, nor indeed have I ever had the opportunity to develop it, as for most of my life I have been served at college. That evening's meal was good. I remember it because of the company perhaps? But both discussion and dishes define good meals.

The starter came on a long, white gilt-edged plate with the Trinity Arms in full colour on the rim of the porcelain. The chevron between three barbed roses, under a lion passant gardant, between two closed books. The shield of my life. As with the roses, the salmon was in triplicate: one white wine confit with a coarse texture, one hot curl of fish in bread and finally a mousse-filled strip of salmon rolled onto a small salad of watercress and chive mayonnaise with pink peppercorns. Vinegars had been added to each portion and we ate, for only a moment, in silence before Burgess could not contain himself any longer.

'Cyprian, do you know whom that is up on the end of High Table?' he asked me, with a nudge of his arm. I looked at the man he was referring to. 'He came up last year,' said Burgess, 'won a doctoral scholarship for a book he'd already written.'

The man was obviously not tall, as his colleague sitting next to him rose past his frame even seated. His jacket was a very thick lightly patterned tweed, over a white shirt unbuttoned and at a strange angle. He had a poor cut to his hair, which flayed above his head like a darkened halo, and his eyes, black and wide, stared into the room, across all our heads and into what seemed to be an eternal distance.

I thought I recognised his face, but unsure, I said to Burgess, 'I'm not certain but he looks familiar. Do you see how he seems to be looking at the eternal?'

'The eternal?' said Maclean. 'A little early for profundity, isn't it?'

'How interesting,' Burgess said, 'and observant in your own way. Well, do you know him?'

I had to admit that I didn't and so said, 'No, should I?'

'You should,' he said, 'that's Wittgenstein.'

The main course was a rabbit risotto. 'This college's food is, I must say, more adventurous than our poor fare at Trinity Hall,' said Maclean.

'Well, I did tell you it was a tired little place,' said Burgess. 'Anyway, our chef has, shall we say, travelled a great deal.'

'Do you know him?' I asked, slightly surprised that Burgess would have ever met the college staff, never mind actually spoken to them.

'Oh, he knows all the staff, if they're attractive anyway, don't you,' said Maclean.

'How indiscreet,' said Burgess. 'I've only spoken to him once.'

'Once is enough for you,' said Maclean with a grin.

I looked down at my rabbit. It had clearly been roasted, as small black crispy pieces were mixed into the rice with longer, more succulent parts. After roasting, the meat had been stripped from its bones and pinched into the *al dente* blend. A few peas had been added for colour, although they also had a fairly strong taste. The rice had been cooked in cider as well as stock. On the whole, it was a passable idea, but risotto was not something I'd seen before nor a dish I would choose again. Burgess claimed, with an outlandish smile, that it at least, as he put it, proved the chef had '*been* to Italy.'

'When did Wittgenstein come to Cambridge?' I asked Burgess.

'Oh, he was here a few years ago apparently, but after teaching in some dismal little primary school in Austria, Ramsey convinced him to come back last year.'

'Teaching?' I said. 'I thought he was supposed to be a genius.'

'Oh he is, well, old Bertrand Russell thinks so anyway, that's why they gave him a doctorate and a Fellowship without anything more than a discussion over a glass of port.'

'I must say,' said Burgess, uncharacteristically slowly, 'I'll miss him; Ramsey, that is.'

'Has he left Cambridge?' I asked.

'No, he never will now. God help him, he's dead and buried at St Giles.'

'What from?' I said.

'Well, he had problems with the liver, but for someone who learnt German in one week and lies dead at twenty-six, I have my own theory.'

'As ever,' said Maclean.

'Yes, well,' Burgess said sharply, 'he lived life too fast. Lesson for us all there, in my not so humble opinion.'

We all seemed to need to dwell on this, and paused while the pudding was placed in front of us. Trinity meals are of a good quality but they don't last long. Well, not the food at any rate. This was another trio. In fact I've had so many dishes at college echoing our naming that I've forgotten most of them. Not this one though. Not that night.

A blackberry parfait rested on a rich coulis of the same fruit with one blackberry beside mint leaves as a garnish. This was adjacent to an apple sorbet on an impressively thin brandy snap biscuit, and then finally a small blackberry and apple pie on crème anglaise.

'This is the finest course yet,' exclaimed Burgess, 'just right for first night of term, although perhaps a little autumnal, don't you think?'

'Signs of things to come,' said Maclean, with a forced ominous tone. 'What do you make of your first Trinity meal, Cyprian?' he said.

'I think it will be very memorable,' I said.

'Oh?' said Burgess. 'You've changed your tune. What is it about tonight then, meeting us?'

'Frankly,' I smiled, 'yes, but the parfait was wonderful too.' Burgess and Maclean laughed as the servers came to remove our plates.

We stood as High Table rose to leave and listened to the brief closing grace.

Benedicto benedicatur.

'Right, that's it for another night,' said Burgess, 'let's go and get drunk.'

'A class act, isn't he?' Maclean whispered in my ear.

'Oh, I don't mind,' I said, 'I like him.'

'I bet you do,' he said, 'everyone does, but be careful.'

We sauntered out into the twilight. The Great Court stretched away from the steps of Hall in all directions. The largest court in Cambridge is always at its best during two times of the day. At the height of Easter term, the mid-afternoon sunshine and blue sky convey an almost Italian backdrop to the whitened gold buildings. And now, in the late evening, it shimmered from lights in the windows around its circumference and the still air allowed the central fountain to fill the square with the sound of water.

The three of us walked to our rooms. Maclean had been allowed guest status by the porters that night, 'to aid discussion', as Burgess had told them.

'Well, that was as good as you said it would be,' I said to him.

'Not bad for a college effort, is it?' said Burgess. 'Almost as though they cared about us,' he joked.

'Interesting people,' I said, 'more of a mixture than I'd expected actually, I even heard a Scot!'

'Oh, yes,' Burgess said, 'that's Cairncross. Funny sort of chap, keeps himself to himself.'

'Rather coarse accent,' I commented.

'Yes, not a good family, I hear, although he's been at the Sorbonne apparently,' said Burgess. 'Very good with French, as you might imagine. You're about to meet one of his tutors. Well, his Side actually.'

'His Side?' I asked.

'Haven't they told you yet?' said Burgess. 'Your Side is your personal tutor and confidant, depending on which straw you draw,' he said with almost a wink. 'And Cairncross' Side is the shortest straw of them all.'

*

I'd eaten what I can only describe as puréed slop. A faint taste of carrots and lamb had been discernable on the plate, although the great achievement of the home's cook had been to make them look almost exactly the same. Something green had slid about beside this and the only saving grace was the mint sauce. I have always adored it.

'Did you enjoy your lamb?' she said, pushing me up the corridor.

'Er, what I could see of it, yes.'

'Oh, you forgot your glasses again, Daniel?'

I decided to be polite; after all, she wasn't responsible for what might be said to have happened in the kitchen. 'Yes, I'm always leaving them in my room, aren't I?'

'Well, let's get you back there then, dear,' she said. I have often wondered why, good people though most of them are,

35

nursing staff in homes such as these feel the need to patronise us, the elderly. Most of my fellow, shall we call them 'inmates', do not notice, of course, but I do. It feels like a kind of control mechanism for the most part, but secretly I have another theory. If you are able to disarm someone so obviously close to death and treat them as a child, then perhaps your own sense of mortality is pushed back into the shadows.

Elderly people, and I am certainly such a person now, have the capacity to make those who are younger see their own futures. My riddled face, my slow movements, my constant mothed smell, my watered eyes are the destiny of all who push me around in wheelchairs. It must be tempting, or just easier, to consider us to be at a distance. That way, death too is kept at bay.

'There you are, Daniel,' she said as she settled me in front of my desk. 'What are you writing, dear?' she asked, with what I must admit was a kind tone to her voice.

'Oh, just a few thoughts about when I was younger in Cambridge,' I said.

'That's nice,' said the nurse. 'Memories then?'

'Yes,' I said, 'memories.'

She left the room and I leant across the desk to turn on my brass lamp: one of the few items they would let me bring here from college after my heart attack. I have written many books and articles under this lamp. In a sense, it has been a guiding light, if that doesn't sound too trite. As a scholar, much of one's life is spent in solitary confinement of sorts, punctuated by student questions and the odd dinner. As I have never married, although despite inclinations otherwise I have often thought about what it would have been like to be with someone, this lamp has been my companion.

College was busy when it suited me, and quiet when I required it. Here it is always quiet, apart from the occasional shout from some poor bastard who is losing his mind. It is the fear of this that makes me write. I must confess what I observed when I first arrived in Cambridge, before the lights go out.

The Master at Trinity was so good in allowing me to keep rooms long into my retirement. Common enough in Cambridge, I suppose, but still, generous. I write now because I do not want to forget. My books on mathematics, those few contributions to the world of proof, are in the past.

The aspect of my time at Cambridge that fascinates me now, because it is so long ago, is also about proof in a way, or perhaps evidences, testimony and confirmation in my own mind of what happened. In retelling my observations at Cambridge in that twilight before apocalypse, I wonder how much is memory and how much is remembrance. The difference between the two seems to me that the former must be true, and the latter not necessarily so. To remember is not to recall facts; it is to picture those you loved in whatever way best suits them.

They used to say that the lamps were going out all over Europe regarding the Great War. When I was a student at Trinity, we fervently believed that the same unlit brutality was again inevitable. We were right, of course, but also desperately wrong.

*

We climbed the steps up to our rooms and met a tall, rather gaunt and slightly older man than ourselves. 'This is Anthony Blunt,' said Burgess, running up to him and then embracing Blunt for what seemed to me to be a long time.

'Hello,' I said, 'Cyprian,' and shook Blunt's hand. That was the first time and I noticed his long fingers seemed to match his face. He turned to greet me but did not smile as such; rather, he widened his lips slightly and kept his mouth closed.

Burgess said, 'Unlock the door, Cyprian, there's a good chap.'

I took the key from my pocket and held it for a second in my hand. I had a strange sense of things moving more slowly than was usual. Perhaps it was the wine. I pushed the key into the lock and turned it for the door to swing open.

Our sherry glasses were still on the table and Maclean said, 'Oh yes, starting early were we?'

Burgess looked at him and said, 'Of course, darling.'

I had not before heard one man use this term to another. It stayed with me for the rest of the evening. I had been told of such things by my father, but only by implication and only from the pulpit. I had not yet asked myself any difficult questions. It was oddly liberating, though, to be alone with these men, who seemed to be close but not unwelcoming. Only Blunt, on our first meeting was merely cordial. Burgess, as ever was the direct opposite.

'Pour us some drinks, Cyprian,' said Burgess.

'Good god, Burgess,' said Maclean, 'we're not in school now you know, do it yourself.'

'I don't mind in the least,' I said, and walked over to the drinks cabinet. There was some brandy so I got out four glasses and poured.

'Thank you,' said Blunt, as I passed him a drink. 'How was dinner?' There was a pause in the conversation as I'd turned round and didn't realise that Blunt was addressing me. 'How was dinner, Cyprian?'

'Oh, sorry,' I said. 'Em, it was very good,' I said quickly, 'salmon, rabbit and blackberries.'

'Another Trinity trio,' said Blunt.

'Not together, you fool,' said Burgess, 'although there were trios involved, you might say.'

'You never miss an opportunity, do you, Burgess?' said Maclean.

'I'm glad,' said Blunt, 'couldn't get there myself, had to go out this evening.'

'Where to?' said Burgess. 'We missed you.'

'Never you mind,' said Blunt, 'and anyway, I wouldn't have been sitting with you in the first place.'

'Are you older than us? I mean, are you a tutor?' I asked.

'How sweet of you not to notice,' said Blunt, 'but unfortunately, yes to both. I teach French; what are you reading?'

'Mathematics,' I said.

'Ah, the attempt to *prove* things,' said Blunt.

'Or disprove them, surely,' said Maclean.

'Well, usually it is in the positive,' I said. 'Not much purpose in showing that something cannot be true; more exciting to discover truth.'

'What a remarkable statement,' exclaimed Burgess.

'He'll go far, won't he?' said Blunt.

Maclean got up to put some music on the record player. 'What do we want to listen to?' he said.

'Jazz,' said Burgess.

'Absolutely not,' said Blunt. 'Put some Mozart on, there's a *Zauberflöte* hidden away in there somewhere.'

'How do you know that?' I asked.

'Burgess has eclectic tastes, don't you?' he said wryly.

'But it's mine. I only brought it this afternoon,' I said, unable to hide a certain nervousness in my voice. I mean, how could he have known.

'Oh, really, sorry, my mistake, old man. Can we play it anyway?' Blunt said. 'So much more to it than his blessed jazz. Anyway, Cyprian, do you believe in honesty as fervently as you say you do in truth?'

I felt tired. I had not prepared for an evening like this, so I just said, 'Are they not the same thing?'

'God no,' said Blunt. 'Truths can exist quite happily without us; for example, it is a truth that France would never turn to fascism, whilst honesty is dependent on us.'

'Meaning?' I said.

'Meaning that honesty can only truly, if you'll forgive the expression, exist if we either bring it into being or, as is sadly so often the case, disguise it.'

'He means lying,' said Burgess.

'Yes, I follow that,' I said, perhaps too sharply.

'Oh dear, I think we may have hit a raw nerve,' Blunt said.

'Actually, you have,' I said. 'Sovereign truth is a little close to my father's idea of God.'

'Ah well, God has nothing to do with it,' he said. 'I'm talking about practicalities, truths which can actually influence events.'

'And God cannot?' I said.

'Certainly not! He is allowing Mussolini to run riot, and I've not even begun on Germany,' said Blunt.

'What he means, dear boy,' said Burgess, 'is that there are forces at work in Europe, and elsewhere, that have no concern for your father's God; in fact, they place man at the summit of our experience.' Burgess took a sip from his brandy and dropped his glass through his fingers onto the table.

'Well then, you are right about France, Blunt,' I said.

'Oh, why?' he asked.

'The French would never idolise man; it would always be wine,' I joked.

'Precisely,' said Blunt, 'that's why, civilised though they are, we cannot expect rescue from our fine neighbours.'

'Rescue from what?' I said.

'Haven't you heard a word I said?' Blunt exclaimed.

'Oh leave him be,' said Maclean.

'It's all right,' I said, 'just a bit tired, that's all; you mean Mussolini?'

'Yes, and Hitler,' said Blunt. 'His Nationalsozialistische Deutsche Arbeiterpartei is a rising force in the Weimar Republic.'

'And,' said Burgess, 'when Hitler testified last year in the trial of two officers accused of being Nazis, he persuaded the judges that the Nazis were a friend of Germany.'

'That's not true,' I said.

'Isn't it?' said Blunt. 'Or is it a truth disguised by dishonesty?'

'But a friend?' I said, and moved uncomfortably in my chair.

'Depends on who runs the place, doesn't it?' said Burgess. 'I mean, if Hitler *was* Germany, as he clearly wants to be, then the Nazis would be its friends, wouldn't they?'

'He has to become Chancellor first though,' I said.

'He will,' said Blunt, 'and then who will stop him?'

'I don't know,' I said.

'I do,' said Blunt.

I rose from my chair and walked to the undrawn curtains. Burgess, Blunt and Maclean continued talking behind me, and the high pitches of Mozart's most enigmatic opera punctured their low voices.

I remember that evening as clear as if it were yesterday. It was the first of many discussions late into the night over brandy, with the splendid Great Court outside our mullioned windows. I have looked from those ancient openings all my life, but perhaps no evening was so defining as that one.

I stood at our window in the core of Cambridge, in the heart of England and at the centre of our Imperial world. I stood and thought of what our fathers had fought for in the Great War. A war we had missed. I could hear the hooves of horses thudding in the mud of the Somme. I thought of one man's truth and of another's honesty. I heard the horses galloping, coming closer. I felt their weight.

I closed my eyes.

*

Two – Kissing Hitler

Michaelmas marks the turning of the world towards autumn. It is the most highly coloured term in Cambridge, as greens become orange and brown. Michaelmas marks the defeat of Satan by the Archangel Michael and his ensuing fall into a blackberry bush. The fruit should not be eaten after early October because of the devil's curse as he landed. My father said that if God could create humanity then why not other intelligent beings? Angels and archangels have life as we do.

The autumn term also sees the last of punting. The water is colder and the air crisps from its surface. That year's final push up the Cam saw the four of us joined by one other in the largest punt we could find and make our way slowly to Grantchester.

'Righto, who's punting?' said Burgess.

'You, obviously,' said Blunt.

'You must be joking,' Burgess said. 'Impossible to get any decent drinking done that way.'

'It's all right, I'll do it,' I said, not really wishing to just lie there for the couple of hours it would take to get to the Orchard.

'Good man,' said Maclean, 'always a willing volunteer.'

'Yes,' I said, although I preferred then anyway, as now to watch from a distance rather than be brought into the middle of a conversation, especially when Blunt was around.

'What are we waiting for?' said Blunt.

'Philby,' said Burgess. 'Not right to go without him on the last punt of the year.'

The man I was soon to know, Philby, was running towards us, holding a straw boater on his head with one hand and swinging a large hamper in the other. He shouted, 'Wait for me, you bastards!' and came down to the boat, out of breath but still with an enormous physical presence. Dressed in a blue suit lined in white satin, and wearing very fashionable shoes, he could have been mistaken for someone posing for the British Railways posters, which hang in King's Cross enticing Londoners to come to Cambridge for the day. Perfect, immaculate, he appeared almost engineered to appear British.

'You're late,' said Blunt. 'We said eleven o'clock.' As he finished this sentence the clock on the Trinity Great Gate began to strike eleven. 'Ah,' said Blunt.

'Don't underestimate me,' said Philby.

'Have I ever?' Blunt said.

'Once, and you know it,' smiled Philby.

'Right, that's enough arguing,' said Burgess. 'If we don't get going, we'll be viewing Grantchester in the dark, and exciting though that may be, it'll make picnicking rather difficult.'

'Quite right,' Maclean said. 'Push off, Cyprian.'

The four men made themselves as comfortable as it is possible to do so in a punt and I pushed away from Trinity's bank. I'd been practising all term on the river and had quite got the hang of handling the notoriously difficult craft. We floated into the middle of the Cam and with a strong push on one side I straightened the boat up and we were away.

Perhaps the single most inspiring view of Cambridge is there, from the Backs. The clock tower of St John's in the far distance. The golden symmetry of the Wren Library at Trinity. The graceful frontage of Clare and then the glory and height of King's Chapel. From the river, because movement is so low in the water, all of the university appeared to tower over us. I loved it then and I love it now. My ashes, floating on this part of the river, will ensure the Chapel delivers on its promises.

'Don't you just hate all this,' said Burgess.

'That's a very aggressive word,' said Blunt. 'I think hate is too strong.'

'I do,' Burgess said, 'it seems so complacent,' and he took a long drink from a bottle of white wine. I noticed it was French.

'I think you may be complacent, Burgess,' said Philby.

'Oh yes, I'm complacent, complicit, complicated... anything you want me to be,' Burgess said.

'You're many things, but you're not complacent,' said Blunt.

'Thank you,' Burgess said sternly.

'Lazy yes, complacent no,' said Blunt with a wry smile.

'I'll take that as a compliment,' said Burgess.

I listened. I heard every word. I still did not comprehend what the four of them were saying. I wondered why, when these four seemed so close, that they were including me. They were all older than I was then, by some way in Blunt's case. Despite this, I felt included in some way. This meant a great deal to me in my first term at Cambridge, as it would to any young student.

They were judgemental people, Burgess, Maclean, Blunt and Philby. They laughed at others readily and seemed dismissive of the opportunity life had so obviously given to us all. Cambridge is an intellectual luxury. It is opulent to be in a place of both learning and beauty. It has protected the persons and interests of a class in England for hundreds of years. Royal patronage for generations has provided it with status and with wealth. Even Cromwell left it relatively untouched. His own college, Sidney Sussex, holds his beaten, tarred head in its safe. Silver melted elsewhere was largely protected here as the university again ensured that in whatever battle raged across or beyond the nation, it was to be found, at the end, on the winning side.

And there we were, that fine chilled morning before the collapsing world, aimlessly punting up river to a place of extraordinary prettiness. Grantchester had been the stage not long before, where famous writers drank tea under the shade of its bounteous orchard. We drifted upwards towards the village, propelled occasionally by my pole in the browning water as early rains pushed silt from the surrounding meadows.

The men, and I'll call them friends, although that I suppose is the beginning of a confessional tone, chatted and ribbed. Infrequently they would bring me into the conversation, asking perhaps my opinion from what Blunt always called, with a slightly haughty quality in his voice, 'a mathematical perspective'.

They were especially interested in what I thought of Wittgenstein. As I recall now, his name was mentioned regularly in those early discussions. His fame would allow for this, of course, but it was as often in relation to his upbringing as it was to his ideas. Burgess seemed most engaged with his personal life.

'He has a boyfriend, you know,' he said.

'Oh, who doesn't?' said Blunt.

'Me, for one,' said Philby.

'There's always time, darling,' said Burgess.

'Oh, bugger off,' shouted Philby.

'Is that a pass?' Burgess quipped.

'Yes, of course,' said Philby, 'there's nothing I'd like to do more than…'

'Leave him alone,' Blunt said. 'Anyway, he's taken.'

'He should be,' said Philby, 'out and shot.'

Philby smiled at this last retort of his, but for a brief second the others looked genuinely shocked. In the water, I noticed hundreds of early fallen leaves drifting past and under the boat. The sun had risen to its low autumn position and was flooding through a willow tree, dripping into a bend in the river ahead. A crow launched itself with a loud cry from the branch of a tall chestnut tree in the middle of the passing field and flew towards, then directly over us.

Perhaps the rare occurrence of none of them talking, even for such a short time, has lodged that memory with me? Whatever it was, I felt something I now recognise only too quickly. The simple act of violence suggested by Philby as a joke provoked in the other three an immediate and undisguised fear. Alarm can be etched on any face. It does not matter how skilled the deceiver. It may only be fleeting, perhaps even go unnoticed, but it will be there. Ultimately, everyone has an honest face when afraid.

'So, regardless of Philby's unfortunate gloom,' said Burgess, 'shall we enjoy ourselves?'

'I don't feel gloomy,' said Philby, 'I was only teasing.'

'Well, tease someone else,' said Burgess. 'I don't intend to be shot for anything.'

'Pass me a drink,' I said, 'thirsty work this punting.'

'Shall I take over?' asked Maclean. 'I'm pretty handy at this.'

'All right,' I said. 'I've got us halfway there anyway at least.'

'You've done us all proud,' said Blunt. 'Go on, Maclean, give the boy a rest.'

Maclean climbed down the boat and stepped onto the till, where I was standing. I handed him the pole and made my way to the ruffled rug where he'd been sitting. Although the temperature was cool, the river was calm and a light breeze came through the trees onto the water. I let my hand run in the water where I'd been holding the pole and the slight redness that the wood had given the skin by friction began to subside.

Next to me, Philby was rummaging in his hamper for another bottle of wine as Burgess had more or less commandeered the first one.

'I hope we don't run out,' I said.

'It'll be fine,' said Philby. 'There's plenty more in the pubs at Grantchester anyway.'

'So,' said Blunt, 'what do you make of Michaelmas term so far, Cyprian?'

'I'm enjoying myself,' I said, 'you know, working hard, putting up with Burgess.'

'Same thing, aren't they?' said Burgess with a smile.

'Let's say, some of your habits take a bit of getting used to,' I said.

'Such as?' he said with a grin. It was nearly impossible to actually annoy Burgess. Either he was fairly carefree or the always-at-hand drink would make him affable.

'Well, for a start, there's your singing,' I said.

'That's a very fair point,' Blunt said. 'The singing is not good, but in my opinion neither is the musical preference.'

'Very unfair,' said Burgess, 'just because I don't weep at the sound of some over-strung soprano…'

'Precisely,' said Blunt, 'you have no taste.'

'Ha,' said Burgess, 'ask Cyprian what he thinks, *he* likes jazz.'

'He has no choice,' said Philby, 'he lives with it.'

'To be honest, I like variety, a bit of both,' I said.

'You mean you like everything?' said Blunt.

'Yes,' I said.

'Which is another way of saying you love nothing,' he said.

'Not exactly,' I responded, sensing that this was going to result in yet another grilling by Blunt.

'So, what would you say is the precise difference between liking everything and loving nothing?' he asked, leaning forward in that accusatorial manner I had already grown to dislike since meeting him.

'I suppose…' I started to say.

'You suppose?' said Blunt, 'Rather an imprecise premise already, wouldn't you say?'

'I propose,' I said sharply, 'that the difference may be defined if the person who likes everything is *passionate* about nothing, but if a person *loves* something inanimate, such as a piece of music or an ideology, then it might follow that the person is *too* passionate.'

'Too passionate?' said Blunt.

'Yes,' I said. 'I mean, passion is surely driven by one's feelings towards another human being.'

'But what if, for example,' said Blunt, 'my passion for Mozart originates in the memory of sharing an experience, an opera, with someone?'

'Well, that must be someone other than me,' said Burgess.

'Or,' Blunt continued, 'a passion for an ideology is not for the concept itself, but rather for its effect on real people?'

'I hadn't thought about it like that,' I admitted.

'No, you hadn't thought at all,' he said. 'Well, let's be kind: you have not yet thought enough.'

'I didn't realise we were going up river for a supervision,' said Philby.

'Oh,' Blunt said, 'what do you think you're at Cambridge to do? Punt?'

'To be frank,' said Philby in his charming way, 'yes.'

The cross-examination left me a little sore and I turned away from them for a while. The boat moved slowly through the water and gave time for me to make some of my own early judgements on the group of men who were to be my companions at university.

Philby, although I had not known him for more than a day, seemed very engaging. Handsome and slick, he moved his body effortlessly, though with great consideration for his appearance. I knew by then that he liked women and I was sure the feeling, should he ever choose to put himself in their way, would be mutual. Despite these positive characteristics, I saw one I did not like. He often shifted from confidence to arrogance and turned this on the university. I do not believe he thought for a minute that he was fortunate to be at Cambridge. Rather that it drove him, through a combination of narcissism and egomania, to a point where he convinced himself that he could alter everything and everyone around him.

Maclean was difficult to read. I knew him to be clever, but because he was so much less showy than the others it perhaps put him in a dim academic light. But those with dimmer lights are often most skilful at hiding them under bushels. He was not an attractive man. His face was a little long for my liking and his hair not well kept. Maclean's family, I think, were rather demanding of him, especially his father, the government minister. He had the air of someone silently rebelling.

Blunt intrigued me just as he annoyed me. He talked a lot, and not just when interrogating someone. I think he perversely enjoyed the fact that he was slightly older than the rest of us. Already a tutor and Side at the college he literally and metaphorically sat above us at dinner but seemed happy to mix with us socially, although always on his terms. He had the capacity to hold opposite opinions during debate with equal strength, which is why, as I lay in the boat that late morning, I found it a little rich that he was picking up any idea of hypocrisy in my own statements. I believed him capable of considerable self-delusion, but also grandeur of the most irritating kind. He had been told when young, I was certain of it, that the world owed him a living. This assumption, which was almost impossible to catch him actually holding, made it very hard to win an argument. He probably would not have been listening in any case.

Burgess, my room companion and root in Cambridge, was of a different class to the others in my eyes then. Equally deft in social settings as Philby, he seemed more honest, perhaps because the reckless cannot be dishonest. This was not all on account of his drinking. He had an edge to his voice that sounded at once like enjoyment and desperation. In an immense, flamboyant but ultimately generous way he appeared to be pushing himself through Cambridge by refining his natural brilliance and a forced need for acceptance at the same time. The result was a person whose company one enjoyed but which left one exhausted. Living with him that first year put me in the firing line.

*

'Would you like tea this afternoon, Dr Cyprian?' said an unfamiliar voice. I turned from my desk and saw a new young member of staff standing at my doorway in front of his trolley.

'I think I will,' I said. 'I don't usually, but you're new, aren't you?'

'Yes,' he said, 'I've started working here to put myself through college.'

'Oh, good for you, good for you,' I said. 'Which are you at?'

'Trinity,' he said, and smiled as he poured the tea.

'What's your name?' I asked.

'Michael,' he said, and quietly placed a cup of tea on my desk before leaving the room.

Having changed punts rather fussily under the Silver Street bridge to move from the middle to the upper river, Granchester came into view around a bend in the river. The fenland reaches Cambridge on this side like a swaying coast of reeds. Only two miles from Trinity are distances of water hidden by the plants. From within their forest I could hear warblers and the remarkable sound of a bittern, calling almost like a lost ship in its inland sea.

'I'm hungry,' said Burgess. 'I always forget how long it takes to get here. We should have bicycled.'

'Are you quite mad?' said Blunt. 'This is far more civilised.'

'Civilised yes, quick no,' said Burgess.

'You need instant gratification, don't you, Burgess,' said Blunt.

'What I need is lunch,' said Burgess.

'Well, we're nearly there now,' I said.

'Oh, the kraken awakes,' said Philby. 'You've been in a world of your own.'

'Sorry,' I said, 'just drifted off, you know, the water and that.'

'I shouldn't have been quite so hard on you,' said Blunt.

'Don't worry,' I said. 'What's the point of being at Cambridge if I can't be picked up on every point of order.'

'Oh, let it go, Cyprian,' said Burgess, 'he's just being…'

'What exactly?' said Blunt, 'what am I *being*, as you put it?'

'There you go again,' Burgess said. 'Come on, we're there now, and this looks like a reasonable spot.'

Maclean manoeuvred the boat towards the bank and brought us to a halt on a small landing place. 'We'll not even have to get our feet wet,' said Burgess.

I got out first and Philby followed me, then the others. 'Hand me the hamper,' Philby said to Burgess. He dragged it off the boat and pushed it towards Philby. 'Careful old man,' Philby said, 'that's my mother's and she doesn't even know I pinched it over the summer.'

'At least I've brought another one,' said Maclean. 'Managed to sneak a few things from the college kitchens this morning.'

'Trinity Hall food?' said Burgess. 'We are slumming it today.'

'At least I did bring something,' said Maclean.

'I brought wine,' said Burgess, 'and there's plenty more where that came from.'

We climbed up the bank and found a spot under a creaking tree to lay down the rugs. It was a day to keep jackets on, but otherwise, now the morning had passed into early afternoon, the weather was surprisingly good. Burgess lay down and put his hands behind his head, crossed his feet and pulled his hat over his face. 'Shall I be Mother?' said Blunt.

'When are you anything else?' mumbled Burgess from beneath the hat.

'Well then,' said Blunt, 'let's see what we've got.'

Blunt began to unpack the two hampers and carefully laid out the contents on the rug. It was an odd selection of items but would probably do until we found a pub later. Overhead, I thought I saw the same crow from earlier in the journey circling us, his black shape occasionally crossing the sun. The reed beds were so plentiful that even from a short distance they could be heard as the light wind ran through the drying stems.

'*Je plie, et ne romps pas,*' announced Blunt.

'I beg your pardon,' said Burgess.

'Jean de la Fontaine,' said Blunt, '*The Oak and the Reed.* God, didn't you learn anything at school?'

'You know I didn't,' smiled Burgess.

'Didn't Midas have something to do with reeds?' asked Philby.

For once, I answered before Blunt. 'Yes, when Apollo turned Midas' ears to those of a donkey, Midas swore his barber to secrecy.'

'But he couldn't keep the secret?' said Maclean.

'No,' I said, 'the barber ran to a meadow, dug a hole and told the secret into it. From that moment the reeds that grew there could be heard whispering the secret in the wind.'

'As famously painted by Palma il Giovane in *Apollo and Marsyas,*' said Blunt, with the usual knowing look.

'How ridiculous,' said Burgess.

'Really?' Blunt said. 'Don't you think these reeds hold secrets?'

'All reeds hold secrets,' I said.

'Good man,' said Blunt. 'I hope you can.'

'So, what's "God" like then, Cyprian?' said Philby.

'Ask my father,' I said.

'No, not the imagined version, the real one,' he said. 'Wittgenstein.'

'I've not had a supervision with him yet,' I said, 'only a couple of lectures.'

'Yes, well?' he went on.

'All right then, the first impression I received of him was confusing. He walked up to the lectern, held up a photograph and kissed it. Then he turned the picture to face us.'

'Remarkable,' said Blunt. 'Who was in the picture?'

'It was difficult to make out, very faded. It was a man with a small moustache. He said the picture meant a great deal to him, but in itself meant nothing,' I said.

'And?' said Philby.

'Well, someone called out to ask him who it was,' I said. 'Wittgenstein stared straight at the other student and asked him to guess, but to hold the name in his mind.'

'Then?' said Burgess.

'Then he asked the student to shout out the name he had in his head,' I said, 'but the student hesitated and said that he didn't want to. After a little encouragement he shouted "Hitler" loudly into the room.'

'And was it?' said Blunt.

'Wittgenstein looked pleased,' I said, 'and then explained that, although the picture looked like Hitler, indeed might even be of Hitler, it could not actually be Hitler because he would not have kissed it.'

'So who did Wittgenstein say it was?' said Burgess.

'He said that in his mind he was interpreting the picture to be of Charlie Chaplin, who he admired, and then he kissed it again,' I said.

Philby burst out laughing and asked, 'What does that prove?'

'I'm not sure what it proves exactly,' I said, 'but I think he was trying to say that because the picture was indistinct then he was interpreting it, and went on to embarrass the student even further by teasing him for his reading of it.'

'I'm not sure I follow,' said Burgess.

'You're many things, Burgess,' I said, 'but logical is not one of them. He was showing that meaning couldn't exist of itself, in that the picture has no meaning, but that it lies in interpretation, in language. Pictures only have meaning as part of our language game.'

'You mean culture, of course,' said Blunt.

'Yes,' I said, 'culture is a game, a fiction created by mass agreement.'

'Truth can only come into being if everyone accepts the same statement,' said Blunt.

'And therein lies the danger of accepted truth. You cannot hide or destroy an idea as you might a photograph,' I said.

'So what if you want to fight an idea?' said Philby.

'You have to play the game,' said Blunt. 'If we all say that, for instance, the sky is blue…'

'It barely is today,' said Burgess.

'Anyway, let's say it is blue,' continued Blunt, 'then it is only blue because we all agree as to what *blue* is.'

'Exactly,' I said. 'Meaning is only meaningful if we all agree on a form of words.'

'But what if I disagree?' said Burgess, and he stood up, pointing at the sky. 'The sky is purple.'

'But it isn't,' said Maclean.

'In my interpretation, in my own little world it is,' said Burgess.

'It isn't possible to be solitary and make statements with meaning,' I said. 'Talking to yourself, without reference to agreed normality, has no purpose.'

'Logic only exists in a crowd,' said Blunt, 'or, to be balanced, also the absence of reason.'

'You imply we only mean something when we are together?' Burgess said, sitting down on the rug again.

'Yes,' I said. 'If you had spent your entire life believing the sky to be purple, and never spoken with or met another human being…'

'Like the Master?' joked Burgess.

'No, Burgess, be serious,' I said. 'If your world was entirely isolated you would not be able to describe that as a form of life.'

'What would I be?' said Burgess.

'A life-form,' I said.

'There you are,' he said, 'that is the Master!'

'And you are studying all this in mathematics?' said Maclean.

'Yes,' I said. 'Mathematics is only logic numerically proposed. Wittgenstein isn't really a mathematician, but he is interested in the true and the false, which amounts to the same thing.'

Burgess had clearly lost interest in the conversation by this point and wandered back down to the river. I watched him throwing sticks into the water and wondered if his short attention span actually proved the opposite of how it appeared; that, in fact, he was the cleverest of the whole bunch. He certainly made me feel, following such answers, that I was not talking about the real world, no matter how strongly Wittgenstein proposed that language is everything. I felt, at that moment on the Grantchester meadow, that Burgess was showing me that I was missing something more fundamental, perhaps even physical or real.

I looked down at the contents of the hampers that now lay across the rugs. Philby had been, as I grew to realise, typically generous and when combined with the stash from Trinity Hall, appropriated by Maclean, we had quite a feast out on the fens. There was jellied chicken, mayonnaise, lettuce sandwiches in brown bread, cream cheese sandwiches, large stuffed olives, stuffed celery, salmon sandwiches, hard-boiled eggs, cucumber sandwiches, shredded cabbage salad, a choice of cut hams and, most memorably, veal birds. These were fried chicken thighs wrapped in thin slices of veal. They sat in a cold cream and white wine sauce and went very well with one of the white wines we had brought: a Chateau Sisqueille Rivesaltes Languedoc.

'The veal birds are delicious,' I said. 'Where did you find them, Philby?'

'I brought those,' said Maclean.

'Good god,' said Burgess, 'Trinity Hall food isn't as bad as I thought! You must invite us for dinner.'

'Consider it done,' said Maclean.

We ate into the picnic and I remember feeling warmer as the sun reached its autumn peak and the food and wine began their release.

'I think it's time to visit the Orchard,' said Blunt. 'Cyprian, be a good man and help me pack all this away.'

'Help?' said Burgess. 'That's a first.'

'I'm in a good mood,' said Blunt.

'Righto,' I said. 'Burgess, you know they won't let you drink in there, don't you.'

'What the eye doesn't see the heart does not grieve,' said Burgess. 'We'll sit far from the house; it's best down by the river anyway.'

The Orchard sat as it has always done, on a bend in the road through the village that ran in parallel with a bend in the Cam. On this arc of land poets, philosophers and students who would become both have gathered for tea since the 1860s. It is a place rich in its links to the university. May Balls became popular, particularly after the Great War, as many also came here to remember Rupert Brooke, like my father a Kingsman, and resident of Grantchester for a while. We left the boat where it was, Philby hammering a second stick into the mud to tie it. We placed the hampers under a rug on the wooden slats of the floor and walked the short distance into the village.

'Remarkable little place, isn't it?' said Burgess.

'Yes, beautiful,' I said.

'Not quite the glamour of Cambridge, though,' said Philby. 'I couldn't possibly live here, could you?'

'No,' said Blunt, 'I would go quite mad within a week.'

'Most people who live here do exactly that,' said Maclean, 'if they're not already mad to begin with, of course.'

'Such as?' I said.

'Well, Augustus John for a start,' said Maclean.

'Oh yes,' said Blunt, 'the naked portrait artist.'

'Lived in a caravan here, didn't he, in Brooke's day?' said Maclean.

'Yes, with two wives,' said Blunt, 'at least two by all accounts.'

'I've always liked his paintings,' said Burgess.

'You would,' Blunt retorted. 'He was like you, forever being thrown out of Cambridge pubs.'

'I've never been thrown from a pub in my life!' said Burgess.

'Not for want of trying,' I said.

'Well, who cares?' said Burgess. 'If it's good enough for old Augustus, it's bloody well good enough for me.'

We walked down the main road in the village and through the gates of the Orchard. To the right, the meadow sloped down to the river. There were already strong signs of fruit on the trees, a promising harvest. The colours stood against one another like oils. I could see why so many painters came here, but to paint this scene seemed pointless, capturing it impossible.

I could not see what Blunt saw. He had a genuine gift for interpreting art works. This was something within him that was not a lie. He could read paintings as others do a book, or some perhaps even when listening to music. He referred to paintings readily, almost as his life's totemic images, using them as fables or warnings. His ability to discuss works of art in this way certainly enabled him to enter into conversations, even relationships that may have been closed to him otherwise. He once promised he would take me to see a particular painting by the greatest artistic influence in his life: Nicolas Poussin. It is called *Dance to the Music of Time*, and would be locked into my life one afternoon as it had always been to Blunt's own.

*

There was a knock at my door just as I finished my tea. 'Yes?' I said, probably too loudly. 'Come in.' Michael entered to collect my cup and saucer.

'Did you enjoy that, Dr Cyprian?' he asked.

'Oh, just call me Daniel,' I said. 'I won't be tutoring you.'

'You're a don?' he said, sounding a little surprised.

'Yes,' I said, 'and there's no need to look quite so astounded,' I added in as friendly a tone as I could manage. 'I taught at your college for years.'

'Oh great,' said Michael, with a genuine look of pleasure in his eyes. 'So you know the college well then?'

'Every blade of grass, every step, every legend,' I said. 'And you're just starting.'

'Yes, and I certainly don't know the grass,' he laughed.

'No, well, all good things come to those who wait... and who work,' I added. 'What are you reading?'

'Philosophy,' said Michael.

'Ah, the attempt to answer everything with nothing,' I said provocatively.

'Well, I wouldn't accept that, of course,' said Michael.

'Why do you say "of course", Michael?' I asked.

'I think we are able to consider ideas of concrete human experience,' he said. 'I mean that philosophy is about more than conceptual thinking but also feeling, living.'

'You mean you're a young existentialist?' I asked.

'If you imply that I look at what has happened in my life and consider its confusion in terms of pain or guilt, then yes, I am interested in the philosophy of more than language,' said Michael, taking great care over his words.

'Don't worry,' I said, 'you're not in an examination with me.'

'What did you teach?' he asked.

'Why do you use the past tense just because I'm no longer paid to do it?' I said.

'Sorry,' said Michael, 'I didn't mean to offend you; of course, I should say what is your field?'

'A much better question,' I said with a smile. I paused, then said, 'I suppose you could say I taught mathematics, but my discipline, to answer the better question, is mathematical philosophy.'

'Oh dear,' said Michael, 'you aren't going to agree with my overly emotive starting points then? Just a minute...' He put his hand to his mouth and stood silent for a few seconds. 'When I was briefed by the Sister here on the residents in this corridor, we were, forgive me, told your age. Were you at Trinity in the 1930s?'

'How clever of you,' I said, 'you happen to be right.'

'You were taught by Wittgenstein then?' he asked.

'He probably wouldn't have called it that, but yes,' I answered.

'So you wouldn't be interested in people who lose hope?' said Michael. 'If something had happened that forces you into despair?'

'Those are disproportionate words in someone so young, surely?' I asked.

'No, I don't think so,' said Michael, walking back to his trolley with the tea things. 'I don't think so.'

'Meaning?' I said.

'Meaning, if you want to use such a loaded word,' he said, 'that I cannot escape my past, well,' he added quickly, 'no-one can, I suppose.'

'Why would you want to?' I asked. 'Although I do agree with you on that point.'

'Cambridge is a way out for me,' said Michael. 'It's a means of escape, or as much as possible anyway.'

'Escape from what?' I asked.

'I've got to go now,' he said. 'Can I come and see you for a while later? When my shift finishes?'

'Yes, of course,' I said. 'If I'm lying down don't assume I'm dead.'

Michael laughed and left the room. I had not had a conversation with a young student like that for some time. He was so definite. I felt that he was struggling against a great deal in his life. I have considerable experience of seeing students like that, especially when they are also so obviously capable. It is almost as though there comes with ability a greater sense also of vulnerability.

I closed my eyes.

*

'Let's ask for scones as well as tea,' said Blunt.

'Tea be buggered,' said Burgess, 'I only want wine, and I have my own supply.' Burgess ran down towards the river.

'Elegance personified, isn't he?' said Philby.

'Well, I'd like tea,' said Blunt, and walked up to the house to arrange it.

'Shall we find a good spot?' asked Maclean.

'How about down there under one of the willows?' I suggested. 'A bit of shade would be good after the picnic.'

'It has got rather warm, hasn't it?' said Philby, removing his hat to fan himself.

'Have you all been here before?' I said to the group.

'Yes, well, I came here a few times last year,' said Maclean. 'It's an interesting place, although one tires of more than a single afternoon. Blunt said earlier he could manage a week, but I doubt that.'

'I would have thought it would be nice to stay over in one of the pubs though,' I said, 'just for the night, I mean.'

'Yes, I suppose so,' said Philby. 'I'd still miss Cambridge even then, to be honest.'

We walked down to where Burgess was lying happily in the grass beside the river. The shade was certainly welcome and the only sound was of water and a wood pigeon repeating its call over and over.

'Absolutely *everyone* has been here though, haven't they?' I said. 'Woolf...'

'Oh god, old Virginia, yes,' said Burgess, 'but this is her sort of place you see, with a river running through it.'

'Oh, he lives!' exclaimed Philby.

'How do you know?' I said to Burgess, who remained under his hat.

'Julian told me she loves water, apparently,' said Burgess. 'That's why she and Leonard bought Monk's House in Sussex. It's close to the Ouse.'

'Who is Julian?' I asked.

'Have you not met him yet?' said Burgess. 'Quite a thing he is, and he's got *quite a thing* for our Blunt too, by all accounts... finds him fascinating, apparently.'

'Good god,' said Maclean.

'Exactly,' said Burgess. 'Probably what Blunt thinks of himself come to it.'

'He's not at Trinity, is he?' I said. 'I would have bumped into him surely.'

'No, King's,' said Burgess. 'Actually, there's a couple of interesting people at King's this year. I suppose if you're not at Trinity it's the next best thing,' and he laughed.

'Apart from Trinity Hall,' said Maclean.

'Oh, come on, dear boy, there are limits and you know it,' said Burgess.

Blunt came back with a tray of tea and scones. 'It's quite busy in there,' he said. 'Half of the college must be down for the day.'

'Well, we're fast running out of summer,' said Maclean.

'True,' said Blunt. 'Most people seemed to have cycled down to Grantchester. Trust us to take the slow boat.'

'Much more civilised, wouldn't you say though?' said Burgess.

'Oh yes,' said Philby, 'and you can bring more with you.'

'We were just talking about Julian Bell,' said Burgess with a smirk.

'Oh, yes,' said Blunt in a disinterested voice. 'What of him?'

'He's Virginia Woolf's nephew, isn't he?' I said.

'Yes,' said Blunt.

'Do you know him well?' I asked.

'I should say he does,' said Burgess.

'Yes,' said Blunt, 'I do, as a matter of fact. He's an interesting young man: very passionate, very poetic.'

'Does she ever come to visit him?' I said, trying to sound calm.

'Yes, occasionally, although I hear she doesn't like Cambridge at all,' said Blunt.

'Oh, why not?' asked Philby.

'It's run by men,' said Blunt. 'Too stuffy and probably too structured for her.'

'I wouldn't say Cambridge is structured, per se,' said Burgess.

'That's only because you ignore the structures,' I said.

'Oh, I don't,' said Burgess, with a hurt look on his face. 'I just bend them a bit.'

'You can say that again,' said Philby. 'You'll be caught one day, mark my words.'

The afternoon was still warm as we sat beside the river, under the shade of the willow tree. I looked at my companions and wondered why they seemed close. On the face of it, there was not a great deal in common, except perhaps a shared derision for their backgrounds. They were careless in this respect.

It was a constant, barely hidden aspect of any conversation with them that, at any moment, all their prosperity, the trappings of strong schooling or the golden buildings of the university could be thrown into question. Or rather, thrown out as useless. I believed they knew how lucky they had been to be born into homes where Cambridge would be seen as a natural progression in life. I did know some people, although admittedly not too many, who had come up without the kind of background of these four.

I talked at some time during my first term to one, a young man in the same court as Burgess and myself, who had worked to gain a scholarship from his school. He told me there had been only one that year, as in every year, and the competition was not especially hard. Not many people in his school had parents who would see university as anything other than an expense, a waste, and a luxury. He had come up from London, and not the part of London Burgess would talk about crashing parties in either. The north, a respectable but not affluent suburb, which would have housed a school, perhaps, with a headmaster who knew what Cambridge might mean to at least one boy per year.

By chance, the four friends with whom I spent that first year at Trinity were very different. I do think, though, that only Blunt had come from a home where Cambridge could have been described as an assumption. Maclean's father was an MP, which probably meant he had been intended to go up to Oxford. Philby's father sounded extraordinary to me. Also a Trinity man, he worked for the Colonial Office in India; apparently obsessed with birdlife, he was also a great linguist. I don't know how often Philby saw him, or his mother, but that is why he was nicknamed at college. Being born in India has a certain cachet. Burgess's father was a Navy man, a commander I think, rather strict, which explains a lot. I know everyone thought Burgess to be brilliant. I remain one of them.

'He's drifted off again,' said Burgess, nudging me in the ribs.

'Sorry, I do that,' I said.

'We'd noticed,' said Blunt. 'No matter, perfectly natural on an afternoon such as this, the wind in the trees, the water trickling...'

'The wine not flowing,' said Burgess, holding up an empty bottle.

'You can't have finished that all by yourself,' said Blunt. 'God almighty.'

'He may very well be,' said Burgess, 'but I want a pub, not a church, so shall we scoot along?'

'He's right,' said Maclean. 'The time for tea has passed; let's finds something stronger.'

'There's a pub up the road,' said Philby. 'We passed it on the way from the boat.'

As we walked back up the small hill in the centre of the village, I could tell that the temperature was dropping. The evenings at this time of year did not hold the heat as those of summer do. Even with an afternoon that had been warm, the wind soon betrayed its Suffolk coastline entry onto England. Before that, it had swept over the waves of the North Sea, and before that still, Russia.

We walked in an unusual silence through the village and towards the small pub. It had indeed become windy and this, with the collective feeling that such weather marked the end of summer, surely kept our thoughts internal. For myself, I was struck on that walk of the unexpected chance I had to perhaps become something with these men. For the first time that first year, I was glad I had not chosen my father's college. I was also glad I had not decided to do things entirely differently from him and go to Oxford.

Their way of being together seemed more than convivial. It appeared close. There was a less than masculine nature about this. The chatter of what is recorded here was mostly about others, as women of the time might talk. All four, but particularly Burgess, were very interested in the lives and habits of our contemporaries at Cambridge. That they included me within their circle began to play on my mind.

In those first few months I did not fully understand what was happening. When the busy babble turned, as it did inevitably to politics, or art, or to things more conceptual, there were real arguments: relatively safe, but real.

'What would you like?' Burgess turned to me and asked.

We had reached one of his favourite places in the world: the bar. 'I'll go for a pint of Younger's No. 3,' I said.

'Ah, a bit of the old Scotch bitter,' said Burgess. 'Good idea. In fact, I think I'll get us all one of those to begin with.'

'Not for me,' said Blunt, 'as large a glass of red wine as they'll give you.'

'What a surprise,' said Burgess sarcastically.

'I don't like beer,' said Blunt. 'There's simply no need to drink it when there's wine in the world.'

'Excuse us,' said Burgess with a smile, and ordered the drinks from a slightly worn barman. He had clearly seen more Cambridge students than he wished to.

I found a corner of the pub as far from the bar as possible. This group would probably only confirm the barman's suspicion of students as pretentious good-for-nothings. It was a convivial spot. Comfortable, faded green upholstered benches looked out over the meadows and a fire had been lit in the grate. The flames were low and flickered across new coals with blue hearts. Over the fireplace an indistinct inscription had been written under a stopped clock. The time said ten to three.

Burgess brought the drinks over on a battered wooden tray. 'Here we go; enough of riverbanks and tea,' he said.

'For once I agree with you,' said Blunt. 'It is good to get inside.'

'It is getting colder, isn't it?' said Maclean.

'Yes, and welcome too,' said Philby. 'I can take as much heat as the next man but England is wonderful in the autumn.'

'I agree,' I said. 'The summer is certainly something to look forward to but I couldn't live anywhere too hot.'

'I could probably be forced to live in Southern France, if the opportunity arose,' said Blunt.

'Will it arise?' said Burgess.

'Not for a long time,' Blunt said, 'sadly.'

'Why not?' I asked.

'There are things happening in Europe that make me want to stay on this island,' Blunt said. 'Many things.'

'Such as?' said Burgess. 'I mean, we all hear the news, of course, but perhaps your great insight…'

'There's no need to be facetious, Burgess,' said Philby. 'Anyway, I feel Blunt is right.'

'Thank you,' said Blunt.

'I'm not sure I follow,' I said. 'I mean, I know that Italy is becoming more interesting.'

'That's not exactly the word I would use,' said Philby.

'Nor I,' Blunt said sharply. 'Italy will lead to violence, mark my words.'

'Why?' I said.

'Violence always leads to more violence,' said Burgess in an unexpectedly serious tone.

'That's what I was just about to say,' said Blunt.

'I know,' said Burgess, 'I'm quoting you.

'Why is it inevitable?' I asked, in a more innocent way than I should have, as father had warned me of similar things recently over dinner.

'We will be cast, individually and as a nation, into the judgement of Solomon,' said Blunt.

'The judgement of Solomon?' I asked. 'What do Bible stories have to do with Italy?'

'Actually,' said Blunt, 'I wasn't thinking of the story so much as the painting, by Poussin; do you know it?'

'No,' I said.

'Well you should,' said Blunt. 'For one thing it's a masterpiece, and another it has a lot to say about falsehood and truth. You should be aware of it. It's like a pictorial equation.'

'Solomon had to decide between the impossible, didn't he?' I asked, although I obviously knew the story from childhood.

'Yes, two women both claimed that one child was theirs. In the painting, Poussin shows one poor woman acting aggressively and another more finely dressed one, appears to be inconsolable,' Blunt explained.

'And how is Solomon depicted?' said Philby.

'He sits in the middle,' said Blunt, 'almost Christ-like, actually. The poor woman is holding a dead child with the same colour skin as her own. The woman who appears wealthier is of a purer skin and standing over her is a soldier...'

'About to cut the live child in half,' interrupted Burgess.

'Precisely,' said Blunt. 'The child is being held upside down by the soldier, who is braced to attack him with a sword.'

'What happens?' I asked

'Interesting use of tense, Cyprian,' said Blunt. 'Art's ultimate intention: to depict action. Anyway, for years I have thought that the poor woman must be the liar because she seems to be careless of the child's impending death.'

'Surely the other woman's action signifies real feelings?' I said.

'If you were in Solomon's position it would be impossible to tell,' said Blunt, 'but when you look at the painting carefully you can see he is showing his decision by raising his hand for the poor woman and against the otherwise convincing richer one.'

'Why is it depicted in reverse like that?' I said.

'I believe Poussin is accurately showing how true and false might appear in extreme situations,' said Blunt. 'The clue is not with the women but with the live child. It is easily missed but as clear as day when pointed out. The child is stretching towards the poor woman so she must be his mother.'

'Where is this painting?' said Philby.

'In London,' said Blunt. 'We'll see it one day, although actually there's another of Poussin's I want Cyprian to see.'

'Why?' I said.

'It'll become clear when you see it,' he said.

'So how does the judgement relate to us now?' said Maclean.

'If we think of ourselves as Solomon, who might the women be?' said Blunt.

'I don't know,' I said.

'Who is acting and who is telling the truth, and in so doing creating chaos for those watching?' asked Blunt. 'Like the crowd surrounding Solomon,' he added.

There was a short pause before Burgess said, 'Mussolini and Stalin.'

'Very good,' said Blunt.

'But how do we know which is which?' I asked.

'Well, that's a good question,' said Blunt, sitting back against the bench and taking a sip from his glass of wine. 'Do you have an answer?'

'Truth or falsehood does not give us the option that neither are right,' said Philby.

'Yes,' Blunt said, 'but in the case of Solomon, as in our modern dilemma, that is irrelevant. One of them *is* right.'

'Are you sure?' I asked.

'Without a doubt,' said Blunt. 'Either Stalin or Mussolini is offering hope to a living child, in this case, us.'

'Well,' I said, 'when you put it like that I would have to choose Stalin.'

'Why?' said Philby.

'I think Blunt is talking about reversing the rules…' I said.

'Exactly,' said Blunt. 'In Poussin's Solomon we are led to believe that the richer woman, the less aggressive character, must be telling the truth because we expect her to do so, whereas…'

'Whereas the game is given away in the detail,' I said. 'It's all in the detail. Leave out the crucial one, the regard by the living child for its real mother, and you make a mistake.'

'Precisely,' said Blunt. 'An easy mistake because that is exactly what Poussin wants you to do, to be as confused as Solomon was initially.'

'A mistake?' I asked. 'Like assuming Wittgenstein was kissing Hitler?'

'Yes,' Blunt said, 'and a deadly one at that. If our country is the living child, who do we decide is its real mother, who will protect it?'

'Or us, for that matter,' said Burgess.

'Yes, things are happening in Europe that our government is powerless to stop,' said Blunt, 'even if they recognised them for what they are.'

'So we cannot make a mistake, Cyprian,' said Philby.

'No, indeed,' said Blunt, 'and I never do make mistakes.'

That evening I decided that I would stay with these four men. The beer kept coming until closing time and we decided we would walk back the couple of miles across the Grantchester Grind, rather than try and punt in our current state. We would bribe a porter in the morning. The light was still in the sky, perhaps one of the last evenings of the year when that would be the case. Although the talk had been serious, it had also been enjoyable. Even Burgess had contributed greatly, and I could see that Blunt was fond of him.

As the others chatted on the walk back towards Cambridge I was as usual left thinking about what had been said. Could Blunt be right in his assertion that Stalin was the best bet for Britain, for all of us? I knew him to be cruel, but then the true woman in the painting had been depicted as less than desirable. I sometimes felt that Blunt expressed life through art in too strained a fashion, but there was something in his conviction that attracted me and made him compelling.

The towers of the colleges came into view as dusk fell across their ancient ornamentations. We walked more slowly along the Backs, admitting with some sincerity that King's Chapel did look magnificent, even though it wasn't our college. We crossed the river at Trinity gates, passing the Wren Library in its darkened elegance, and fell into our rooms.

For the first time, after we had gone to bed, there was a knock at my door and Burgess opened it. He came and sat on my bed at first, and I remember we talked, then lying next to one another. His hand occasionally brushed mine, but I thought nothing of it. I was happy that in my company he seemed calmer.

*

There was a knock at my door and Michael came in. 'Hi,' he said.

'Hello,' I said, 'have you finished your shift?'

'Yes, all done,' he said. 'Have you been asleep? I was knocking for a while.'

'Yes,' I said. 'Did you think I'd snuffed it?'

He laughed uncomfortably. 'You shouldn't joke about it, you know,' he said kindly.

'Listen, Michael, when you get to my age you have to joke about it,' I said. 'Anyway, everyone I know is dead, so it takes the edge off it somewhat.'

'What are you writing?' he asked, glancing at the desk.

'I'm writing about the dead,' I said. 'Funny you should ask.'

'Who are they?' he said.

'I don't think you came in here to talk about me, did you, Michael?' I said quickly.

'No, I suppose not,' he replied.

'You were going to tell me from what you need to escape,' I reminded him.

'Pain,' he said, almost as though he had said something less personal, less profound.

'That word is both strong and enigmatic,' I said. 'Do you want to tell me more?'

'I have no one,' he said quietly, but quickly. 'My entire family was involved in a car crash when I was three years old.'

I took a moment to allow him to continue, but he didn't. 'Were you in the car at the time?' I asked.

'Yes, I watched them die. My mother was first. She was terribly injured. We crashed into a parked lorry that was carrying steel rods. They came through the windscreen. One penetrated her chest, went through the seat and into my older brother behind her. He couldn't move. My father was driving. Another rod shot through his body but it went into the seat rather than me. I was too small.'

'Oh my god,' I said.

'They all died in front of me, but it took several minutes to happen because the injuries were like punctures. Air just left them. It was so slow. They could say goodbye. They all said they loved me. Then they were gone.' He dropped his head.

I looked at him and thought about what to say. 'Do you have a photograph of your family? I said finally.

'Yes, of course,' he said, and produced one from his wallet. It was small and had discoloured slightly, probably from being held in the light too often. 'They're fading already,' he said.

'The photograph itself has no meaning,' I found myself saying. Michael looked angry for a moment. I saw this and said, 'No, I'm saying the object does not have meaning.'

'It does for me,' he said defensively. 'And should for you too.'

'No, you don't understand, Michael,' I said. 'Describe it to me, the actual object.'

'OK,' he said, 'but this is a bit strange. This object is about three inches across and two inches in height. It is pliable. It has many fingerprints on its surface; almost all of them are mine. There are figures depicted on it. They are all smiling. They are standing in the shade because the picture captures a very hot day. The paper is smooth and thin. The object is almost weightless.'

'Good,' I said. 'Now close your eyes.' Michael closed his eyes. 'Now, bring the picture into your mind,' I said. 'Have you done that?'

'Yes,' he said.

'Are your family still or moving?' I asked.

'They are moving now,' said Michael.

'What are they doing? I said. 'Tell me how you have instinctively seen them. You see, it's not the object but those within it that are meaningful.'

'They're wandering around,' he said. 'I think they are picking blackberries.'

We talked that first evening for some time. He is a comfort to me. I believe he considers me similarly. His surname is remarkable, giving him Michael Gabriel.

Three – Liberum Arbitrium

Christmas was approaching at the end of my first term. The long evenings of late summer and early autumn had been replaced by dark falling on the city like a shock. I have always been susceptible to losing track of time. For some reason, a life spent at Trinity has not required the close observance of time passing. It just happens. Careful marks in the university calendar serve to steer wayward dons in broadly the same direction through the year.

I am dependent on such markings and even now can only think in terms of the academic calendar, from summer to summer, like a migrant bird.

Cambridge in my undergraduate years was not the pulsing centre of start-up companies, sparkling hotels and brand-conscious shopping centres it has become as I have aged. College dinners then were more than a formality; they were necessary because there was nowhere else to eat. It was a small place, an ancient island in the fens where everything remarkable occurred in the courts. I admire what it has become: a technology powerhouse with medieval rites remaining as its engineering.

It was at a party that first Christmas that I met the most intricate person I have in the recollection-bank of my life. Alan Turing walked around the edge of the room, holding a glass of wine in a clenched fist. He looked nervous and quick. His jaw was sharp and he seemed to use it to keep people at a distance. No one was talking to him before I summoned the courage to ask him his name. We were hosting a party at Trinity and a network of people I then knew little about had invited guests from King's to 'see what they're made of', as Blunt had put it that morning.

'Alan Turing,' he said, in answer to my first question. It struck me for a moment as odd that he would give his full name in this way.

'I'm Cyprian, Daniel Cyprian,' I said, and offered my hand. He looked at it for a second and then placed his in mine. It was exceptionally hot.

'Do you want to get some air?' I said, 'you seem rather warm.'

'Actually, I would appreciate that,' he said. 'Is it always this balmy at Trinity?'

'Well, I've never really thought about it, but I suppose it is,' I said, 'not least when we're all packed into this shabby room.'

'Oh, this is palatial compared to King's,' said Turing, 'at least you have some decent furniture.'

'Well, Trinity isn't exactly short of cash,' I said. 'Mind you, neither is King's.'

'I wouldn't know,' he said.

We walked out into the court, into the snow. We could hear the party going on upstairs and it gave us a pleasing sense of isolation together.

'Why did you talk to me?' Turing said, stopping and then kicking some of the snow.

'Well,' I said, 'it's a party, isn't it? We're supposed to mingle, even if you are from King's,' I joked. Turing did not smile.

'Yes, but why me?' he said.

'You looked interesting,' I said carefully. 'You were holding your glass so tightly I thought you were nervous.'

'Well, that's a better reason,' said Turing, 'but you have friends in there, don't you? Why not just stay with them?'

'Well, I see them all the time,' I said, a little annoyed at the accusatory tone in Turing's voice. 'I was trying to be welcoming.'

'Well, don't do it again,' he said, and then walked away.

'Hold on,' I said. 'Look here, why are you being so aggressive? In fact, why did you agree to come anyway?'

'I'm looking for people to argue with,' he said flatly.

'You're going about it the right way,' I said.

'No, not to have an argument with,' he said, 'argue with, about things that matter.'

I put my hand on his shoulder and turned him quite forcibly around to face me. 'You know what this party is for, don't you?' I asked him.

'No, I thought it was a tradition at Christmas,' he said.

'It is, but it's got precious little to do with Christ,' I said.

'Good, I don't like Christ,' said Turing, 'far too cruel. So what is it for then?'

'To be perfectly honest, I'm not absolutely sure,' I said. 'Blunt told me... do you know him?'

'Yes, he introduced himself to me this evening,' said Turing.

'Well, Blunt said something about the Apostles, but I wasn't really listening to him and I'm not sure what he meant anyway.'

'Good god,' said Turing, 'you mean you've not heard of them?'

'I have heard of them,' I said, 'just didn't realise it had anything to do with tonight.'

'Well, neither did I,' said Turing. 'God, you don't think they're considering us as members, do you?'

'If they are, you know what they'll refer to us as now... embryos,' I said. 'I always wondered why they wanted to keep my company.'

'Oh I don't think that's the only reason,' said Turing, smiling for the first time since we'd come outside.

He seemed to relax a little after we'd shared a moment of confusion. We began to walk again together around the court. Trinity was full of life that night. There were many parties in warmly lit rooms. Voices, laughter, toasts could all be heard. Yellow light from the buildings filtered onto the vast white court. It was near the time to break, where we all returned to families in towns not even close to being as beautiful as this one. Most were thinking of the reclaiming of their time by parents in grey drawing rooms, or scratching away at conversation with aged relatives like archaeologists, desperate to find something to discuss.

Cambridge glittered, not only in its effortless confidence and ancient beauty, but in the sense it provided of freedom; the autonomy of equal associations.

'When you said you were looking for arguments, what did you mean, Turing?' I asked.

'I expect you'll find out soon enough,' he said. 'We're to be in the same tutorial next term... with him.'

'Who?' I said, although I already knew of course.

'Wittgenstein,' he said.

'Yes, I thought that was who you meant,' I said. 'So you're reading mathematics as well?'

'You mean you are too?' he said, slightly surprised.

'Yes, although I'm not sure about anything I've heard yet,' I said.

'You must be good then,' said Turing. 'I mean, we're not here to absorb facts, are we?'

'Facts?' I said, smiling. 'You believe in such things?'

'I believe they can be either true or false,' said Turing.

'But you would have to prove that either way, surely?' I asked.

'That implies a final solution,' he said. 'I believe it is enough to have tried to produce an answer. I'm working on something now; have you heard of the German mathematician, Hilbert?'

'Yes,' I said, 'but only in lectures.'

'I think he's wrong to say there are no unsolvable questions of truth and falsehood,' said Turing.

'Why?' I asked. 'Because some problems do not have a solution?'

'Partly,' said Turing, 'but it's more to do with the fact that true and false statements are not confined to mathematics.'

'How else can they be defined?' I said.

'As good and evil,' said Turing, 'my own version of the Entscheidungs-problem.'

'Alas, my German is not what it should be,' I said, realising that the wine I had been drinking with Burgess earlier was beginning to take effect.

'The decision-making problem,' said Turing, sounding a little frustrated. 'It's Hilbert's idea that all problems must have solutions.'

'I still can't see how that isn't the case,' I said.

'Look,' said Turing, and then after a moment his tone changed to be more gentle. 'It's about machines. Hilbert says that some sort of automatic process would eventually be able to determine the truth or falsity of any mathematical problem.'

'And what do you think?' I said.

'At the moment you're the only person who seems to care what I think,' said Turing.

'Well?' I asked again.

'Logic says that not all problems have a resolution,' said Turing, 'so, I am interested in machines that might on one hand solve a problem…'

'And on the other?' I said.

'God, you really are listening to me, aren't you?' he said.

'Of course, but it is cold; do you want to go back inside?' I said.

'Fine,' said Turing.

We turned and began to walk around the court. Suddenly, Turing bolted away from me and ran right across the hallowed, now whitened Trinity lawn. 'Stop, the porters will see you!' I shouted.

'I don't care,' he shouted back. I ran after him, feeling elation at chasing him, and at being on the lawn, a feeling I had not had in my life before. I caught him at the door of our building.

'On the other hand?' I said, very out of breath.

'On the other hand,' said Turing, now smiling, 'the same machine might meet a problem, which is genuinely unsolvable. In which case it would go on forever trying to find an answer.'

'What would be the point of that?' I asked.

'To try to solve a problem is enough to determine whether it is true or false, don't you see?' he said.

'Yes, of course,' I said, although the idea was, I must confess, beyond me.

'I'm glad we came outside, Cyprian,' said Turing, as we ascended the staircase back to the party.

'So am I,' I said. 'The air was good. Would you say that was an argument?'

'No, you'll have to try harder,' Turing said, and patted me on the shoulder. 'Come on, let's get another drink.'

We rejoined the party and I was still reeling from the conversation with Turing when Burgess sidled up to me. 'Where have you been?' he asked.

'What's it to you?' I said, slightly defensively.

'Oh, well, excuse me,' Burgess said. 'I'm only asking, not interrogating; well, not yet anyway.'

'I went for some air,' I said.

'By yourself?' said Burgess.

'No, with that rather surprising chap, Alan Turing,' I said, finding it difficult not to smile with a sense of achievement at having met someone before Burgess had managed to ingratiate himself as usual.

'Where is he?' said Burgess.

'He's over there,' and I pointed at Turing, who was slouched on a settee with a glass now familiarly gripped in his fist.

'Oh, he looks interesting,' said Burgess, 'must be at King's?'

'Yes, both,' I said.

'Well, aren't you going to introduce me?' he said.

'I suppose so,' I said, although that was the last thing I wanted to do at that moment.

We walked over to Turing and he got up. I remember now, and I will always remember him as having a sort of shine about him. He had extraordinary personal energy, his eyes played on you and he seemed to possess an epic quality I only observed in one other person that year. I brought them face-to-face and then introduced them: 'Alan Turing, this is Guy Burgess.'

They shook hands and Turing's charisma immediately began to work. Burgess became unusually serious and welcomed Turing to Trinity. 'So you're at King's?' he asked.

'Yes, reading mathematics,' said Turing, 'or what passes for it here anyway.'

'Same as Cyprian,' said Burgess.

'I've just learnt more in one conversation with Turing than in the whole of the rest of this term,' I said.

'You didn't say that to me,' said Turing, sounding surprised.

'I didn't need to, did I?' I said. 'You already thought that yourself I expect.'

'Correct,' he said.

'Well,' announced Burgess, 'another mathematician; it *is* getting crowded.'

'Do you want me to leave?' said Turing.

'Good god no,' said Burgess, 'that's not what I meant at all. You're a bit jumpy, aren't you?'

'I'm sorry,' said Turing, 'just a lot of new people, that's all.'

'Of course,' I said. 'Let's get you a refill.'

Blunt sidled up to me as I poured the drinks. 'I see you've met the sparkling Alan,' he said in a conspiratorial tone.

'Yes, interesting, isn't he,' I said.

'For a Kingsman, certainly,' said Blunt.

'My father is one too, you know,' I said.

'Yes, precisely my point,' he said.

I lifted the two glasses and moved to return to where Turing and Burgess were still talking. 'You didn't tell me this party was associated with the Apostles,' I said, looking Blunt straight in the eye.

'Actually I did,' he said, 'but you didn't seem that interested.'

'I'm very interested,' I said quickly, 'just didn't think they'd be interested in me.'

'Oh, Cyprian, it's not "they", it's "we". We are interested in you,' he said.

'Why?' I asked.

'You want to discuss things properly,' he said. 'That is attractive to us. Also, you have a sense of judgement, of passing judgement I mean. That is an essential characteristic of an Apostle.'

'Is it?' I said, somewhat surprised.

'Oh yes,' said Blunt. 'If you're not prepared to pass verdict on important matters, on people perhaps, or if you were without opinions, we would be far less inclined to talk to you.'

'I try to avoid doing that actually,' I said, 'my father disapproves of it.'

'The truth will out,' said Blunt.

'I didn't realise such a habit could be regarded as a positive aspect to someone's character,' I said.

'Well, I suppose in ordinary people, it wouldn't be,' said Blunt.

'And the Apostles aren't ordinary people?' I asked, raising my eyebrows slightly.

'Oh no,' said Blunt immediately, 'we are extraordinary.'

Blunt told me to keep our conversation to myself for the moment and then swaggered off in that way he had, walking as if he were using a cane. He almost danced that year in Cambridge. I remember him then as supremely confident, enjoying a somewhat prefectoral role, an older brother and a mixer, someone who made things happen.

Handing Turing's glass back to him, I said, 'Take a drink, you're going to need it.'

*

I awoke with the strange feeling of someone's hand on my shoulder. It has been so long since I haven't woken alone that it disoriented me for a moment. I lay there, awake for a few seconds before opening my eyes, letting the sensation of touch transport me back to other hands, earlier awakenings. 'Dr Cyprian?' his voice said.

I turned on my side awkwardly and saw Michael standing there. Michael Gabriel. He had the sun behind him and it lit his hair, filtering light to orange at its edges. Dressed, as they all are, in white, he was almost smiling, almost. His head was at a slight angle, investigating me. I forget how old I must look, how vulnerable, at the edge of life. I have looked at my face many times in the last few months and thought what a distance it has travelled from my heart.

'Dr Cyprian?' Michael said again, and I realised how slow I had been to respond.

'Michael,' I said, 'good morning.'

'And to you, Dr Cyprian,' he said.

'Please call me Daniel,' I said, 'but don't tell any of the others I told you to do that.'

'OK,' said Michael. 'I have coffee, Daniel.'

'Ah, perfect, and toast?' I asked.

'Yes, as it says on your notes,' said Michael.

'My notes,' I said. 'I wonder what it doesn't say on those.'

'I suspect a few things,' he said.

'You construe correctly, young man,' I said, pulling myself up to sit in bed. 'Do you have a newspaper for me?'

'No, should there be one? This isn't a hotel, you know,' he said, smiling.

'It'll be in the Sister's office I expect,' I said. 'I have an arrangement with her.'

'I'll fetch it for you,' Michael said. 'I'll come back later to wash you.'

'I can manage that myself,' I said.

'Not according to…' he started to say.

'I know, the notes,' I said. 'See you later then.'

I needed to think. My mind was at its most fluid in the mornings, which started early in the home. Michael had brought me coffee at seven thirty a.m., which I would not have had until later in college. It was almost as though these places needed to remind you, that by making the day as long as possible you had precious few of them left.

The coffee tasted bitter but good as it entered me. I got up and put on a dressing gown. It struck me again, as is the case with most mornings, that this really was my favourite period of the day. There is a sense of relief; if I wasn't writing so much it might be called laziness, in not having to lecture. My days of running across court to a theatre were over now. I miss some aspects of that life, but the mornings are now an unbroken quietness: the isolation of coffee and the window, the view of fields in an early grey light. My notes scattered across the desk, looking as though a poker game of memories had ended too abruptly.

I stood and looked out from the window. In the distance I could hear a commuter train on its way into London. It is now the turn of other people to make something of their lives each day. To make journeys. My time is almost spent. It is my turn to listen to the trains. I could almost feel their repetition on the tracks, like distant horses. Life truly is circular.

There was a knock at the door and Michael returned. 'Sit down, please,' I asked.

'I was just coming to collect your breakfast things,' he said.

'That can wait. I want to ask you a question,' I said.

'Yes,' he said, 'anything at all.'

'Where were you brought up, after the accident, I mean?' I said, as gently as I could.

'I wouldn't describe it as that,' he said. 'I brought myself up.'

'But someone must have taken care of you? You were so young,' I asked.

'Yes, an aunt and uncle, although I don't think they had planned for such an event,' he said.

'I'm sure they hadn't,' I said.

'No, I don't mean the accident. I don't think they had intended a child to be in their lives; they never gave me the impression I was very much wanted,' he said.

'Even after such a terrible accident?' I asked.

'Precisely because of it,' he said. 'I think my uncle would rather my father survived than me. They sent me to boarding school at the first opportunity.'

'That could've been worse,' I said. 'Did you like it there?' Michael shifted in the chair a little and crossed his legs. He was tall and quite powerfully built, which seemed to make sitting comfortably a little difficult.

'Actually, I did,' said Michael. 'It was lonely for a while, but I met someone brilliant called Christian Moorcroft. He was as good at mathematics as I was, better probably, we used to do what we called research together.'

'On mathematics?' I asked.

'Yes, and physics, and astronomy,' said Michael. 'Something about the profundity of what we discussed helped me deal with my loneliness.'

'And Christian himself helped too?' I asked.

'Oh yes,' said Michael. 'It wasn't only that he loved mathematics as I did. In our own way we loved one another. We were very close friends.'

'Why are you using the past tense?' I said. 'If he was that good, did he not come up to Cambridge as well?'

'He wanted to,' said Michael, 'but he died of a brain tumour. It was there, dormant from childhood, apparently. It grew with him. There was nothing anyone could do.'

'Good grief,' I said, 'death stalks you, doesn't it, Michael?'

'Oh yes,' he said. 'I can almost feel it. That's why I started running.'

'Running?' I asked.

'Yes, it was always the only sport I was any good at,' he said. 'Now I use it deliberately. People think it's because I like to keep fit. In fact, it's because I want to stay alive. I'm fast. I'm safe when I'm running.'

'Do you miss Christian?' I asked.

'Yes, every day,' said Michael. 'Sometimes, though, it's almost as though I can see him ahead of me, when I run. Almost as though he's beckoning me somewhere.'

'You don't really believe that, do you?' I said as kindly as I could manage.

'I only believe what I can see,' said Michael. 'I'm at Cambridge because of him. I know he's dead, but I also accept that some bonds are very strong, maybe enough to hold him near.'

'And you feel that when you run?' I asked.

'I feel nothing when I run,' said Michael, 'that's why I do it.'

He got up and started to collect my breakfast things onto a tray. 'Are you sure you don't need any help in having a wash?' Michael asked.

I hesitated for a moment, wondering what I might really want to happen. 'No,' I said eventually, 'I can manage.'

'OK,' said Michael, 'but you know where the call button is if you need anything?'

'Yes,' I said, 'thank you for offering.'

After he left the room I returned to the window. There was something familiar about Michael Gabriel. Even the way he moved seemed almost to be an echo of someone, years later, as if one person stirred in the past and it rippled into another time. I pulled the chair from the desk to the window and sat down. The sky had filled with clouds, great grey giants shifting imperceptibly over me. I tried to mark their movement, but it was impossible to trace between such close distant colours.

I closed my eyes.

On the edge of the cliff in my imagining I saw Michael standing there. He was looking down. I could sense his angst, not fear, which he could have controlled, but the existential knowledge that if he jumped he could blame no one. The inevitable nothingness that would be his meeting with the rocks filled him with dread. The absurdity of how much he had lost in life, and his ability to make decisions presented itself in his mind in its sheer free will. *Liberum Arbitrium.*

The values by which he tried to exist seemed inconsequential in the face of his loss. He was trying to focus on the concrete, on his hand touching his face, to force himself away from the edge in spite of the absurd. Anything was possible when viewed from the edge of a cliff.

I opened my eyes.

I got up from the chair and walked a little around the room. I knew I would have to confront Michael with what I had seen. I needed time to piece together what I was building in this deadening room. I must continue to write. Washing was first and I picked out a towel from the pile left for me. I filled the sink with water and then filled my hands with it. The water drew me in. I pushed my face, eyes wide open, into it and held my breath. It was so quiet.

*

The room was all but empty when I arrived. A couple of students chatted quietly in the corner waiting for Wittgenstein. We all waited. Then Alan arrived, red-faced and sharp-jawed. 'What have you been doing?' I asked him.

'Running,' he said.

This was to be the last supervision of the Michaelmas term and as our examinations were finished, its purpose was to prepare us for the full series following Christmas and the New Year. Outside, it had hardly become light. A December attempt by the sun had failed and, instead, the smoke from one of the student's cigarettes hung in a dusky haze. The room was on the second floor of Nevile's Court. Wood-panelled walls promised ghosts. The rug on the floor was worn. A fire moved in the grate. A sparrow landed on the windowsill outside, cocked its head and vanished. A clock ticked on the mantelpiece. Its pendulum swung against the dying light of winter.

That was the first time I had seen Wittgenstein. He dressed as though embarrassed, a sort of unsuccessful neatness. His hair appeared to be caught searching for a path, absolutely still in many directions. His eyes were the most striking aspect of his appearance. They found their targets, whether objects or people, like bright blue arrows, taut then released at great speed. Wittgenstein's eyes were impossible to avoid.

He stood in front of us for what seemed like many minutes in silence, before pulling a chair towards him and sitting down. 'So you are all interested in the truth?' he said.

'Not necessarily,' said Turing, very quickly. We all turned to look at him.

'Are you saying you are not interested in truth?' said Wittgenstein.

'I am interested in establishing the undecidability of the first-order predicate calculus,' said Turing.

'Really,' Wittgenstein said, and then immediately, 'so you believe truth does not have to be proved?'

'Absolutely not,' said Turing. 'It can exist without proof; indeed, an eternal process of trying to find proof might prove the existence of a truth.'

'Gentlemen,' said Wittgenstein to the rest of us, 'we have here a rare beast. Someone who wishes to talk about mathematics rather than perform it.'

The rest of us sat in the dusty room, stunned not only by the physical presence of Wittgenstein but also by Turing's fearless poise.

'The proof-theoretical,' Wittgenstein continued, 'metamathematics, or as it might be termed, nonsense.' Wittgenstein turned to Turing and stared at him.

'I'm talking about syntactic completeness,' Turing said, 'and I think you know I am. I am not saying that a formula is provable if it is valid.'

'What are you saying then?' Wittgenstein asked.

'If a formula cannot be proved and its negation cannot be proved either, then it is undecidable, not false,' said Turing.

'You are talking about intuition,' said Wittgenstein accusingly.

'Indeed I am,' said Turing. 'Do you not believe there are things above even mathematics?'

'No,' said Wittgenstein. 'You are giving language to things that do not need description, things, life, that are merely detours.'

'I am interested in detours,' said Turing.

'You are distracted by them rather than finding them interesting,' Wittgenstein said.

'You are ignoring them rather than dismissing them on logic,' Turing said.

By now, the rest of us had given up any thought of contributing to the supervision.

'Plato banished poetry from the world of truth, did he not?' said Wittgenstein.

'Yes, but that was not because he thought it false, only inaccurate,' said Turing.

'It's the same thing,' said Wittgenstein.

'I do not agree,' said Turing. 'Mathematical propositions are truths; even unproven, they still avoid falsehood.'

'No,' said Wittgenstein, 'mathematics is not philosophy; only grammar, social convention and demand can create truth, or avoid it.'

'Then why are you teaching philosophy in a mathematics supervision?' asked Turing.

'I am not teaching anything,' said Wittgenstein.

I thought for a moment of raising my hand and entering into the debate. I thought again and decided against doing such a thing. The two men had clearly reached something of an impasse and left the rest of us far behind some time ago anyway. Wittgenstein left the room. It was hard to gauge his mood as his mannerisms were so exaggerated and his voice relatively calm that he appeared to be struggling to maintain a single temper.

Outside, and again in the cold, I said to Turing, 'Why did you go at him like that?'

'He thinks he knows everything,' he said. 'He thinks that logic is all-pervasive.'

'He is very compelling though, don't you think?' I asked.

'Yes, he has astonishing eyes,' said Turing, 'but he forgets that the things he refuses to speak about may have meaning for other people.'

'For you?' I asked, slightly fearful of the answer.

'Yes,' he said. 'Two and two may well equal four, but it does not eliminate free will.'

We parted company with a handshake and I walked back up to my rooms. The supervision had left me with a cold feeling that was only intensified by the ice on the path. I placed my feet carefully on the cracked surfaces. Concentrating in wind this cold took all my willpower. It was as though each successfully realised step was a defeat of chance. So much was against me getting across the court without slipping that I practically forgot how odd I must look, moving at glacial speed across the ice.

'Hey, hurry up!' shouted Burgess from the window of our rooms. 'I've been waiting ages for you.'

I looked up and shouted back, 'Sorry, didn't want to fall.'

'I'll give you a fall if you don't get up here,' said Burgess.

I accelerated my walking by adding some not unimpressive slides and then ran up the stairs to our rooms. Burgess was waiting in the doorway. 'Where have you been?' he asked. 'You were supposed to be finished an hour ago.'

'Our supervision turned into something of a debate,' I explained. 'I didn't realise it had gone on this long though, I must say.'

'Between whom?' asked Burgess.

'Turing and Wittgenstein,' I answered. 'Turing decided he would try to puncture the great genius's ego.'

'Good god,' said Burgess, 'and did he succeed?'

'Hard to say,' I said thoughtfully. 'Probably not, on balance.'

'What were they arguing about?' asked Burgess.

'Oh, the nature of truth,' I said.

'Bloody hell, you mathematicians think of nothing else, do you?' he said.

'Well, it is really the root of everything, isn't it?' I said in a slightly annoyed voice.

'All right,' he said, 'no need to get huffy.'

'Sorry,' I said, 'it's just that I didn't really appreciate what they were saying, and also it faintly annoyed me that none of the rest of us got to say anything.'

'Well, if you didn't understand it, what could you have said?' asked Burgess.

'That's a fair, but equally annoying point,' I said. 'Anyway, what's the rush?'

'Have you forgotten?' said Burgess.

'I think I'm going to have to admit that yes, I have,' I said. 'What do we have to do?'

'That's a good way of putting it,' Burgess quipped. 'We are all invited to the Master's Lodge for Christmas drinks.'

'Oh,' I said, having genuinely forgotten, 'isn't that odd? I mean undergraduates receiving an invitation?'

'This one likes undergraduates,' said Burgess. 'J.J. Thompson not only discovered the electron but he also likes students.'

'Extraordinary man,' I said.

'Yes,' said Burgess. 'He's a bit stuffy but at least he's providing the drinks. Come on, let's get over to the Lodge.'

The Master's Lodge appeared almost like a small castle captured not by marauding hordes but by the intelligentsia. Draped in the now-frozen reaches of that summer's wisteria, it seemed a place of secrets, like brushing away giant cobwebs at the entrance to a cave. Officially a Royal residence, it is a remarkable house. Burgess and myself made ourselves known to the porter at the door, removed our coats and stepped inside.

'Good god,' said Burgess, 'this looks livelier than I expected.' All around the room the Master had arranged for extravagant decorations to be hung. The main reception rooms reminded me of my mother's favourite shop in London, Fortnum & Mason's, at this time of year.

'I agree,' I said. 'Very jolly, isn't it? Oh look, there's Blunt.' Blunt came up to us and presented his hand in that rather dripping way of his.

'Hello, you two,' he said. 'Doesn't this all look simply marvellous.'

'I thought you were against excess,' I said with a grin.

'Oh, darling,' he said, 'everything in its place, and in this place everything looks good.'

'It is a fine house, isn't it?' Burgess said. 'Cambridge understatement yet again.'

'It has quite a history,' I ventured.

'Bugger the history, darling,' said Blunt, 'let's get sozzled.'

'Here, here,' said Burgess. 'There appears to be a delightful little man over there with a tray of drinks.'

'Well let's start with him then,' said Blunt.

I was already beginning to enjoy myself when Philby arrived. 'Hello, old man,' he said to me, 'enjoying the Christmas spirit?'

'Yes,' I said, 'very much actually.'

'Are the others here too?' he asked.

'Oh yes. Burgess has a source for drink and Blunt is overwhelmed by the décor.'

'All's well with the world then,' said Philby, 'and what about you, Cyprian? What have you found?'

I was still a little preoccupied with the supervision that morning so just said, 'To be perfectly honest, Philby, I'm not entirely sure.'

'What do you mean, old man?' he said.

'I had my first supervision with Wittgenstein this morning...'

'Say no more,' said Philby.

'No,' I said, 'I mean he was sort of extraordinary but it wasn't only him. Do you remember that young chap from King's, Alan Turing?'

'Yes, from the party the other night?' he said.

'Precisely, yes, him. Well, he got into an argument with Wittgenstein,' I said.

'Crikey,' said Philby, 'I thought no one did that.'

'I suspect that would be Wittgenstein's view,' I said. 'I think he prefers people just to listen to him.'

'I bet he does,' he said, 'but why has it got you worked up? Isn't arguing what you mathematicians enjoy doing?'

'When it's purely about numbers, yes,' I said, 'but this seemed to go much further.'

'Meaning?' asked Philby.

'Well, it wasn't really about mathematics,' I said. 'It was pretty clear that they disagreed about truth.'

'Ah, your pet topic,' said Philby. 'Well, I wouldn't worry about it.'

'That's just the thing,' I explained. 'I used to worry about it. I mean, I was brought up by my father to put truth before all else.'

'And now?' Philby said.

'Now, I'm not sure it's just quite so necessary,' I said.

'Well, you have learned a lot in one term, haven't you?' said Philby.

'I'm not sure,' I said.

'Precisely. If you're no longer sure about truth and falsehood you're going to be a great deal more interesting next term,' Philby said. 'Now, let's get a drink.'

'This is Professor Thompson,' said Blunt, almost lifting my arm for me so I could shake the Master's hand.

'Good evening, sir,' I said.

'Oh, we don't need to be formal on an occasion like this,' the Master said, 'just call me J.J.'

'Well, er, righto,' I said.

'Are you enjoying the party?' he said. 'Now what was your name again?'

'I didn't give it before,' I said.

'Well, you're rather confident,' said the Master. 'I shall call you Icarus.'

'My name is Cyprian, sir, I mean J.J.,' I said.

'Fine, then Icarus it is,' said the Master. 'Far more suitable. What are you reading anyway?' he asked.

'Mathematics,' I said.

'Good,' said the Master, 'the basis of everything.'

'Yes, I believe so,' I said.

'Well, you'll have to do more than just believe it, won't you, young man? You'll have to prove it,' said J.J. with a laugh, and then just before turning away, 'Now if you'll excuse me, Icarus, I'll go and mingle.'

'Yes,' I said, 'of course, sir.'

J.J. Thompson wandered away in the crowd of dons and students. I sensed great warmth from him, for which he was well liked by all at the college. It was rare to find someone so eminent to be so open with his younger colleagues. I turned to Blunt and said, 'He is remarkable, isn't he?'

'In his way, yes,' said Blunt. 'I do find him a little overbearing though, didn't you?'

'No,' I said, 'I was pleasantly surprised. I wouldn't have thought someone so important would speak to me like that.'

'Well,' said Blunt, 'despite his position I must say I like him, but his importance is only temporary. I want you to meet someone genuinely interesting.'

Blunt took hold of my arm in that way of steering people that he seemed to do all the time and brought me across the room. He tapped a quite smartly dressed don on the shoulder. 'Maurice, I'd like you to meet someone,' he said, and then to me, 'Cyprian, this is Maurice Dobb.'

'Good evening, Cyprian,' said Dobb, 'I've heard a lot about you. I understand you know Kim Philby?'

'Yes, indeed,' I said. 'Blunt introduced us at the start of term.'

'Did he indeed,' said Dobb. 'Well done, Blunt, well done. Are you enjoying the Master's drinks affair?'

'Well J.J. certainly is, isn't he?' said Blunt.

'Yes,' said Dobb. 'I think J.J. is the cleverest old duffer I know, even in Cambridge.'

'Why do you say that?' I asked.

'Well, he found the electron and they gave him a Nobel Prize,' said Dobb, 'but he doesn't know the first thing concerning what is happening in the world.'

'Oh?' I said.

'Good god no, man,' said Dobb, 'J.J. is of the past, one of those at Cambridge for whom Cambridge is the world.'

'But he is such a great physicist,' I said.

'Physics merely describes realities,' said Dobb. 'It plays no role in change, it is about the minutiae of life, and occasionally the universal, but it is not concerned with living.'

'Gracious,' I said, 'if physics is irrelevant to life, I don't know where that leaves mathematics.'

'An entirely different question,' he said. 'Mathematics at least reflects the greatest human debate.'

'Which is what, precisely?' I asked.

'That between truth and falsehood,' said Dobb, 'the attempt to prove one or the other, regardless of the consequences.'

'I am interested in the consequences,' I said.

'Are you indeed, Cyprian, are you indeed?' said Dobb.

There was a pause as the three of us looked around the room. The drinks were moving from glass to body with what seemed like greater speed. It struck me that the people in this room had little regard for Christmas or for Christ. It was a ritual, conveniently placed in winter to provide a reason for drinking and for questioning. I noticed then that Blunt and Dobb exchanged a knowing glance as they looked at me. I had for the first time the sense of being watched, judged. The conversation was so engaging, the surroundings so carefully constructed to provide an air of authority to everyone's words, that I knew it would be hard to resist being drawn into their collaboration. I turned to Dobb and Blunt and said, 'Dr Dobb, what is your opinion of *Liberum Arbitrium*?'

'What an extraordinary question?' he said.

'I did tell you about him, Maurice,' said Blunt.

'What do you mean, Cyprian?' he asked.

'Well, you say that truth and falsehood are definable, that they should be followed or accepted regardless of their effects?' I said.

'You could put it like that,' said Dobb.

'In that case, we lose our free will, do we not?' I said. 'I mean that if we find something to be true then we must accept it, regardless of what that might mean personally.'

'I believe so,' said Dobb.

'But that is my point,' I said. 'The difference between mathematics and the real world is that numbers require proof; everything else is opinion.'

'Such as?' asked Dobb.

'Well, God springs to mind,' I said.

'God has nothing to with reality,' said Blunt.

'Quite,' said Dobb. 'Where is God in Hitler's Germany?'

'So if not God,' I said, 'where do you believe the truth to lie?'

'In the one force that can protect us from the Nazis and give freedom to the greatest number of people,' he said.

'You mean communism?' I asked.

'That is precisely what he means,' said Blunt. 'Now this little argument has gone on quite long enough.'

'Oh don't worry,' said Dobb, 'it's good to see an embryo with a mind of his own.'

'Thank you,' I said, 'and I intend to keep it that way.'

'Absolutely,' said Dobb. 'We wouldn't want you to become an automaton, now would we? Ah, there's Philby, I must go and say hello,' he said. 'Blunt, might we meet later? Cyprian, I look forward to another argument next term.'

Dobb walked away to where Philby was standing, engaged in what appeared to be a much more light-hearted conversation with the Master's wife.

'You're on form tonight,' said Blunt.

'Why did he call me an embryo?' I asked. 'What have you said to him?'

'I think you know why,' said Blunt, 'and as for what I've said to him, that's for another occasion.'

'But I need to know what you think of me,' I said.

'Oh dear, suddenly lost our confidence, have we?' said Blunt.

'No,' I said, 'I just don't like the thought of being talked about.'

'Oh, I think you'll just have to get used to that,' he said. 'Come on, let's go and find Burgess.'

The rest of that evening passed pleasantly enough. There was the usual atmosphere of a college about to go into rest, but also another, more elusive sense that the wider world might not be considerate of our life in Cambridge. Maurice Dobb had got under my skin somewhat, which was no doubt what he had sought to achieve. Blunt seemed pleased with himself for the rest of the evening, and I was left after the party with unease for the coming term. My father had considered that he had prepared me for Cambridge, for college life. Certainly, I knew how to act, but he had not prepared me for the inquisition that being with these people constituted. Turing, Wittgenstein, Dobb and my four associates, all believed they knew what was right, that they knew how to deal with the world, and yet they were all filled with questions.

I decided then to commit to the comment I had made to Dobb, that I intended to remain my own man, that no matter the trappings of their close membership, I would observe rather than transform in the company of Burgess, Blunt, Maclean and Philby. It would not be easily achieved. Their conviviality and cleverness were attractive and, in addition, I was surprised and complimented by their interest in me.

If the truth lay anywhere within the people I had met that first term at Cambridge, the closest I had come to it, I was certain, was in Turing. He possessed penetrating decision-making ability. It was as though he genuinely did not care for the outcomes of formulae between falsehood and truth. He cared only for their workings. In this, he was the most honest man I ever met. His free will was intact because nothing could influence him. If I could use Turing as a balance to the searing self-belief of my friends, I would stand a chance. I could retain my identity. I would not have to lie.

*

Apostle
Lent

Four – Nimrod

The first morning back, following Christmas and New Year at home, was spent making plans to visit London with Blunt. We were all aware that there was trouble brewing in the capital, and although I would rather have stayed in Cambridge, Blunt in particular was keen that we should make the trip. 'Things usually happen in London first,' he said, 'before moving to the rest of the country.'

'What is attracting your interest?' I asked him, as we sat with tea.

'Mosley,' he said. 'Ever since he left the Labour Party, he's been sounding increasingly angry.'

'Why should that interest you?' I said.

'Angry men are always interesting,' said Blunt,' they tend to make things happen.'

'I'm not sure I approve of what he is, as you say, making happen,' I said.

'I'm certain I don't either,' said Blunt, 'but I'm equally certain I want to know about it.'

Cambridge in the depth of winter is a strange scene. The summer is filled with life, even for a small place. Its yellow-stone colleges glint in the sun and the river seems as though made of green treacle. In winter, the city is a blue-grey. Viewed from the top of any building, the ancient courts and silent, still chapels, halls and gatehouses seem to take on the appearance of a vast graveyard. The fen light is low and moves from the coast like fog, eventually embracing the standing stones of the colleges in a distant spell. Cambridge in the winter appears as a skilfully carved memorial to itself. This city is its own *memento mori*, alive and richly coloured in the summer and a still, misted skeleton below in winter. Its annual migration from yellow to grey is a journey of remembrance, a constant returning.

Blunt and I sat with tea in the bay window of one of the college halls at Trinity. My mind was drifting between our conversation and thoughts of the city. 'You see,' said Blunt, 'it's all because Ramsay Macdonald has made such a damn mess of the financial crisis. He's been thrown out of the Labour Party and formed some harebrained national coalition.'

'Well, I know there's trouble,' I said, 'but surely the Commons will work to the greater good?'

'You are mistaken,' said Blunt in an unusually dark tone. 'All our politicians want to do is to work to their own good. Why do you think the Liberals are split between those who want Cabinet seats and those who think the whole thing is ridiculous?'

'Where does Lloyd George fit in?' I asked. 'He seems to me to be a sensible sort of chap.'

'He is, comparatively,' said Blunt, 'but he hasn't the faintest idea what to do about the depression either.'

'Who does?' I said.

'No one,' said Blunt, 'not one of them, and while England burns, or should I say withers, Hitler is on the rise. I'll tell you now, Cyprian, that it's not the depression that depresses me, it's fascism.'

'Surely they aren't linked that closely?' I asked.

'Of course they are, man,' said Blunt. 'When the money dries up, so do the jobs and then the man on the street starts to look around for someone to blame. The politicians got it in the neck last October, but it won't stop there.'

'Because it isn't really their fault?' I said.

'No, because it's not violent enough,' said Blunt. 'That's why Mosley is one to watch. He's reacted very aggressively. He doesn't blame a system. He blames parts of society. Believe me, he says he wants to help Britain, but I think it's clear that he wants to align us with dark forces on the Continent.'

'He couldn't do that, could he?' I said. 'I mean, he's a baronet.'

'Simple boy,' said Blunt, rolling his eyes to the ceiling, 'that's where his frustration comes from. He's just like Hitler, believing in a kind of new medievalism with himself in control of the Round Table. Fascism isn't a political movement, it's a fairy story in which the demons live happily ever after.'

'Oh, don't be daft,' I said.

'Daft is it?' said Blunt. 'Then why does Hitler make reference to the distant past, the master race? He believes we originate in Atlantis.'

'We?' I asked.

'Well, of course,' said Blunt, 'we are Germanic, well Anglo-Saxon, just as he is.'

'I don't think I've considered such a thing before,' I said.

'Well begin considering it,' Blunt said. 'I certainly don't take Hitler's admiration of our Empire as a compliment.'

'No, of course not,' I said, 'but I don't believe in a master race.'

'According to Hitler you don't have to,' said Blunt, 'you're already part of it.'

I took a sip of tea and looked out the window. We sat in silence for a while. I thought about what Blunt had just said. I did enjoy posing as someone ignorant of the contemporary world, and I knew that Blunt equally took pleasure in acting as a man of it. What he said made sense when I looked at the achievement of my surroundings. Cambridge was not and never would be Nietzsche's school, or perhaps more precisely, Hitler's version of it. However, it was at the centre of Britain's global reach, its power, and its ambition. Did this mean those of us watching fascism's growth had a responsibility to address it?

'I know what you're thinking,' said Blunt, suddenly breaking the silence. 'You're trying to imagine what part we should play in all this.'

'Very perceptive,' I said. 'Yes, it was more or less along those lines.'

'It's very simple,' Blunt said. 'We must do everything we can to halt the rise of fascism in Britain and everything we can to intervene in its growth in Europe. It was on the wireless this morning that Mosley intends to take a trip to Italy this month, to meet Mussolini.'

'That'll be nice for them both,' I joked.

'Quite,' said Blunt, 'but not so good if the dots begin to be joined up.'

'Meaning?' I asked.

'Meaning that Mosley has only a little support in this country, but unless people wake up to the threat of Hitler then we will be looking at a much stronger Far-Right in Britain,' said Blunt.

'I agree that would be a bad thing,' I said, 'but surely we are a long way from Germany or even Italy?'

'Yes, in a sense,' said Blunt, 'but financial difficulty can quickly result in social changes. If you are out of work you have little to lose, especially if you perceive the usual political parties as not being up to the job. The real threat of Mosley is that he could come back with evidence of Mussolini's success in getting people back to work.'

'Well, he has been successful, hasn't he?' I asked.

'Yes,' said Blunt, 'but at what cost? His people don't ask questions of his fascist leanings specifically because they can give bread to their families.'

'Yes, I see,' I said.

'And the same is the case in Germany,' Blunt continued. 'Hitler can do almost anything he wants because he has given his people what *they* wanted most.'

'What is that?' I asked.

'Their dignity,' said Blunt.

'Italy and Germany are one thing surely,' I said, 'but Britain is different. I mean, the English won't be taken in by that sort of thing?'

'Fascism is not a force confined to any one nation,' said Blunt. 'We can just as soon be taken in by it here as anywhere else. The characteristic markings of fascism are the curtailment of individual and minority liberties, the abolition of private values and the substitution of state life and public values.'

'That's patriotism, isn't it?' I asked.

'In its worst form,' said Blunt, 'because from it follows militarism.'

'You're not a pacifist are you?' I asked him.

'Certainly not,' he said, 'but I do oppose the prevalence of mass-values and mass-mentality that is always seen in fascism. Additionally, the falsification of intellectual activity under state pressure is required to manage the masses.'

'I didn't think you gave a damn about the masses,' I said challengingly.

'Not for their own sake, of course,' said Blunt, adopting a more familiar haughty tone, 'but I believe the rise of fascism can only be halted by something equally as large, if not larger.'

'Blunt,' I said, 'are you trying to tell me you are a communist?'

'Of course I am,' he said.

Blunt sat back into his chair. He crossed, uncrossed and then crossed his legs again. He looked out of the window and in profile I thought he seemed to resemble a ghost. It was as if I was talking only to a spectre of the man, a dead version. He turned his head and stared at me, searching my face for a reaction to what he had said. If he found one, it was not judgemental, for I did not possess the knowledge to make so fundamental a condemnation of another man's beliefs, no matter how Blunt regarded my ability to judge as regards joining the Apostles.

'What are you thinking?' he said at last.

'I was thinking that your description of fascism sounds rather similar to my understanding of communism,' I said quickly.

'You have no such understanding,' said Blunt.

'I beg your pardon?' I said.

'Don't want to appear rude, old man,' he said, 'but you haven't the slightest idea what communism is.'

'I know, as you said about Hitler and the like, that state pressure is applied to the masses,' I said.

'Yes, but for a different reason and in a different way,' said Blunt. 'Fascism is focused on the leader, "the Duce, the Fuhrer"…'

'And Stalin?' I asked.

'Stalin is a member of the Party,' said Blunt, 'he is not the party embodiment; and what's more, I believe him and the Red Army to be the only real obstacles to Hitler's vicious ambitions.'

I left Blunt to his tea and decided to go back to my rooms. We had agreed that a visit to London was long overdue, regardless of his interest in Mosley. Blunt was keen to show me a painting in the Royal Academy that was by the same painter who had so gripped me when he last took me to the Fitzwilliam Museum in Cambridge. He had said he was intrigued by my reaction to the Fitz's painting and wanted to show me an equally intimate portrait. The painting I had by then already grown to love at the Fitz was by Sir Lawrence Alma-Tademer and was called *94 Degrees in the Shade.*

I walked across the court in a biting January wind. On the far side of the lawns I could see the warm lights of my rooms, already required on this dark grey morning. Despite the cold, I did not walk quickly. Blunt, as was usually the case, had given me much to think about. Leaving a conversation with Blunt could not be dissimilar to leaving one with the Oracle of antiquity. He seemed so knowledgeable and self-assured that one left with a parallel sense of one's own comparative ignorance having been somewhat modified and enriched.

I did not, however, feel the same as he did about communism. I did not necessarily agree that the only person who could stop Hitler, if there had even been agreement that he needed to be stopped, would be Stalin. I looked at my college and, standing in the snow, turned a full circle, forming another with my shoes. There was a sense of reticent power here. I wondered if Stalin's brutality would ever be enough in any case. Surely the force that would halt the Nazis would more likely come from this quiet, ancient place of intellect and ingenuity.

I got to the small door to my staircase and kicked the snow from my shoes. I climbed the staircase and pulled out my key, which was deep inside the pocket of my woollen trousers. Inserting the key, I turned it and pushed the door open. A bedder had lighted a fire for me, and I breathed in the smell of burning wood. It was warm and the lamp behind the settee beckoned me to sit and read. I went over to my bookshelves and cast my eyes along the spines. For some years at school I had harboured the idea of becoming a librarian. The combined aspect of knowing a collection and yet at the same time, being acutely aware that I would be a mere ephemeral interpreter of it, had always seemed attractive.

Cambridge is a city of words, a metropolis of collections. The librarians of that city remain its police, its judiciary and its government. The collective noun for librarians is, I believe, a stack. Other examples are a pity of prisoners, an eloquence of lawyers, a goring of butchers, a prudence of vicars, a malapertness of peddlers, a scolding of seamstresses, a decanter of deans and a disguising of tailors. Perhaps we should refer to a promise of librarians. They hold so much.

I was to choose a life at least close to them, as an academic. At that moment, though, all I had to do was select a book. The fire crackled behind me and as I stood there I could feel its heat on my back. I pulled a copy of the Bible from the shelf, almost without thinking. I went to put it back and then thought again. These were fine stories. In the warm dim light of the table lamp I sat and opened the book. It fell open in Genesis and at the story of the Tower of Babel.

*

It was so quiet. I held the old Bible in my old hands and turned to Genesis.

And the whole earth was of one language, and of one speech. And it came to pass, as they journeyed from the east, that they found a plain in the land of Shinar; and they dwelt there. And they said one to another, Go to, let us make brick, and burn them thoroughly. And they had brick for stone, and slime had they for mortar. And they said, Go to, let us build us a city and a tower, whose top may reach unto heaven; and let us make us a name, lest we be scattered abroad upon the face of the whole earth. And the Lord came down to see the city and the tower, which the children built. And the Lord said, Behold, the people is one, and they have all one language; and this they begin to do; and now nothing will be restrained from them, which they have imagined to do. Go to, let us go down, and there confound their language, that they may not understand one another's speech. So the Lord scattered them abroad from thence upon the face of all the earth: and they left off to build the city. Therefore is the name of it called Babel; because the Lord did there confound the language of all the earth: and from thence did the Lord scatter them abroad upon the face of all the earth.'

I closed my eyes, remembering the years that have passed since first reading of the tower. It seemed that Blunt had been complicit in an attempt to destroy another Babel, but in fact had merely been shoring up a dark alternative.

I opened my eyes.

Michael Gabriel came into the room. I looked up at him and decided at that moment that what I had he should have, starting with the book. 'Michael,' I said, 'I want you to have this Bible.'

'I, er, don't really go for that sort of thing,' said Michael, 'all a bit didactic for me.'

'Don't be ridiculous,' I said, 'it's perfectly acceptable to own this, regardless of your views of God.'

'Why bother owning it at all then?' he said in a relatively gentle voice.

'These are stories first and religion second,' I said. 'In this book lies answers to human problems. If some choose to take it further and make a deity from it then that is their own business.'

'My difficulty is that so many of those people choose to meddle in other people's business based on what is in that book,' he said.

'True,' I replied, 'but does that mean they have a monopoly on the stories?'

Michael stood for a moment and then came to sit next to me. I was on my bed and I noticed that his weight affected the mattress so much more than did mine. I was close to a skeleton and his body was that of someone far more alive. I closed the book and held it out to him. 'Here,' I said, 'you take it.'

'No,' said Michael, 'you hold on to it until…'

'You mean until I'm dead, don't you?' I said. 'It's fine, Michael, we all know why I'm in this room.'

'Sorry,' he said. 'I just meant you might want to have it for a while longer.'

'All right,' I said, 'I'll keep it on one condition.'

'What condition?' he asked.

'That you let me talk to you about one of the stories,' I said.
'Only one?'

'Yes,' and it's one you'll think you know already,' I said.

Michael moved across the room and pulled a chair over towards the bed. 'You mean you have time now?' I asked.

'Yes, I've finished today,' he said. 'Do you want me to run downstairs and get us some tea? I could get changed as well. I can't relax in this uniform.'

'Fine,' I said. He left the room and seemed to be gone for a long time. I felt comfortable, lying there on the bed with the expectation of his returning. Why did he make me sense possibility in this way, a prospect of friendship I had not experienced for many years. I could not have expected an opportunity in one so much younger than myself, and yet, for reasons unclear, there it was, the distinct awareness of a forming confidence.

I lay back on the pillow and closed my eyes.

*

I lay back on the settee in my rooms content in the knowledge that I would be seeing Blunt and the others later. The fire glowed now, releasing less heat but creating a source of comfort instead. There had been parts of the conversation with Blunt that had disturbed me a little, but then there always were. He had a notable intensity just beneath his polished poise. It could be draining and I was glad to be back in my rooms.

I finished the story of Babel, noticing that of course the name of the city remains unrecorded in the biblical version. I could recall in my own childhood, hearing my father preach of the tower: his stern warning echoing that of God's, that humanity should not attempt to reach heaven by its own accord, nor should it make idols to be worshipped. His Anglican view had little space for differing interpretations.

I had spoken with him one evening, following a discussion in school about the tower. We had learnt of its many resonances in other literatures, both religious and secular. He was actively disinterested, telling me that there was only one truth. I have never been able to accept such a view. He did at least agree with those more eminent than himself that the name Babel is derived from the Hebrew 'balal' meaning to jumble, a reference to God's punishment of multiple languages.

The tower is found in Judaic and Islamic religious texts, in addition to the Christian Bible, which is also true for the Flood. Each religion has its own reason for altering aspects of each story, but the stories themselves remain. Blunt's discussion of a master race came into my mind. He seemed convinced that Hitler was intent on the concept, that it was the very idea of a pure strain of humanity that gave the Nazis their purpose.

As I lay pondering all of this, there was a knock on my door and without waiting for me to answer in came Burgess. 'What are you doing?' he said.

'I'm reading, if you must know,' I said.

'Why?' said Burgess.

'Because I'm at Cambridge,' I said.

'There's no need to be flippant,' Burgess said, 'I was only asking.'

'Sorry, Burgess,' I said. 'I was just thinking when you came in, a little distracted.'

'Thinking?' he said. 'Oh yes, you've had tea with Blunt this morning, haven't you?' He smiled. 'That explains it. What were you thinking about?'

I sighed. 'Do you really want to know?' I said. 'I mean wouldn't you rather talk about something more interesting?'

'I don't know yet whether what you were thinking about is interesting or not, do I?' said Burgess, falling into the chair opposite where I was sitting. Burgess hung his legs on one of the arms of the chair, folded his arms and looked at me impatiently.

'Oh, all right then,' I said. 'I was thinking about whether there could be an association between the tower of Babel and

Hitler's apparent determination to create a master race.' I paused. 'There,' I said, 'I knew you wouldn't be interested.'

'No, no,' he said, 'actually I am interested, but what is a mathematician doing thinking about theology and politics?'

'It's all connected for me,' I said, 'in the pursuit or invention of truths.'

'Bit early for all that, isn't it, old man?' said Burgess.

'There, I knew you weren't really interested,' I said.

'No, I am, honestly,' said Burgess. 'What is the basis of this great thesis then?'

'It's not really a thesis, as such,' I said, 'more of an emerging idea. You see, I am also interested in words, in language, not simply numbers.'

Burgess swung his legs back to the floor and, stretching them out, crossed his ankles together. 'Go on,' he said.

'Well,' I continued, 'the dictator must be absolutely convinced that he is right. Hitler might be a dictator...'

'Some say he is already,' said Burgess.

'Yes, well, there you are then,' I said. 'Mussolini is in the same camp, is he not?'

'Has to be, old man,' said Burgess.

'And Mosley?' I asked.

'You have been talking to Blunt, haven't you?' said Burgess.

'Yes, Blunt is convinced that Mosley will try and move on Britain the way Hitler and Mussolini have in their countries.'

'I'm not so sure,' said Burgess. 'I mean, would we really fall for all that claptrap?'

'I don't know,' I said, 'but it's a terrible risk we're taking if we just ignore what he's doing.'

'I agree with that,' said Burgess, 'but I wouldn't really believe that the British would accept fascism the way the Germans and Italians do.'

'Surely not all of them?' I said.

'I don't know,' said Burgess. 'They're voting pretty conclusively for it, and there are even darker things rumoured.'

'Yes, I know,' I said. 'Anyway, the idea that a master race is preferable to, for example, multiple human races has to start somewhere, does it not?'

'And you suggest it is Babel?' asked Burgess.

'Well, I'm coming round to the idea,' I said. 'After all, it is written…'

'It is written?' exclaimed Burgess. 'Now you sound like a vicar!'

'Remember my father is one,' I said.

'Of course,' said Burgess, smiling. 'It explains so much, dear boy.'

'All right then, the biblical version of Babel is a description of how the world changed from a powerful, unified race of people with one language into a confused, disparate and multi-lingual number of races.'

'And?' said Burgess.

'Well, Hitler may see his ultimate aim as a return to the days before the destruction of the tower.'

'And himself as Nimrod?' said Burgess

'Precisely, leading a world of like-minded brutes such as Mussolini,' I said.

'And Mosley?' asked Burgess.

'Perhaps, if he is not watched,' I said.

'And who would do the watching?' asked Burgess.

'I don't know,' I said, 'but I think Blunt has an idea.'

'Oh really,' said Burgess.

'Yes,' I said. 'Er... can I be open with you, Burgess?'

'Always, dear boy,' he said cheerily.

'Has Blunt ever talked to you about communism?' I asked.

Burgess shifted uncharacteristically in his chair. He rested his chin on his fist and looked around the room. I could hear the sound of the clock ticking and of the fire, as though someone were treading carefully over dry sticks. The cracks were of almost exactly the same pitch as the clock. Burgess looked at me and smiled slightly. He was obviously considering how to answer, which of course in itself was a kind of answer. He moved his chin from one fist to the other. He uncrossed his ankles and sat upright in the chair. He placed a hand on each knee and exhaled slowly.

'He has spoken to me about it,' he said, 'but I don't quite know what to make of it.'

'What is there to be made of it?' I asked. 'Surely he's only asking a question?'

'I don't know,' said Burgess. 'I mean, I'm pretty sure he's had similar conversations with Maclean and Philby too.'

'Really?' I said, slightly surprised. 'I wouldn't have thought Philby would be in the least bit interested in all that, far too many girls to keep him busy.'

Burgess laughed and said, 'There's more to Philby than meets the eye, I'm sure of it. I mean, he's a good chap, but I do get the sense that he might be planning something.'

'And Maclean?' I asked.

'Oh he'll go along for the ride,' said Burgess.

'But all this can't be Blunt's idea, can it?' I said. 'I mean, I know he's terribly bright…'

'Oh terribly,' said Burgess, 'and he'd be the first to say so too.'

'True,' I said, 'but even so, he seems so… so proper, if you know what I mean. I can't imagine him being caught up in anything as distant from a tea party as communism.'

'I think,' said Burgess, 'that he might believe communism to be the only guarantee of more tea parties.' He sat back in his chair. 'You were talking about the biblical version of Babel,' he said.

'Indeed,' I said, 'there are many others.'

'Many other truths?' Burgess asked.

'Quite possibly,' I said. 'It's difficult to get away from the fact that with so many versions of the same story there must be an element of truth hidden amongst them.'

'Compelling,' said Burgess.

'So, returning to Nimrod?' I asked him.

'Yes, in fact, between you and me I once saw a picture of some statue or other of him and I was very impressed,' said Burgess with a grin.

'Impressed by what?' I said.

'Frankly, dear boy, if you need to ask that question then perhaps it should be me telling this story,' said Burgess.

'Ah,' I said, uncomfortably, 'I see what you mean. I mean, I think I see what you mean.'

'Never mind,' said Burgess, 'do go on.'

We talked for about an hour longer before Burgess decided he would, as he put it, 'have a lie down'. I had observed that even by mid-morning he smelt of drink, probably whiskey. I had not yet tackled him on the issue and wasn't sure whether to or not. He seemed, at least on the face of it, relatively happy, which was a state I admired, whatever its source.

I had spoken of Nimrod as someone who defied God and Burgess took the story in a serious frame of mind. He'd said that any attempt to reach God for whatever reason interested him. The tower stood for him as a symbol of aspiration. Of the many versions of Nimrod's life, Burgess responded to the story where, undeterred by the collapse of Babel, Nimrod tries to reach Heaven in a chariot pulled by birds.

I watched Burgess walk to his room and close the door. I got up and went over to the window to look at the snow on the court. There was a distinct draft between the ill-fitting ancient lead catches and I took a couple of steps back. The college was at its quietest. The only sound was a distant clanging from the kitchens as the staff prepared us our lunch.

I walked back to the bookshelf and replaced the Bible, perhaps a little more carefully than how I had removed it. The fire had gone down during our conversation and already the temperature in the room was beginning to drop. I didn't mind keeping it going, but Burgess and Blunt insisted on ringing for a bedder. There were some logs piled in a basket next to the fire and I picked one up. It felt slightly moist in my hand and as I turned it the green moss stained my fingers. I threw it on the fire with two or three others and went back to the chair.

I slumped down in it and watched the fire gradually take hold of the wood. I thought of Abraham walking unscathed from the fire set by Nimrod to murder him. I heard my father telling the story from the pulpit, gradually increasing in volume as he raised the pitch of his voice for effect. I looked across the congregation. My hand moved on the arm of the chair and I returned to fire watching.

*

I could feel the edge of the bed with my hand and became aware of the room just as Michael returned. He was in a T-shirt and jeans, a white T-shirt. I was beginning to recognise his movements. They were certainly an echo, of those of an earlier friend, now dead. He pushed the door open with his foot as he was carrying a tray of tea.

'I brought us some biscuits too,' he said, with a smile.

'Goodness, Michael, what did I do to deserve you?' I said.

'Nothing yet,' said Michael, 'you'll have to owe me.'

'I doubt I have anything of interest to you,' I said. 'What can any old man give to a young man?'

'Interesting question,' he said. 'How about age itself?'

'What do you mean?' I asked.

'Well, I don't mean you make me feel older,' he said, 'but rather that you seem to know so much. Knowledge is an attractive characteristic.'

'Is it indeed,' I said. 'Might I propose it is only so when carried lightly?'

'Good point,' said Michael. 'Now, what were you going to tell me?'

'I want to talk to you about something other than mathematics,' I said. 'I am an old man now, as you've so kindly pointed out, but something I have learned is that not all truths necessarily are found in science.'

'Really?' asked Michael. 'Where else then?'

'Stories too,' I said. 'Many years ago I once talked to a friend about the story of Nimrod.'

'In the Bible?' asked Michael.

'Well, yes, on that occasion it was the biblical version,' I said.

'You mean there are others?' he said.

'Yes,' I said, 'many others, in fact, Nimrod appears in Christian, Judaic and Islamic texts.'

'Does that make his story more true?' asked Michael.

'I think it might,' I said. 'It is a little like finding corroborating evidence at the scene of a crime.'

'Go on,' said Michael.

'Well, the Koran mentions Nimrod's orders for Abraham to be burned to death, and his desperate reaction to Abraham walking unhurt from the furnace,' I said.

'Really?' said Michael. 'I didn't even know Abraham was an Islamic figure.'

'Well, this is the point, dear boy,' I said. 'We are a world of too many languages.'

Michael turned to pour the tea. I watched his hands. He was careful in his movements, and despite the error of pouring in the milk second to the tea he produced a strong, dark cup. He passed it over to me and then handed me a small plate. Rather typical of this place: our plates did not match. I've always suspected that the crockery is an accumulation of that previously owned by those who have died here. There is the distinct sense that others, now gone, have used the plates and cups. On occasion, I have been handed a fine piece of porcelain and wondered how a person of relative wealth could end their days in these white rooms. I suppose I have become used to fine pieces such as that, but never actually owned any of it myself. The college always provided.

Michael offered me a plate of biscuits, and although I have never been especially fond of biscuits I took two. 'Thank you,' I said.

Michael came to sit on the chair he had pulled close to my bed earlier. 'Please continue, Dr Cyprian,' he said.

'Daniel, please Michael,' I said, 'do call me Daniel.'

Michael smiled.

'You see,' I said, 'it's the very fact that Nimrod is to be found in many texts that makes his defiance of God interesting.'

'Why?' asked Michael.

'Well, because the stories are so similar, but they are with us now in texts at the root of religions that for hundreds of years have been at war with one another,' I said.

'I think I see what you mean,' said Michael.

'I mean,' I continued, 'that for much of modern history, mankind has fought over the same truths, or rather slightly differing interpretations of them.'

'Well, yes,' said Michael, 'I know that, but I've never really thought about it.'

'This is what Cambridge will do for you,' I said. 'It's not about reading around your subject but rather reading outside of it, far beyond it, indeed.'

'But how is religion linked to mathematics?' he asked.

'Oh, dear boy, you have a lot to learn,' I said. 'Now, let me read you something. Pass me the notebook from the table there.'

Michael walked across to the table and lifted a large black notebook from it. Handing it to me he said, 'What's this?'

'Just sit and listen for a while,' I said. I had been wondering about how to begin to share with Michael what I knew, indeed what I had observed. I felt the best way would be to allow him into my final project, the last book I would write. In that way I might hope not only to be less lonely in my fading months in this place, but perhaps also to help him. Michael Gabriel. I opened the notebook and began to read:

'As I lay in the warm grass I could sense the future. I closed my eyes and listened to the summer sing. In the next field I heard horses beginning to gallop and then felt an echo in the soil coming up through my chest. I could feel their weight, hitting the ground and entering me. I felt their strength transmit into my body, pushing vigour through me, giving me speed. It went on...'

I saw Michael closing his eyes.

*

Burgess came back into the sitting room and slumped in an armchair. He stared at me for a few seconds and then said, 'I hope you haven't been keeping that fire going by yourself?'

'Of course I have,' I said, 'why shouldn't I?'

'You know I prefer the bedders to do that for us,' said Burgess, 'keeps everyone in their right place.'

'What an appalling comment,' I said.

'Not at all,' said Burgess. 'They need to know where they are just as we do; helps to make the world go around.'

'I'm not so sure,' I said. 'It seems to me that a lot of what made the world go round fell apart after the last war, and good riddance to it.'

'What an extraordinary thing you are,' said Burgess, smiling. 'Honestly, I am impressed and humbled,' he said, almost with a wink.

'Don't get too carried away,' I said. 'I'm still glad someone else is making us luncheon.'

'Excellent thought!' exclaimed Burgess. 'Shall we go across to Hall?'

Lunch was very good, as it generally is in the richer colleges. My love of the detail of food had no real precedent in my family. Father had absolutely no interest in the subject as food for him came close to the baser instincts of life. Like sex, he regarded eating as something simply to carry out as quickly as possible and with little personal involvement. My mother, perhaps typically, was more complex on both issues, not that we ever talked about sex, of course, but she was a more outwardly passionate person than my father and so I can assume she was also more psychologically honest. She enjoyed cooking and eating but even she did not have a particular care for culinary investigation. She had usually finished a meal before giving herself the chance to understand what was before her.

We were served a terrine as a first course, coarse in texture and collapsing under the knife. It appeared to have at least three meats, probably rabbit, pheasant and perhaps boar. The portion was large and sat over one centimetre high on the plate, alongside which was a light green salad with a simple vinaigrette dressing. The dressing was too strongly flavoured with herbs for my taste but Burgess liked it.

'Come and join us,' he called over to Blunt, who was arriving uncharacteristically late to lunch.

'Oh, I thought it would be the two of us today,' I said to Burgess.

'Really?' he asked. 'Oh well, never mind, you can have me all to myself later,' he said with a smile.

'Good afternoon, gentlemen,' said Blunt as he rather awkwardly stepped over the bench we undergraduates were asked to sit on for meals. 'I don't often get to sit down here for lunch,' he said. 'My true place, of course...'

'Never mind the one-upmanship,' said Burgess, 'tell us what you've been doing this morning... and why you are late.'

Burgess was always able to make a simple question sound like intrigue.

Blunt was brought a portion of the terrine and quickly polished it off. The main course was braised beef. As it was lunch the serving was modest and the ring of beef rested on mashed potatoes. There were only green vegetables, long beans, which I believe were slightly over-cooked, dark kale and a sprinkling of bright peas around the plate. The sauce was a powerful reduction that retained its wine and as I cut the beef it fell perfectly into the gravy.

'Well,' said Blunt, 'I saw this young man,' he said, gesturing to me, 'over tea this morning.'

'Indeed,' I said.

'And we decided to go to London after Easter,' he said definitively.

'Did we?' I asked. 'I didn't realise we'd set a date.'

'Well, I set a date then,' said Blunt, 'but you've agreed to it...'

'How have I done so if I wasn't there to agree?' I asked.

'Because you weren't there to disagree,' said Blunt. 'Now, don't be so pedantic.'

'Well, excuse me,' I said.

Burgess interrupted. 'If you two could stop bickering like a married couple, Blunt, might you indulge me and actually answer my question?'

'What was the question?' said Blunt.

'Oh for god's sake,' said Burgess, 'you were going to tell us what you've been up to this morning.'

'Oh yes,' said Blunt. 'I had a rendezvous.' He said the last word as though he were chewing a toffee at the same time, as if he were being forced to pronounce it slowly.

'Oh, how exciting,' said Burgess, with a slightly childish clap of his hands, 'and what did this rendezvous,' he mimicked, 'present by way of opportunities?'

'That's a surprisingly good question,' said Blunt, 'because, as a matter of fact, it did, as you say, present an opportunity, I believe.'

I had finished my beef whilst the other two played verbal tennis, and so was in a position to continue Burgess's interrogation without obstacle. 'What do you mean, an opportunity?' I asked.

'Well,' said Blunt, 'let's just say you should keep this coming weekend free.'

'You can't leave us hanging like that,' said Burgess.

'Oh I can,' said Blunt, 'and I will,' and he refused to answer any further questions on the matter.

The dessert was named for our college: Trinity Burnt Cream, which, of course, has a famous French cousin. Rather typically of the French indeed, they claim to have invented this mix of hard sugar and soft custard, but we would have none of it. In Trinity was this created and we agreed that was the end of the matter.

We walked out into the cold and winter court and agreed to meet for dinner. I had lectures to attend and so did Burgess, although he did not appear to be minded to go to them. He walked off quickly towards our rooms and waved his arm cheerily without turning around. Blunt went to walk away, but I caught his arm.

'Will you really not say what you have planned for the weekend?' I asked him.

'No, Cyprian, I will not,' he said, not unkindly, 'but you will find out soon enough.'

I accepted this and let the matter go. I had the more immediately enticing prospect of another lecture by Wittgenstein, and I was looking forward to sitting beside Turing again. I was also coming to the realisation that I desired such a scenario more than I had previously understood.

*

When telling stories there is more than one way to recount the truth. Even time itself is of no consequence. Accuracy is for historians. In art people are freed from recorded moments to be recast as the storyteller chooses. This enables the creation of fairytales.

*

I saw Turing sitting further back in the lecture theatre than he had done previously. I waved and he smiled slightly, appearing to give the impression that he wanted me to join him but did not wish to appear too keen. I took this as a good sign and climbed the steep stairs up to where he was sitting.

'I've been making some notes,' he said to me, almost in a whisper. 'I've been thinking about truth: does it imply the provable or can it exist regardless?'

I chose to move closer to him, using what I later realised was the cover offered by his lowered voice. Turing smelt very clean; of soap, in fact. I noticed that his fingernails were immaculate.

'If it can exist regardless,' I whispered, 'then God may too exist?'

'Precisely,' he said, 'and very good to see you, Cyprian, by-the-way.'

I was taken aback by his quick change of emphasis from God to me. 'Same for me, to you, er, same here,' I blundered. Turing did not notice.

'Gödel is about to publish his doctorate, you know,' said Turing. 'Have you heard of him?'

'Yes, he's only about our age, isn't he?' I said. 'Someone was telling me about him in a seminar last term.'

'He is very interesting,' said Turing. 'He has finished his work on incompleteness theorems… very interesting indeed,' he said, as he turned to look out of the window.

'I think Wittgenstein is going to discuss it this afternoon,' I said.

'Really?' said Turing, in a suddenly much louder voice. 'Thank god I prepared something.'

'You are going to let someone else in the class say something this time, aren't you?' I asked in as polite a way as I could muster.

'Why should I?' said Turing. 'He will only want to argue with me.'

As astonished as I was by the sheer unbridled confidence of that statement, I found no way to respond to it. Turing was right.

Wittgenstein entered the room as if he had just run from the train. He as much as threw his battered briefcase onto the long lecturer's desk before pulling out a chaos of papers. He plied them into a pile out of a fashion and lifted his head to speak. He opened his mouth and then appeared to think better of it. He looked down again at the papers and began rearranging them. Some minutes passed without any other sound in the room. I could feel Turing becoming restless beside me. His right leg was bouncing up and down silently and he was doodling on his notebook. He had covered a whole page with formulae before Wittgenstein finally broke the silence.

'Gentlemen,' said Wittgenstein firmly, 'I have decided to lie to you. There, what do you think of that?'

We all looked around the room to see if anyone had the nerve to respond to a question that would quite clearly lead to a supplementary one of a complex nature.

Turing was still doodling and appeared not to have heard the question.

'Turing,' said Wittgenstein, 'you appear to be rather busy. Would you mind terribly listening to me?'

'I am thinking about whether machines might be able to lie, not you,' said Turing.

'Ah, so I do have the rare pleasure of your attention,' Wittgenstein said. 'Do you have an opinion you want to enrich the rest of us with?'

I had no idea that the two men had developed the ability to converse so candidly with one another.

'Let me ask *you* a question,' said Turing. 'Rather than describe something as a lie, can we use the word contradiction?'

'That is a very fair question,' said Wittgenstein. 'Think of the case of the liar. It is very queer in a way that this should have puzzled anyone, much more extraordinary than you might think... because the thing works like this: if a man says "I am lying" we say that it follows that he is not lying, from which it follows that he is lying, and so on. Well, so what? You can go on like that until you are black in the face. Why not? It doesn't matter... it is just a useless language-game, and why should anyone be excited?'

Turing almost rose to his feet as he answered. 'What puzzles me is that I usually use a contradiction as a criterion for having done something wrong. But in this case I cannot find anything done wrong.'

'Yes, and more,' said Wittgenstein. 'Nothing has been done wrong. Where will the harm come?'

'The real harm will not come in unless there is an application, in which a tower may fall down or something of that sort,' said Turing.

Wittgenstein said, 'The first question is, why are people afraid of contradictions? It is easy to understand why they should be afraid of contradictions, etc., outside mathematics. The second question is, why should they be afraid of contradictions inside mathematics?'

Turing placed his notebook on the narrow lecture desk in front of us and quite obviously was thinking very hard as he paused. I could hear birdsong beyond the window and wondered what kind of bird would sing in winter.

Turing said, 'Because something may go wrong with the application. But nothing need go wrong. And if something does go wrong, if the tower falls down, then your mistake was of the kind of using a wrong natural law.' Turing continued, 'You cannot be confident about applying your calculus until you know that there are no hidden contradictions in it.'

'There seems to me an enormous mistake there,' said Wittgenstein. 'Suppose I convince Cyprian there, sat next to you, of the paradox of the liar, and he says, "I lie, therefore I do not lie, therefore I lie and I do not lie, therefore we have a contradiction, therefore $2 \times 2 = 369$." Well, we should not call this multiplication, that is all...'

'Although you do not know,' said Turing, 'that the tower will fall if there are no contradictions, yet it is almost certain that if there are contradictions it will go wrong somewhere.'

'But nothing has ever gone wrong that way yet,' said Wittgenstein, and with a raised hand he halted the argument. Even Turing was not then confident enough to continue speaking.

After the lecture, if such an epithet could be applied to what again had become a debate even though it was not a supervision, I walked out into Trinity Court with Turing. We decided we would take afternoon tea in town. As we left the college and came out onto St. John's Street, I said to Turing, 'You know the tower you were using to say that contradictions can both exist and have practical consequences?'

'Is that what I was saying?' he said, smiling cheekily.

'I thought so,' I said. 'In any case, I have interpreted it like that.'

'Fine,' he said, 'what of it?'

'Well,' I went on, 'Wittgenstein said two things that I found interesting in relation. Firstly, he appeared to be saying that lies are just a language-game, and secondly, that nothing has gone wrong, to use his phrase, in the way that you suggested yet.'

'He did propose both of those ideas, yes,' said Turing. 'Why do you bring them together though?'

'I have been thinking of Nimrod recently,' I said. Turing stopped and turned to look at me.

'What of him?' he asked.

'Well, he built a tower and effectively brought the ultimate language-game crashing down on himself,' I said. 'He had constructed a lie that was also a truth, in that in essence its truth was a lie and so on, just as Wittgenstein said.'

'You mean, something has gone wrong in the way that I suggested?' said Turing.

'Precisely,' I said. 'And what's more, I think there is a modern parallel.'

We continued walking down towards King's Parade, past Gonville and Caius and then out onto the street opposite the Senate House.

'I've been talking with Blunt about this, and Burgess actually,' I said.

'They aren't interested in logic, are they?' said Turing.

'Well, not as such,' I said, 'but they seem to be deeply interested in pursuing some kind of truth, and in so doing are using a kind of logical process.'

'What kind of truth do you discuss with them?' he asked.

'It's only truth in their opinion, of course,' I said. 'I don't know that I quite agree with them actually. I think they are both of the opinion that the only way to oppose fascism is by aligning oneself with communism.'

'Well, they aren't alone in thinking that,' said Turing.

'You mean you agree with that way of thinking?' I asked him.

'To be perfectly frank,' he said, 'I do not know yet, but no, I suspect I do not.'

'That is exactly how I feel,' I said, 'but regardless, my idea is that there is a comparison between Hitler and Nimrod... they have both been constructing a tower towards a kind of god.'

'Interesting idea,' said Turing. 'Certainly they are both full of contradictions.'

'They are indeed,' I said, 'and if Hitler claims that 2 x 2 = 369, then that becomes true as far as I can see. His master race is Nimrod's god.'

'You are a very intriguing person,' said Turing.

'Oh, why?' I asked.

'You do clearly understand logic,' he said in a tone of voice that would have been patronising had I not already accepted his superior intellect, 'but you also employ intuition, a very human tool and one I cannot ever see being performed by computational devices.'

'Well, I am not a device,' I said, laughing.

'I can see that,' said Turing. He turned to me just before we went into the café opposite King's College and put his hand on my arm. 'Have you ever been in love?' he said.

*

Michael opened his eyes.

'Let me ask you a question,' I said to him. 'Forgive me, it's a little personal.'

'No problem,' he said.

'Have you ever been in love?'

*

When I got back to our rooms, Burgess was lounging on the settee with a cigarette in one hand and what looked like sherry in the other. He was listening to *Don Giovanni*.

'What are you thinking about?' I asked him.

'My father,' he said.

'Inspired by this?' I asked, 'he must be quite the devil.'

'Only partly,' said Burgess. 'Sometimes he's even worse than that,' and then, as if to wrong-foot me as usual, he added with a smile, 'but I like him like that.'

'Are you going to stop playing games and have a drink before dinner?' I asked.

'I'm already having one,' he said, waving his sherry glass.

'I meant another one,' I said. 'I don't think I've ever been quick enough or early enough to offer you your first drink of the day.'

'There's no need for comments like that,' Burgess said.

'Sorry,' I said, for despite everything I had already grown fond of Burgess. Everyone was fond of Burgess.

I took his glass and refilled it from the cabinet. I walked carefully as neither of us liked spilt drinks and passed it back to him. He was staring right into my eyes as a doctor might when checking for a complaint. I stared back.

'Your eyes are those of an observer,' he said, 'not a participant.'

'A participant in what?' I asked, 'and that's a ridiculous thing to say in any case.'

'Is it?' he said. 'No matter, we'll soon find out what you're made of.'

'Meaning?' I asked.

'Meaning, that you will be offered an opportunity very soon that could alter the course of your life,' said Burgess.

'How enticingly dramatic,' I said, a little curtly.

'I'm being serious, Cyprian,' he said. 'There's a group of us who think you're sound.'

'Who does?' I asked, even though I, of course, knew the answer.

'Blunt, Maclean, Philby, even though he doesn't know you too well, and myself, you fool,' said Burgess. 'We think you might be one of us.'

I took an indecently long sip of sherry and looked at Burgess. Another habit of his was to leave a theatrical silence after such an utterance. He had swung his legs back onto the settee and now lit another cigarette. The Mozart had reached a critical point in the drama and was building to the scene where his ghostly father meets Don Giovanni. I couldn't have continued talking over it even if I had wanted to, so I sunk back into the chair and listened for a while.

Watching Burgess reminded me of the pleasure I had of watching our large friendly dog in my parents' house. He moved occasionally on the settee towards greater comfort and seemed to be able to almost immediately enter his own mental world. For someone so engaging he was certainly, at times at least, able to be self-sufficient in this way. I was growing to admire him.

Whilst Burgess readied himself for dinner I took a walk in college. It was still too early in the year for the light to have changed much and the early evening was almost dark. Despite this, I had already developed an attachment to the college that, of course, would last the rest of my life. I moved from court to court and stood for a while finding pleasure in the symmetry of the Wren Library. I walked under the cloisters and along the lines of columns that supported the building and its collections. I nodded to those I knew and caught the eyes of others. My shoes had metal caps and their taps echoed on the stone. It was an elegant sound for a graceful time.

Trinity provides for its undergraduates a sense of immediate success. To be there, felt as though one could achieve everything or become anything. It was this sense that drew out such possibilities in us, in them. They were extraordinary people, those four men. They believed in things. They were certain they could change the world. They thought they were untouchable and unrestrained and right.

They were building their own tower even while warning of another.

*

Five – Images Oubliées

Michael looked at me and said, 'Yes, I have been in love.'

I smiled and took a sip of tea. I looked at him. He clearly had experienced pain; indeed, it retained its impression upon him. 'Did being in love make you happy?' I asked him.

'Oh yes,' he said.

'And was it with your friend at school?' I asked, 'Christian Moorcroft?'

'Yes,' said Michael, rather coyly.

'This is the first time you've told anyone that, isn't it?' I said gently.

'Yes, but how do you know that?' he asked.

'We've all been young once, Michael,' I said, 'and these things never really change; well, they haven't yet in any case. How did he make you feel?' I said.

'Well, as you say, he made me happy, although I don't think either of us realised really what was going on,' said Michael.

'Did you talk about how things were different with him?' I asked.

'Oh yes,' he said. 'One time in particular we were just spending the afternoon together, listening to music, when he reached across to me as we lay on his bed. He would never kiss me but in every other way he was affectionate. He said I was the only boy he found attractive.'

'How did that make you feel?' I asked.

'A little confused, to be honest,' said Michael. 'I mean, I had noticed him looking at me about a year earlier after sports but I wasn't sure,' he continued. 'Christian always said he liked girls generally but also liked me. It was as if I was somehow safe, like a controlled environment for an experiment.'

'He made you feel like an experiment?' I asked.

'In a way, yes, and even though I enjoyed it, I felt very vulnerable, as though I was giving myself to someone who would never give as much back,' he said.

'That is difficult,' I said.

'Actually,' said Michael, 'I started running before he died. I told you before that I run in order not to feel…'

'Yes,' I said.

'Well,' Michael went on, 'in a way I was already not feeling when I was with him. It was as if somewhere inside of myself I was preparing the defences I would need when I lost him; it's just that I didn't know I would lose him like that.'

'How horrible,' I said.

'I thought he would walk away at some point, but that we might be able to be friends even if he got married,' he said, 'but of course, he vanished completely.'

'Not completely, remember,' I said. 'You still see him in your dreams.'

'Yes,' said Michael, 'but the whole experience of being with Christian feels as though it were a dream now.'

'Well there you are then,' I said, 'what's the difference?'

'I wish I could accept that, as a principle I mean, that immortality is achievable for him by closing my eyes.'

'And why isn't it?' I asked.

'His skin is unreachable,' said Michael. 'His skin was what made him animal and close.'

'We must work on that,' I said.

'Dr Cyprian, sometimes I think the only way I can join him, and see my family again too, is to put myself in my dreams,' said Michael.

'How would you do that?' I said.

'Anything seems possible when viewed from the edge of a cliff,' said Michael.

He got up and walked across to my desk. He moved a couple of the papers around and rearranged my pens. I thought this an intrusive but trusting action so I said nothing. Immediacy had very quickly entered our relationship. He was remarkably open with me and I needed to consider how to respond to it. I felt I should make a decision either to back away from this raw, unguided young man or move closer to him. I had been in this position before and regretted my decision then. But now, now I had so little time left and my work was important. I had to finish my writing.

Michael turned and smiled at me. I thought for a moment and decided to respond to him rather than to reject him.

'Michael,' I said, 'would you take me for a walk around the gardens?'

*

The light had changed in the evenings at college. The buildings of Trinity were now a golden red at about six o'clock and the glass in the chapel windows appeared on fire. I stood with Burgess as he smoked a cigarette, waiting for Blunt. They had asked to see me after dinner to discuss an invitation.

Blunt came round the corner into the court, walking quickly with his robes flying behind him. 'I cannot apologise enough,' he said, 'I was caught talking to someone and the time just disappeared. Are you gentlemen ready for dinner?'

The repetitive nature of college life has always attracted me. It is like a universe expanding and exploding and expanding again. Trinity, as is the case with all of Cambridge's more prestigious colleges, believed itself to be its own universe, its own endless galaxies, and its own cycle.

'Yes, of course,' said Burgess, 'we've been waiting for you.'

'Very pleasant time, though,' I said. 'Look at the sun in the windows, Blunt.'

'Crikey, Cyprian, you are the romantic aren't you?' he joked.

'Oh, I wouldn't go as far as that,' I said, blushing slightly. 'I just thought you might appreciate their colour.'

'Indeed I do, Cyprian,' he said, 'indeed I do, and how would you describe the colour of the chapel windows, Burgess, fire? Caesarean gown? Royal-carpeted?'

'Let me see,' said Burgess, 'how about red?'

'And there is my final evidence,' announced Blunt. 'He actually is just a pretty face.'

'I'd rather be that than an—' started Burgess.

'Now, now,' said Blunt, 'let's just go in for a swift pre-dinner drink.'

We went into the college bar and chose gin and tonics, taking them to a group of armchairs over by the mullioned windows. I chose to sit facing the window, which meant that Blunt was required to take the chair with his back to it. In the setting sun his hair was framed in light and he seemed to be a wizard watching us, or perhaps a medieval king holding court. Whichever it was, he clearly enjoyed the attention it brought him as the sun lowered in the sky. I could see him using the chance to catch the eyes of people he knew.

The bar began to fill with the college community. I could hear the voice of J.J. Thompson and a number of others. It was still relatively cold in the evenings so the fires had been lit, and no doubt also had been in the hall. I could smell the burning wood, mixed with the unmistakable mixture of scents applied by these Cambridge men for an evening's socialising. I let my hand rest on the arm of the chair and noticed a slight fraying, unusual in our college. It was under the centre of my palm, where so many others had rested their hands, perhaps whilst balancing a drink as they made an important conversational point.

Blunt and Burgess were talking quietly to one another, not exclusively but clearly not wishing for me to hear precisely what they were saying. They alternated from comparatively serious frowns to light chatter. I was content in their company and in the presence of this academic set: an intellectual wolf pack that appeared relaxed around each other but, having spotted someone weak, or not to their liking, would rapidly circle and attack.

I was only then beginning to understand that Cambridge could be as hostile as it could be homely, as dangerous as it could be pleasurably distracting. It was in effect a kind of large club, where one was welcome if you only rebelled in a particular kind of way. That way was well within the confines of English society, which considered off-the-cuff remarks about King and Country acceptable only if it were known you would still fight for both. This was the heart of the Cambridge establishment, which encouraged originality within similar boundaries to those on a cricket pitch.

As I looked round the room I could see that there was, in reality, a lack of original men about me. My benchmark had already become Turing, who although quiet, save for the times he was anywhere near Wittgenstein, had such a compelling mind that drew one away from the world. There was a falsity about so much self-knowing brilliance amongst most of the others I knew at Cambridge. Their rebellion was nothing more than youth itself, pure energy that would quickly dissipate into Parliament, marriage and the cigar-smoked rooms of their London clubs.

As I sat in the armchair thinking, I wondered what had become of my lack of criticism of my fellow undergraduates when I'd first come up to college. The time I was spending with Burgess and Blunt in particular, but also to a lesser extent with Philby and Maclean, had made me not more observant as such, but certainly more judgemental. I remembered that Blunt had told me last term that he thought I had potential as someone who judged others and that I had inwardly rejected the idea. Perhaps he was being proved right after all. I was certainly condemning many in the room that night.

I felt that even in their black-tied, gowned confidence they were already lost. If only they could see that darkness was coming. Their glasses glittered in the light of candles and of the fire. They smiled and talked and moved round the room with ease, yet remained oblivious to the encroaching threat. They thought themselves wolves in command of their ancient forest, but the trees on its edge were already on fire. Soon flames would encircle us all.

'Cyprian?' said Burgess, 'are you all right, old man? You were miles away.'

'Oh, er, yes, sorry,' I said, 'you two were talking and I was so comfortable here. I must have drifted off thinking about things.'

'About what things?' asked Blunt.

'Oh. never mind that now,' said Burgess. 'There will be time for all that later. Let's go and eat.'

That evening Blunt went to sit with his fellow graduates, leaving me and Burgess to entertain Maclean who had joined us for dinner again, proclaiming the food better at Trinity than Trinity Hall. He was, on reflection, rather a dull man, although almost anyone would appear so when compared to Blunt and Burgess. However, the dinner passed pleasantly enough.

'How are your studies going, Cyprian?' asked Maclean.

'Well enough,' I answered. 'I'm learning more from watching others engage in lectures than from most of the lecturers.'

'Welcome to Cambridge,' pronounced Burgess. 'That's the whole point, old man, we are not here to listen, we are here to joust.'

'Oh you would say that,' I said to him. 'Not all of us belong on that particular field, you know, Burgess, some of us belong in the audience.'

'I wouldn't be so sure about that,' said Burgess. 'You've been making a bit of a name for yourself, you know.'

'Amongst whom?' I asked.

'Oh, that would be telling now, wouldn't it,' he said leadingly.

'No, really,' I said, a little annoyed that my careful attempts at remaining in the background did not appear to be working.

'Blunt has noticed you,' said Maclean.

'So what,' I said, in a perhaps overly defensive manner.

'Oh, have we touched a nerve?' said Burgess. 'There's nothing to worry about on that front, Cyprian. Most people would take it as a compliment to be noticed by Blunt... in that way.'

'Well, I don't take it so,' I said, 'and what do you mean by "in that way"?'

'He means,' said Maclean, 'that Blunt thinks you're clever.'

'Indeed,' said Burgess, 'and with being noticed will come responsibilities.'

Our first course was a simple enough salad acting as a bed for a large slice of cold ham. Around the meat were bright radishes, which complemented the yellows and greens of the salad very attractively. A sharp dressing lifted the leaves.

'Did Blunt talk to you about our invite for later?' asked Burgess.

'He did indeed,' I said, 'although I'm not entirely sure what it is concerning.'

'Oh, just a little club we would like you to join,' said Burgess.

'No one has ever asked me about joining any club,' interrupted Maclean.

'Well, they wouldn't, would they?' stated Burgess. 'You're not at the right college.'

'Oh,' asked Maclean, 'and what would be the right college?'

'Either Trinity or King's,' said Burgess. 'We seek no lower, and there aren't any higher.'

'Charming,' said Maclean.

'Well, I don't make the rules,' said Burgess, 'I just enjoy them.'

I burst out laughing at that point. 'You've never enjoyed playing by the rules in your life, Burgess!'

'On this occasion and this occasion only I do play by them,' said Burgess, with a kind of faked seriousness.

The main course was served. A small jug of gravy bubbling with onions accompanied a pile of mashed potatoes with three sausages per person resting on it. Around the mash in an exactly alternating sequence was placed broccoli and cauliflower. If anything could be noted of the vegetables it could be said they were slightly over-cooked, however not to the point of being inedible. The mash was heavily laced with butter and parsley and the sausages, rather reassuringly, were fat and peppery. As standard college fare it was good, although it did not take a great deal of time to get to the bottom of the dish. I was left with two puddles of gravy, which I had predicted and prepared for by also carefully leaving two large pieces of sausage. I dipped the first piece into one part of the gravy, and then repeated the exercise with the second. My plate was finished precisely and in almost exactly the amount of time I had mentally calculated before taking the first mouthful.

'Do you always eat like that?' asked Burgess.

I was surprised anyone had noticed my activity and even more surprised that it was worth commenting on. 'Yes,' I said, 'what would your point be?'

'Oh, no point,' said Burgess.

'My sentiments exactly,' said Maclean.

Dessert was a selection of fruits, which are my least favourite foodstuffs. We are encouraged to eat them, of course, but I feel cheated by them as an ending to a meal, as though the kitchen had run out of ideas. I ate an orange, hating the pith and pips and enjoying the flavour even less.

'I've had enough of this,' I said, pushing the fruit away from me. 'Is it yet time to leave?'

'Good idea,' said Burgess, adding, 'See you soon no doubt, Maclean.'

'Oh, you weren't joking about me not being invited then?' said Maclean.

'Not joking in the least,' said Burgess. 'Come on, Cyprian.'

I left the table feeling rather embarrassed by the way in which Burgess had spoken to Maclean, but he reassured me that Maclean would be fine, and in any case didn't really mind. We caught Blunt's eye as we were leaving and he gave a small nod from high table to the end that we would see him presently. It seemed that when Burgess wasn't drinking he was smoking, so we walked back out into the court for him to do so. It had grown dark, and lights had been switched on in most of the rooms around the court. The buildings appeared very attractive and, as we stood and talked, I sensed a rare moment of calm around Burgess. Perhaps it had been the effect of dinner, or just tiredness, but he was not quite his usual self.

'Are you quite all right?' I asked him.

'Yes, old man,' he said, 'quite all right, thanks; just a bit pensive that's all.'

'That's unlike you,' I said, not quite sure what the reaction would be.

'I was just thinking about what I said to Maclean at dinner,' said Burgess, 'about him not coming from the right college and all that.'

'What of it?' I asked. 'He seemed to take it in good spirits.'

'Oh yes, it's not him I'm thinking about,' he said, 'it's me.'

'In what way?' I said.

'I sounded like the very people I despise, old man,' said Burgess, 'and not just the people either, the whole system.'

'Really?' I said.

'Yes, do you remember that first afternoon last term when I took you punting?' he asked.

'Of course,' I said. 'I'll never forget it.'

'That's very sweet,' he said. 'Do you remember me saying that all of this,' he swept his arm across the court as he spoke, 'all of this must change?'

'Yes, but I didn't know what you meant,' I said. 'I still don't really, as a matter of fact.'

'What I meant was that at some point Cambridge will be swept away; well, perhaps not Cambridge, not if we can help it, but at the very least what it stands for,' he said.

'Do you really want that?' I asked.

'Part of me does and yet another part of me doesn't,' he said. 'I'm not sure whether to protect Cambridge and all it stands for or to undermine it.'

'What a predicament,' I said, still not quite grasping whether he was in a genuine dilemma or not.

'What I mean is,' he continued, 'that I think it may be under a terrible threat in any case.'

'Arising from what?' I asked.

'From nazism,' said Burgess bluntly.

'Ah,' I said, 'Blunt has the same idea.'

'I know,' said Burgess, 'that's where I got it from.'

We walked back to our rooms, being careful not to step on the lawns. Once inside, Burgess predictably went straight to the drinks cabinet.

'How about a drop of claret, old man?' he asked.

'Isn't it time for port?' I said.

'In normal circumstances it would be,' he said, 'but Blunt will be here soon and you will discover that these particular circumstances are far from customary.'

*

'Are you wrapped up warm enough?' said Michael.

'Yes thank you,' I said.

He had gently lowered me into a wheelchair. I had felt how powerful his arms were as he performed the duty and caught his scent owing to his proximity to me. It was the smell of a person without any kind of added pungency. It was his own smell, still clean but certainly of himself.

'Now, we can take a spin before dinner,' he said, sounding happier than before.

'I think we can leave the spinning out of it, if you don't mind,' I said warily. 'Just a quiet stroll will suffice.'

'I was only joking,' Michael said. 'I'll take care of you, don't worry.'

Michael pushed me along the corridor from my room. The world appears very different from a wheelchair and until you have been bound by one it is difficult to relay its impact on your own perspective and on those looking down at you. Things are lower and you pass them more slowly. It is not relaxing, as some of the nurses here joke sometimes. It is extremely stressful. There is helplessness unique to the experience that I do not enjoy. Indeed, it is one of the aspects of my present life that I actively look forward to leaving, when I do leave this life. Even with the knowledge of Michael behind me, I find the velocity dull and the embarrassment of my age almost too much to bear.

'Now, don't worry about what you look like, or how slowly we are moving,' said Michael.

'How did you know I was thinking either of those things?' I said, genuinely surprised at his perception.

'It's not just you that can observe detail, you know,' he said.

'Well, Michael,' I said, 'we are going to get along just fine if you keep that up.'

'I knew we would,' he said. 'There's something about you that I am drawn towards.'

'Now, be careful,' I said, 'you could get the sack for making comments like that.'

'Oh, I don't think so,' he said quickly. 'I only meant that you are interesting to talk with... what did you think I meant?' he asked.

'Oh nothing,' I said. 'Well, a kind of nothing anyway.'

As we moved round the garden I grew almost immediately tired. There was a time when I would have walked all over Cambridge for hours on end, sometimes with Burgess, more commonly with Turing. We would have discussed everything from Gödel's theories to the end of the world. It all mattered then. Now the only thing that mattered seemed to be finishing my writing, speaking to Michael and telling the truth. All three, it suddenly struck me, were one and the same.

'What did you do during the war?' asked Michael.

'Goodness me, what a question!' I exclaimed.

'Well, people my age should be interested,' he said.

'In principle I agree,' I said, 'but not all of us like to talk about it.'

'I saw something about it in your notebooks while you were asleep,' he said.

Again letting the intrusion go, I focused on the salient point. 'There's nothing in my notes specifically about the war,' I said.

'No, not the war itself,' he went on, 'more accurately, the years leading up to the war. You were very worried about Hitler, weren't you?'

'Well, only idiots were not,' I said. 'That hardly distinguishes me from most other reasonable people.'

'Fair enough,' said Michael, 'but what would you say does distinguish you then?' he asked.

'If you must know,' I said, 'it is probably that in actual fact I was not surrounded by reasonable people.'

*

'Pour the wine then,' I said to Burgess.

'Already onto it, old man,' he said.

There was a knock at the door, and Blunt entered before either of us could get to it.

'Good dinner, gentlemen?' he asked.

'Not bad,' I said. 'The sausages were decent enough, weren't they?'

'Indeed they were, Cyprian,' Burgess said, 'indeed they were.'

'Would you like a glass of claret?' Burgess said to Blunt.

'Well, you've twisted my arm, you scoundrel,' said Blunt. 'I need one in any case, in order to prepare for a toast.'

'A toast to what?' I asked.

Blunt took the glass of wine and motioned for the three of us to sit down. We did so and then he said, 'Listen, Cyprian, we've been watching you.' It was strange how he said it, almost ominous.

'We've noticed that you have potential,' Blunt continued, 'great potential.'

'To do what?' I asked.

'Not to do,' he said, 'but rather to become…'

This was said almost as though he were an actor on stage that had waited the whole play for his great utterance.

'All right then,' I said, 'to become what precisely?'

'I believe the time is right to ask him, don't you, Burgess?' Blunt said.

'Perfect,' said Burgess with a grin.

'Cyprian,' said Blunt, 'we would like you to join our society.'

'There are lots of societies in Cambridge,' I said, 'to which are you referring?'

'Oh you are right,' said Blunt, 'there are lots of societies, but there is only one that is truly worth joining.'

'And which would that be?' I asked.

'I, well, we,' he corrected himself, 'would like to invite you to become an Apostle.'

The room fell suddenly silent. I, of course, knew of the Apostles, even my parents had talked to me about them. I was aware that they considered themselves the ultimate intellects in Cambridge, and when checking once, to see some of the names that were known to have been Apostles, this rather self-assured reputation was supported by evidence. I had not considered myself to be destined to be amongst them.

'Why me?' I asked Blunt.

'It's as I say,' he continued, 'we think you have potential.'

'You mean becoming an Apostle does not mean I have achieved what you call my potential?' I asked rather incredulously.

'Not in the least,' he said, 'it's only the beginning.'

*

'Who were they then?' asked Michael. 'Who were these unreasonable people?'

'It's not that they were unreasonable as such,' I said. 'They just weren't reasonable either.'

'Now you're not making any sense,' he said.

'I am,' I said, 'but it's complicated. Even they didn't really know what they were doing.'

*

'So, a toast?' asked Blunt.

'Well, can I think about it?' I said.

'Absolutely not!' said Burgess. 'You must decide immediately, and we'll only ask this once.'

I looked at the two of them. They looked like conspirators of sorts, as if they were planning something. I moved round in my chair and took a sip of wine.

'So,' said Burgess, 'what'll it be? Do you want an ordinary life or the chance of an extraordinary one?'

'How could I choose the former?' I said with a smile.

'So there it is,' said Blunt. 'Welcome to the future.'

I cannot remember a smile of mine being at a more inappropriate moment than during that toast. I had agreed to become what they wanted me to be. The one other image going through my mind was of Turing, running aimlessly towards his own future. I wanted to run with him, but I had, or so I thought, made my choice.

'Now that is sorted,' said Blunt, 'there is someone else I want you to meet.'

'Who is that?' I said.

'Wait a minute,' said Blunt, and he went to the door of our rooms.

He shouted down the corridor for whoever was out there to come in, and a moment or two later in stepped a blond man who immediately filled the room with light. I had seen him around the college before, but he had never spoken to me further than good morning or good afternoon.

He walked up to me, as I stood up from the chair to greet him, and said in a soft Anglo-American accent, 'Cyprian, it's very good to finally meet. Blunt has told me a lot about you.'

'Really?' I asked, 'and you would be?'

'Michael,' he said, 'Michael Whitney Straight. Good to have the pleasure of your acquaintance.'

'Are you an Apostle too?' I asked.

'Yes, of course,' said Straight, 'and I never made a better decision than to join.'

'Quite right,' said Blunt.

'When did you come to England?' I asked Michael.

'Oh, years ago,' said Straight. 'I was at school here.'

'In London?' I asked.

'Oh no,' interrupted Blunt, 'Michael went to somewhere much more unusual than that.'

'Oh?' I asked.

'Well, yes,' said Straight. 'I was schooled, if you could call it that, at my mother's own school in Devon, Dartington Hall.'

'Good grief,' I exclaimed, 'I've heard my own mother talk about Dartington. She is an educationalist too, you know.'

'Really,' said Straight, 'and what is her view of Dartington?'

'I think she would summarise it as a madhouse,' I said, 'or perhaps more politely, a dangerous experiment.'

'Well, I sure walked into that one,' said Straight. 'You told me he was honest, Blunt.'

'Oh, I didn't mean to offend,' I said quickly.

'That's fine, Cyprian,' said Straight, 'but hey, maybe we should all go down there some time so you can make up your own mind?'

'I'd like that very much,' I said.

'Well, this isn't getting us anywhere,' said Burgess. 'What shall we discuss now our little embryo has become an Apostle?'

'How about the future of Europe?' asked Blunt.

'Ah,' said Burgess, 'I was thinking more along the lines of which wine would best follow this one,' he said, holding up the now empty bottle.

'How about both?' I said.

'The perfect compromise,' said Straight.

'Well, let's deal with the important things first,' said Blunt.

'I agree,' said Burgess. 'Do we move to Burgundy or shall we stay in Bordeaux?'

'Let's stay where we are,' I said.

'Good answer,' Straight said. 'At least we are remaining French. You can always rely on them.'

'Good god,' said Blunt, 'sometimes your American background betrays you.'

'I would never betray anyone,' said Straight, 'least of all you, my darling man.'

'Steady on, old chap,' said Burgess, 'he's spoken for, you know.'

'Oh, I know all right,' said Straight with a smile.

'Now boys, don't let's have a scene,' said Blunt. 'There's plenty for everyone... wine, of course.'

'Oh yes, the French,' I said quickly, glad of the opportunity to avoid what was clearly building towards a confrontation.

'What I was going to say,' said Blunt, 'is that you Americans don't understand the French.'

'Well, we don't like them any more than you British,' said Straight.

'That's not quite the same thing as understanding them,' said Blunt. 'The reason they frustrate me, for example, is that although I do not believe they would stand in Hitler's way, they are the brightest cultural light on the continent, and if that light ever went out it would be a disaster.'

'Surely Hitler doesn't have his eyes on France?' I asked. 'He only seems to wish to bring the German peoples together.'

'Indeed he does,' said Blunt, 'but why stop there? What if a unified German empire, once gorged on the defenceless states, decides to continue an expansionist policy? Where would their natural target be?'

'What about Britain?' said Straight.

'No, I think not,' said Blunt. 'It is my view that Hitler respects Britain, or at the very least our own Empire. I think he would prefer to control Britain by negotiation from a distance rather than directly attacking us.'

'Are you sure?' said Straight. 'What if Britain decided to place itself in harm's way by attacking Germany?'

'We would never be so reckless,' said Blunt.

'No,' said Burgess, 'we could never win.'

'Even that wouldn't be the purpose of it,' said Blunt. 'The only design Britain could have by attacking Germany at some point in the future would be to bring America into a war.'

'Well, there isn't a war,' I said.

'Not yet at any rate,' said Blunt, 'but there is one coming, that at least is certain.'

'How do you know?' I asked.

'I have my sources,' said Blunt, 'and I am reliably informed that the threat is real.'

'How enigmatic,' I said, 'and which are these sources that allow you to speak so confidently of the future?'

'Ah, well, that is why you have joined the Apostles, Cyprian,' said Blunt, 'that is the purpose of it all.'

We fell silent for a few moments. Burgess got up and put more wood on the fire that had been lit by the bedders while he had been at dinner.

'How about some music?' he said.

'Good idea,' said Straight. 'We should listen to jazz.'

'Certainly not,' said Blunt.

'How about Debussy?' I asked. 'Burgess, put on *Images Oubliées.*'

'The perfect choice, if I may say,' said Blunt.

'You may indeed,' I said, pleased to receive Blunt's approval.

'Why do you think it is the perfect choice?' asked Burgess.

'Well, we are discussing the French,' said Blunt.

'Yes?' asked Burgess.

'Well,' said Blunt, clearly a little frustrated that the choice was not immediately obvious to Burgess. '*Images oubliées* is Cyprian's contribution to our discussion, is it not, Cyprian?'

'Indeed it is,' I said.

'Meaning?' said Burgess.

'Meaning,' said Blunt exasperated, 'forgotten images – when France falls, and it will, that is what will be left.'

'France is too strong to fall, surely,' said Burgess.

'The opposite is true,' said Blunt. 'It is too strong, meaning proud, not to fall. France will not allow itself to be destroyed. It would rather capitulate than collapse.'

'Pure speculation,' said Burgess, dismissively.

'For the moment you are right,' said Blunt, 'for the moment you are right.'

'And if *you* are right,' asked Straight, 'how could Hitler be stopped?'

'There is only one force greater than nazism in Europe,' said Blunt.

'The British Empire?' I said, knowing this was wrong.

Blunt crossed his legs and sighed. 'If only that were true,' he said. 'If that were true I would support it, but regrettably it is pure poppycock.'

'Which force is it then?' I said.

'You know full well,' said Blunt.

*

'I'm getting a little cold,' I said to Michael. 'I think perhaps we should go back inside.'

'OK,' he said, and pushed me back towards the home.

'I wonder, were those men quite so unreasonable?' he asked.

'No,' I said, 'not unreasonable, just young.'

'Hey, don't be rude,' said Michael jokingly. 'I'm still young you know.'

'Oh, believe me, I know,' I said. 'You are very talented but you have a great deal to learn. We never stop learning.'

'Learn about what?' he asked.

'Well, me for a start,' I said, and then thought to say, 'If you're interested, of course?'

'Yes,' said Michael, 'I think I would be interested, yes. Where do we start?'

We got to the doors of the home and he pushed me through into the building. We moved slowly along the corridors. As we did so, I caught sight of other people's rooms. Some were empty, but others contained their aged cargo, waiting for shipment to another world. I wondered how many of these lives considered themselves fulfilled. Did all these previously busy people lie in bed now and remember their past as I was racing to do? Did they drift amongst time and beside the young dead as I do?

I have always been terrified of places like this. I have never been afraid to die. I fear for those whose lives contain no parallels, or are purely linear. Mathematics gives only the impression that there is a right answer. At a basic level this can be true. Two times two does not equal three hundred and sixty nine. Two times two results in four, everyone knows that, but at all other higher levels where mathematics meets philosophy the answers are less clear, they are clouded and debatable.

Instinct and opinion accompany any journey made in higher mathematics. It is where science shifts seamlessly, unnoticed like a hunting fox in the dark, into art. It is at this point where I have spent most of my life. Only at the most perplexing mental questions have I found something approaching happiness. All other discussion appears to my mind to be purposeless. At Cambridge, I have been fortunate to be surrounded by the few others on the planet who share this threshold between boredom and adventure.

Most people do not consider their lives beyond progress at work and procreation at play. This is not a broad enough expanse to hold me. I sojourn to collapsing universes too readily. I genuinely fear for the explosion of the sun.

I have always hidden myself to reflect on these things. I have laid myself down in hedgerows all my life, since that summer before going up. My own company has been precious, even as I enjoyed the company of other men, the company of wolves. The delicacy of rest, alone on a summer's afternoon with nothing but books and butterfly nets has sustained me to this point. It has enabled a survivor to tell a story. It has allowed me time to elaborate on other men's lives just before they become forgotten images.

Only I was there with that crowd. Only I truly saw the mistakes being made and the games being played. Only I witnessed so much being done out of love.

'We start as we left off,' I said to Michael, 'with love.'

'I didn't know old people talked so much of love,' he said.

'Of course we do,' I said sharply to him, 'it is all that is left of vanished people.'

He helped me into a chair, saying, 'There's no point you going back on the bed when it is almost time for dinner, now is there?'

'I suppose you are right,' I said.

'Are you looking forward to your meal? You've written a lot about food in your notes,' he said.

Yet again, choosing to forgive the intrusion, I responded, 'No, not really. I seem to have rather lost my appetite recently.'

'That's not like you,' said Michael.

I rephrased deliberately, 'That's not like me,' and then more thoughtfully, repeated it, 'That's not like me. What an odd thing it is to make a statement about oneself in such a way.'

'I think you must be getting tired,' said Michael. 'Perhaps you should have a rest before I take you down for dinner.'

'I don't want to go down for dinner,' I said. 'I just want to think.'

'Well, you've got to eat,' he said, 'otherwise it'll be me getting into trouble over it.'

'Oh well,' I said, 'we couldn't have that now, could we?'

'No,' he said, 'will you let me take you down later?'

'Would they allow you to bring a small sandwich up to me instead?' I asked.

'I don't know,' he said. 'If they do, what would you like in it?'

'Just lettuce, please,' I said.

'Are you sure?' he asked. 'Why just lettuce?'

'I had lettuce sandwiches once on a trip to Grantchester and I feel as though I should have them again.'

'You do live in the past, don't you Daniel?' said Michael.

'I don't live there, no,' I said, 'but it does haunt me.'

'Why so negative?' he asked. 'Surely you haven't lost as much as I have?'

'I have lost more than you realise,' I said.

*

After Blunt and Straight had left our rooms, I told Burgess I was going to go to bed. The conversation had been very draining and I felt I needed to rest, but as I lay there an immense loneliness swept over me. Perhaps the wine had affected me, but it seemed that Burgess was quite able to deal with the fact that Blunt and Straight were seeing one another. Burgess would always be all right, I told myself, and the other two, well, they had each other. As would become common throughout my life, I was left alone, and although I enjoyed the hedgerow I also had a need to feel someone else's skin.

I got up and dressed as quietly as I could, so as not to wake Burgess. As I passed his room I realised that would have been impossible. He was in a drunken slumber, a self-induced hiding place. I crept out into the court and round to the Great

Gate. The porter was also asleep, his feet resting up on a desk and his bowler hat over his face. I unhinged the lock and quietly slipped out, being careful to close the door in the massive gate without a sound.

Cambridge at night was a muffled, dimly lit and unmoving place. I knew where I needed to go. I walked along St. John's Street towards King's College. As I turned onto King's Parade I saw the great chapel foregrounding a half-moon. It was grey and tall, its flower-like masonry reached towards the sky, towards the heavens as intended. It struck me that if God ever died then this chapel would be the length of his coffin. He could rest here forever.

People would come from miles around to view the unchanging deity's body, lying cold in the cold stone. They would stand and wonder how such a thing could have happened and never realise that they were responsible for his death. Their continual questions had taken their final toll. The absence of courage in their firm disbelief gradually wore him down. Eventually, he could absorb no more hate, for that was what drove them. If they could only love him then they would also be required to love one another. This was too difficult for them, and so they chose hate. It was so much easier to hate and destroy, to build towers and make plans to wipe one another out. To make war.

I walked past the coffin of God and got to the last building facing the street. I knew that Turing's room had a view of the road, and I knew which one contained him. I took aim with a small stone and hit his window, not enough to break it but enough to wake him. After a moment he came to the window and opened it.

'I need to speak with you,' I whispered as clearly as I could. I closed my eyes next to his closing eyes.

*

Michael put his hand on my shoulder to wake me. I started a little and then regained my composure.

'I have lettuce sandwiches,' he said proudly. 'The kitchen didn't believe me that you had asked only for lettuce, so they put ham inside as well, but I took it out.'

'Thank you, Michael,' I said. 'That is just enough for me this evening. Would you like to stay while I eat them?'

'OK,' he said, 'but not for too long. I've got to be getting home.'

I took a bite from one of the sandwiches. It was good. I was the only person I knew now who still ate these; we all used to back then, especially on picnics. 'Will you be back tomorrow?' I asked him.

'Yes,' he said, 'I need the money for university.'

'Oh,' I said, obviously sounding a little disappointed.

'Well,' he said quickly, 'and also to see you, of course.'

'Thank you for thinking on your feet,' I said.

'In fact,' he went on, 'I have, in a way, been assigned to you.'

'What do you mean?' I asked him.

'Well, while everyone was having dinner we had a staff meeting, and discussed some of the patients who the doctors feel don't have,' and he stumbled, 'won't be…'

'You mean,' I said gently, 'don't have long to live.'

'Well, yes,' he said.

'And what was the upshot of this happy conversation?' I asked as brightly as I could manage.

'Well,' he went on, 'I didn't realise this, but the nurses were watching me with you today and before and they think I have formed a connection with you.'

'And what do you think?' I asked.

'Well, I think they're right, aren't they?' he said with a smile. 'We do seem to be getting along.'

'We do indeed,' I said. 'So what will this mean for our time together?'

'It'll mean there will be more of it, for one thing,' he said.

'Good,' I responded. 'I would like that.'

'I would like that too,' said Michael. 'I enjoy talking to you.'

We paused while I finished the sandwiches. I could hear distant sounds in the building. There were cries from some poor soul probably woken by their memories. Water was running somewhere. Kitchen sounds permeated beyond the others as the staff cleared up the dining things. Outside, a bird called plaintively in the darkness.

'Well, I really must be going,' said Michael.

'Oh dear,' I said, 'are you sure?'

'Absolutely,' he said. 'I need to go running.'

'Ah,' I said, 'the running.'

'Yes,' said Michael. 'It's better for both of us if I go running.'

'I'll see you tomorrow then?' I asked.

'I told you,' he said, 'you'll see me from now on.'

He collected my plate and left the room with a small wave. I sat back in the chair. Someone would come and help me into bed presently.

The explosion of the sun.

Certainty is a powerful force in mathematics. Its existence is debated now, amongst the theoreticians. I myself have always found it compelling and frightening. Certainty is perfect knowledge that has total security from error. It is a principle applied to numerical activity but also, in philosophy, it is given to mean a mental state that is completely without doubt.

There are those that believe a life without error is impossible and an absence of doubt is unwanted.

Wittgenstein asked why we fear contradictions.

At the end of this universe another will be born. Our greatest contradiction is that we continue despite such knowledge. Turing said that even in contradictions there is perfection. By looking no further than our own actions we are able to determine our fate.

Those we love exist in memory; we hold their image as we held their body. Loss is only so when it becomes an act of forgetting.

Remember him in the sunburst.

*

Six – Tangere

Maurice Dobb entered our Junior Combination Room without any warning. It was highly unusual for a don to do so, not least as it was relatively early in the morning. He appeared to be looking for something and quietly checked under tables and pulled the cushions away from the settees carefully.

'Can I be of assistance, sir?' I asked.

'Ah, Cyprian, isn't it?' he said.

'Indeed, sir,' I said. 'Are you looking for something?'

'Yes, Cyprian,' he said, 'a letter, as a matter of fact. I am sure I would find it in here.'

I ventured to find out more. 'A little unusual, isn't it, sir, for you to lose a letter in the JCR?'

He looked at me for a moment, as if to gauge whether or not to reproach me for what was a question bordering on insolence.

'Yes,' he said, 'it is a little unusual, but there you are.'

'When do you think you lost it?' I asked.

'Oh, a couple of evenings ago,' he said. 'I was in here gassing away with someone until quite late.'

'I'll help you,' I said.

'Em, all right then,' he said, and we both set to work. The JCR at Trinity is a large room with many armchairs and other pieces of furniture. I didn't tend to use it very often, preferring my own rooms with Burgess. However, luck was with me and I found a small white envelope beside a seat cushion, it having almost certainly fallen out during conversation.

'Is this it?' I asked him.

Dobb moved quickly towards me and took the letter from me. As he did so, I recognised the tall, elegant handwriting of Blunt.

'Yes, that's it, Cyprian,' he said, and making a curious small bow to me, promptly left the room.

'The most extraordinary thing occurred this morning,' I said to Burgess as we lounged later back in our rooms.

'Oh, do tell,' said Burgess, with only the faintest air of interest.

'I was in the JCR looking to see if the newspapers had been delivered and Maurice Dobb walked in, as bold as you like,' I said.

'Really?' said Burgess, suddenly more interested. 'What was a don doing in the JCR.'

'It's not what he was doing,' I said, 'but rather by implication what he *had* been doing.'

'Go on,' said Burgess.

'Well, he was looking for a letter,' I said, 'only it was me who found it. It was from Blunt.'

'How do you know?' asked Burgess.

'It was addressed in Blunt's handwriting,' I said. 'How else could I have known?'

'All right, all right,' said Burgess, 'no need to be touchy.'

'Sorry,' I said. 'I just found the whole thing a bit odd, that's all.'

'It's not odd,' said Burgess. 'Dobb is always losing things. Did you know he even lost his dining rights at his old college, Pembroke once?'

'Really?' I said. 'It's almost impossible to do that.'

'I know,' said Burgess. 'Something to do with his divorce at the time I think... and the other thing,' he said with a smile.

'What other thing?' I asked.

'Well, he rather took to Marxism,' said Burgess.

'That hardly distinguishes him around here,' I said light-heartedly.

'True,' said Burgess, 'but I mean he *really* took to it... never talked of anything else, apparently... even lost a lot of students because of it, I heard.'

'Crikey!' I said, 'and now he's at Trinity.'

'Well, yes,' said Burgess, 'slightly more acceptable here though, isn't it?'

'I suppose so,' I said, 'but saying that, what would be classed as unacceptable at Trinity?'

'Acceptance of the status quo,' said Burgess, suddenly more serious.

Burgess would often do that. He was known at Cambridge as someone who didn't take things too seriously, but I always thought that was some kind of cover. He genuinely did behave according to his own rules but that never seemed to be the whole of the man. He was a master joker and, as would appear to be the case with most clowns, the costume hid his private shadows.

'What do you think of him, anyway?' Burgess asked me.

'Who?' I replied.

'Dobb, of course,' he said.

'Oh I don't know,' I said. 'He seems a little strange.'

'In what way?' said Burgess.

'Well,' I continued, 'he looks to be the sort of chap who is a bit forgetful, absent-minded perhaps, but at the same time, very bright.'

'Again, not distinguishing features around here,' said Burgess.

'No, I suppose not,' I laughed, 'but there's more. This morning he appeared quite furtive. I mean, why didn't he wait until no one was in the JCR before looking for a private letter?'

'Maybe he couldn't take the risk of someone else finding it,' said Burgess.

'Well, someone would have stumbled on it eventually,' I said. 'It was only pure chance that I didn't choose that particular armchair,'

'Well, there you are,' he said, 'pure chance, an accident.'

'You know I don't believe in accidents, Burgess,' I said quickly.

'Oh yes,' he said, 'the great code of the mathematical philosophers.'

'Well, it's more a code of the Freudians,' I said, correcting him.

'You're not a Freudian!' exclaimed Burgess.

'I haven't decided yet,' I said. 'Not had enough experiences to edge me one way or another.'

'That's unfortunate,' said Burgess with a grin. 'Where were you this morning then? When I looked in your room it was empty.'

'Oh, I, er was out for an early morning walk,' I stumbled.

'Interesting,' said Burgess, 'I didn't hear you leave.'

'I was as quiet as a mouse,' I said. 'You wouldn't have heard me.'

We went down for lunch, which passed amiably enough. Dobb was at the high table with the other dons and as I caught his eye he gave me an almost imperceptible wave.

'You've caught his attention then,' said Burgess.

Following lunch I intended to spend some time alone before my lecture. I knew that I would see Turing again and I had to prepare myself for the event. As I crossed the court I almost bumped into Wittgenstein. He was with a student who he introduced as Francis Skinner. I had seen Skinner in lectures but, as Turing almost always dominated them, I had not taken a great deal of notice of him.

'Very good to meet you properly,' I said to Skinner politely.

'And you,' he said.

He stood very close to Wittgenstein who appeared not especially interested in talking to me.

'Are you coming to the lecture this afternoon?' Skinner asked me.

'Of course he is,' said Wittgenstein suddenly.

'I was planning to, yes,' I said, trying to stand my ground before Wittgenstein.

'I want to introduce you to Gödel,' pronounced Wittgenstein.

'Oh, I have already heard of him,' I said.

'Really?' he said. 'Francis, we have an expert amongst us.'

I thought it odd that he used Skinner's Christian name but let it pass.

'Yes,' I said, 'someone was talking to me about him last term.'

'Good,' said Wittgenstein, 'then you will be prepared for the lecture.'

'Well,' I said quickly, aware that I may be getting myself into hot water, 'I wouldn't claim to know a great deal.'

'How modest,' said Wittgenstein. 'I have never liked modesty, it seems so purposeless.'

Skinner smiled at me in the way that a man's wife might silently apologise for an inconsiderate remark made by her husband at a drinks party. A natural pause resulted from this comment and Wittgenstein took the opportunity to march away, with Skinner by his side.

*

'Good morning,' said Michael breezily.

'Is it?' I asked.

'It is,' he said. 'It's the kind of morning that lifts the heart.'

I thought this an unusual turn of phrase for someone so young, not least someone young and also unhappy.

'I'm glad you think so,' I said.

'I brought you some tea and toast,' said Michael, 'and you are to take both, nurse's orders.'

'All right,' I said, 'but I'm not my best in the mornings. You should know that by now.'

'I do,' he said, 'but even so, you need to have some breakfast.'

He pulled the sheet and blanket away from my body and lifted my legs to the floor. Even this simple movement was now causing me difficulty and Michael could see that this was the case. He stood back for a few seconds before coming towards me and with some skill, hooked one arm under my right side and, holding my back with his other hand, brought me to a standing position in one easy movement.

'Do you want your tea and toast first?' he asked.

'First before what?' I replied.

'Your bath,' he said.

'Oh god, I haven't time for that sort of thing,' I muttered, 'far too much to do.'

'I'm afraid I'm leaving you no choice,' he said.

'Well, in that case I'll have my breakfast,' I said, secretly hoping such a stalling tactic would mean he would forget about the bath.

He handed me my walking stick and I moved slowly over to my desk, where he had cleared a small area of papers for my cup and plate. Even as a young man I had imagined such a scene. I had known for years that I would be left with more in my mind than in my possession. Indeed, it might be said that I had planned for it to be so. Many of my friends had been afraid of ending their lives in this way. They could not reconcile a life of acquisition with its simple closure.

I had nothing more than was in this room. I needed nothing more, for my mind was calm. I had spent years studying the foundations of the world in numerical form and applying such calculations to fundamentals of the human mind. There is a direct link between the inquiry of higher mathematics and the investigation of happiness, or perhaps even beyond that to contentment.

My father and mother, in their different ways, both firmly believed they had discovered a purpose to their existences. Mother drew all her energy from the conviction that education above all could provide a chance for personal joy. She was right. Father took the view that the church offered such fortuity. In his eyes, only God could, or indeed should, be in a position to deliver such a life.

I took a sip of tea and looked at Michael. He was sitting in the armchair looking out of the window.

In my case, I had taken something from each of my parents. I had spent a life in education, albeit a comparatively comfortable version of my vocation. From my father I learned discipline. I, of course, rejected his monotheistic view of earth and its inhabitants, but the strength of character it required of him to hold such a view manifested itself in me as a continual search for truth.

The search itself is its own truth.

'Can I ask you a question, Michael?' I said, slightly startling him.

'Yes, of course,' he said.

'Have you heard of Pyrrhonism?' I said.

'No, it sounds like a disease,' he joked.

'It is quite the opposite,' I said. 'I discovered it as a young man and it gave great purpose to my mathematical studies.'

'What is it?' he asked.

'It is a form of philosophical scepticism,' I said. 'It means that those who practise Pyrrhonism avoid making truth claims, or similar definitive statements.'

'I thought you were attracted by the idea of truth,' said Michael.

'I am,' I said. 'For instance I do not say that truth is impossible to attain either, as that in itself would be a truth claim.'

'So where does that leave you?' he asked.

'It may appear that it leaves me stranded,' I said.

'That thought crossed my mind, I must admit,' said Michael.

'Ah, my dear boy, that is where you are wrong,' I said.

'Go on,' said Michael.

'If you follow a Pyrrhonist path in life then you spend that life avoiding dogma,' I said. 'In fact, even the statement that nothing can be known is too dogmatic in itself.'

'Aren't these just all contradictions?' asked Michael.

'Precisely,' I said, 'and wonderful ones at that.'

'So what is the result of Pyrrhonism?' he said. 'It sounds as though you do nothing more than sit on the fence.'

'An interesting interpretation of it,' I said, 'but that would not be enough.'

I pushed my chair round from the desk so that I could see him more clearly and he seemed to relax a little in the armchair.

'What do you desire?' I asked him.

'For the pain to disappear and not to be alone,' he said.

'At the edge of the cliff?' I asked him.

'Yes,' he said, 'if you want to put it like that.'

'Well, you see,' I said, 'those very desires are making it more difficult for you to live. You only perceive that upon attaining them you would be happy.'

'Isn't that natural?' he asked.

'It appears so, but it is not true,' I said. 'For example, the judgement you make regarding your state of being alone results in a desire not to be, which in turn results in disappointment and ultimately, unhappiness.'

'But how could I ever stop thinking like that?' he asked. 'I mean, I can't help feeling lonely.'

'It is precisely what you call *feeling* that is propelling the vicious circle,' I said. 'You need to stop comparing being alone with not being alone; after all, your views on this will change over time anyway.'

'How do you know?' he asked.

'Which one of us is closer to death?' I said.

'According to the nurses, you are,' he said, 'but sometimes I'm not so sure.'

'I believe you,' I said, 'but you need to consider the possibility that tranquillity, or indifference to put it more coldly, is only achievable by not making judgements one way or the other.'

'In other words?' Michael asked.

'In other words,' I said, 'the only way to be a whole person is to hold both sides of every desire at the same time. Within this contradiction lies ataraxia.'

'And what is ataraxia?' he asked.

'It is the state of mental imperturbability,' I said.

'Is there a simpler way of thinking about this?' asked Michael.

'No,' I said, 'but you still need to think about it.'

'OK,' he said, 'I'll make a deal with you.'

'All right,' I said, 'what's the deal?'

'I will think about attaining ataraxia if you agree to come for a bath,' he said with a smile.

I have always loved bathing outside, this deriving quite clearly in my mind to the book Burgess asked me about all those years ago, Forster's *A Room with a View*. I have never been overly fond of indoor baths, and I had the added indignity of being unable to perform the rite by myself any more.

Michael pushed me down the corridor to one of the large, uncomfortable bathrooms here. I know they are required to be easy to clean, but it is like taking a bath in a mortuary, you might as well already be dead. He stood me up and began to undress me in silence. He was careful to remain professional of course, but I could sense he felt it to be more potent an activity than it may have been with other residents.

He rolled up his sleeves as I now stood naked before him and swung the chair over the bath towards my body. He took my arms and gently lowered me into it before winding the mechanism to raise me above the lip of the bath. Then, as I hung above the water he slowly released the cords and I descended into the water. It was warm as his strong hands moved across my body.

I recollected the hands of others, all now turned to dust.

*

I held Turing's hand in secret beneath the desk in the lecture theatre as Wittgenstein began his lecture.

'The purpose of mathematics,' he said, 'is purely to determine the truth or falsity of propositions.'

'I disagree,' said Turing, letting go of my hand.

'Imagine my surprise,' said Wittgenstein, 'Turing has a differing opinion. So what is missing from my opening statement?' he asked.

'Mathematical reasoning may be regarded rather schematically as the combination of two faculties, which we may call intuition and ingenuity,' said Turing. 'The activity of the intuition consists in making spontaneous judgements that are not the result of conscious trains of reasoning.'

'Ah, intuition,' said Wittgenstein, 'the great friend of the fluid thinker.'

'Are you not a fluid thinker?' asked Turing.

'Absolutely not,' said Wittgenstein. 'I think in sequence, from one statement to the next. I do not jump around using intuition.'

'Then you may be making a mistake,' said Turing. 'These spontaneous judgements are often but by no means invariably correct, leaving aside, of course, the question what is meant by the word correct.'

'Continue,' said Wittgenstein, sharply.

'Often it is possible to find some other way of verifying the correctness of an intuitive judgement,' said Turing. 'We may, for instance, judge that all positive integers are uniquely factorable into primes; a detailed mathematical argument leads to the same result. This argument will also involve intuitive judgements, but they will be less open to criticism than the original judgement about factorisation.'

'And how does this contribute to our debate on intuition?' asked Wittgenstein.

'I shall not attempt to explain intuition any more explicitly,' said Turing.

'I'm not asking you to explain it,' said Wittgenstein, 'merely to elaborate.'

Turing paused and shuffled in his seat. I could see Skinner looking at us in a less than friendly manner from across the room.

'The exercise of ingenuity in mathematics,' said Turing, 'consists in aiding the intuition through suitable arrangements of propositions, and perhaps geometrical figures or drawings.' He continued in a slightly raised voice. 'It is intended that when these are really well arranged the validity of the intuitive steps that are required cannot seriously be doubted.'

'And what about Gödel?' asked Wittgenstein, 'or am I being too presumptuous in straying close to the intended topic of this lecture?'

'Gödel is indeed very interesting,' said Turing. 'The axiomatisation of mathematics was originally intended to eliminate all intuition, but Gödel has recently shown that to be impossible.'

'Indeed,' said Wittgenstein, turning to the whole class. 'Gentlemen, Gödel had shown that when we see the truth of an unprovable proposition, we cannot be doing so by following given rules. The rules may be augmented so as to bring this particular proposition into their ambit, but then there will be yet another true proposition that is not captured by the new rules of proof, and so on ad infinitum.'

'So what is the question?' said Skinner, suddenly, from the other side of the room.

'The question,' said Turing, 'is whether there is some higher type of rule that can organise this process.'

'And there is such a rule,' said Wittgenstein.

'To an extent,' Turing said quickly. 'An ordinal logic is such a rule, based on the theory of ordinal numbers, in which an infinite number of entities may be placed in sequence.'

'Correct,' said Wittgenstein. 'If Turing doesn't object to me using such a word?' he asked sarcastically.

'Not at all,' said Turing.

'An ordinal logic,' continued Wittgenstein, 'turns the idea of ad infinitum into a precise formulation.'

'Indeed,' said Turing, 'the purpose of introducing ordinal logics is to avoid as far as possible the effects of Gödel's theorem. The uncomputable could not be made computable, but ordinal logics would bring it into as much order as may be possible.'

'And what place does intuition hold in such a process?' asked Wittgenstein.

'I think,' started Turing, and then in almost a single breath said, 'the impossibility of finding a formal logic that wholly eliminates the necessity of using intuition, means we naturally turn to non-constructive systems of logic with which not all the steps in a proof are mechanical, some being intuitive. An example of a non-constructive logic is afforded by any ordinal logic... What properties do we desire a non-constructive logic to have if we are to make use of it for the expression of mathematical proofs? We want it to show quite clearly when a step makes use of intuition, and when it is purely formal. The strain put on the intuition should be a minimum. Most important of all, it must be beyond doubt that the logic shall be adequate for the expression of number-theoretic theorems.'

It was clear that Wittgenstein was, perhaps finally, impressed by this answer. He coughed slightly and then asked,

'You mean to say, as Gödel does, that not all calculations can be performed by mechanical processes?'

'Not yet,' said Turing.

*

It was one of those late winter days where the sky was beginning to turn towards spring. Grey light was gradually being replaced by white or yellow and the city reflected this change. The gravestone colour of Cambridge during the winter, iced with frost and creaking as the sun rose, was shifting towards its summer coat. This would eventually turn the city gold again, the trees bright green, the river dark blue and the low lines of the entire county would again make it hard to distinguish land from sky across the fens.

As I have spent my entire life in this place, my only comparator images have been obtained from visits away. I have never lived anywhere else for long enough to watch how other cities alter with the seasons, but I suspect that owing to the strange light of this low, flat part of England they do not change as Cambridge does. Nothing protects the city from winds that originate in Russia.

It was becoming a little warmer though and I could sense the opportunity we all waited for, like a bird flock waiting to leap into the air in migration. The chains were being pulled from the punts. All winter they had been strung together in the mist and ice, like long ebbing bodies captured by the cold. I have, in fact, always loved looking at punts in winter. They sleep deeply, far from the rush of visiting crowds or released students. They hibernate like most river animals, not snugly but certainly safe. They rest in the reeds and snowfalls during grey days and knife-cold nights.

They too wait for us, I think. Once the resting is done they are ready for jumping bodies and spilt drinks. There is no longer an ice layer across their decks in the mornings and as the boys pulled the chains apart, we all waited for our chance to drift along the Backs.

'Come on,' said Burgess, 'we'll be the first in the water.'

'I don't think so,' I said, 'look over there,' and I pointed to a punt that had already moved down towards King's.

'Who is that?' he asked, obviously annoyed in a childish manner.

'I can't see from here,' I said.

'Well,' he said, 'come on, we'll catch them up.'

It had been many months since that first day, my first day at Cambridge indeed, that Burgess and I had stepped into a punt. He was full of excitement, just as he had been then.

'We'll at least be the first to get to the Mathematical Bridge,' he said.

'You'll have to put your back into it to do that,' I said.

'Just watch this,' he said, taking a swift gulp of something from a hip flask.

'All right, but don't be daft,' I said.

'Cyprian, when have you ever known me to act in a daft fashion,' Burgess said, feigning hurt feelings.

'God help us all,' I said, as we pushed off into the middle river. Burgess turned the punt expertly to place himself at the back in terms of direction and we were quickly moving through the water. It was actually a little colder on the river, so I decided against allowing my hands to run in the water as

I would in the summer months. Instead I kept my eyes on the punt ahead of us. As we came towards Clare College Bridge I shouted up to them, 'Hello, you're the first on the river!'

'Hello!' a familiar voice shouted back.

'Good god, it's Blunt and that damned American,' said Burgess. 'How did they get out here before us?'

'They only just beat us,' I said. 'It doesn't matter.'

'Well, it matters to me,' said Burgess. 'Straight is in danger of getting on my nerves.'

'Why?' I asked. 'Just because he's managed to beat you onto the river?'

'No,' said Burgess, 'it's more than that; it's the fact that he's done it with Blunt in the boat.'

'Why shouldn't he?' I said, a little surprised at Burgess's veer towards jealousy, which was not a characteristic he displayed often.

'*He* knows why he shouldn't,' said Burgess.

We came alongside their boat at King's College Bridge and went quickly past them. I shouted across in an attempt to dispel any awkwardness. 'We'll see you at The Anchor!' I said.

'Who said I wanted to drink with them?' asked Burgess.

'Don't be ridiculous,' I said. 'You do really, and you'll enjoy it.'

We passed under the Mathematical Bridge at Queen's College, with Blunt and Straight not far behind us. Blunt was clearly annoyed to have lost what had, perhaps inevitably, become a race. For a man of what I would consider higher intellect he was remarkably competitive, not that such people should shun the baser urges, of course, but in Cambridge there was a divide between those who cared about racing boats and those of us who, aside from petty but justifiable rivalry with Oxford, liked to consider ourselves above such things.

We pulled in just under Silver Street Bridge, which was being rebuilt to a new design.

'Over here!' I shouted to Blunt, who waved as he and Straight too got out of their punt.

'Well done for being first on the river,' I said to Blunt, as he walked up to me.

'Yes,' said Burgess sarcastically, 'well done.'

'Oh, dear boy,' said Blunt, 'don't be sore. Let me buy you a drink.'

This seemed, at least for the moment, to do the trick and we all went into The Anchor, the tiered public house hanging over the river. It was warm inside and fires had been lit on each level.

'I'll get these in, gentlemen,' said Straight. 'What'll you have?'

'Just wine,' said Blunt.

'Not for me,' said Burgess. 'I'll have a stout.'

'Cyprian, what can I get for you?' asked Straight.

Considering the atmosphere in the room, I could sense that Burgess would regard my decision as taking sides, so in order to attempt a balance I asked for a pint of stout as well, even though personally I would have preferred wine. Burgess smiled and I knew I had made the right decision.

When Straight returned with the drinks I said to him, 'What do you think of the Mathematical Bridge, Straight?'

'Oh, you mean that old wooden one?' he asked.

'Well, actually,' I said, 'it's not that old: that version was completed in 1905.'

'Oh,' said Straight, 'I thought it was much older than that.'

'It was, originally,' I said. 'The first one was built as a bet in 1749.'

'And doesn't it stand without nuts and bolts?' asked Burgess.

'A popular myth,' interjected Blunt.

'He's right, unfortunately,' I said. 'The original had hidden spikes driven into the wood but there is one unusual characteristic.'

'Oh?' asked Burgess.

'Indeed,' said Blunt, 'all the struts are straight lines, even though they create a curve. It's a masterpiece in tangents.'

'I keep forgetting you studied mathematics, Blunt,' I said.

'Yes,' he said, 'I'm not all about art, you know.'

'Well,' I said, 'Blunt is right, it is all about tangents.'

'Do explain,' said Straight.

'Oh god no,' said Burgess.

'Shut up Burgess,' said Blunt. 'You may actually learn something.'

Burgess looked angrily at Blunt. 'I know all I need to know,' he said.

'You most certainly do not,' said Blunt. 'Go on, Cyprian.'

I moved my pint glass into the centre of the table so as not to knock it over. 'Well,' I said, 'the arrangement of timbers is a series of tangents that describe the arc of the bridge, with radial members to tie the tangents together and triangulate the structure, making it rigid.'

'Fascinating,' said Burgess with a grin.

'Actually,' said Blunt, 'it is. Tell him what a tangent is, Cyprian,' he said, obviously enjoying making Burgess feel awkward, perhaps a little too much.

I went on, speaking as quickly as I could so as not to be interrupted by Burgess. 'The tangent line to a plane curve at a given point is the straight line that just touches the curve at that point. Informally, it is a line through a pair of infinitely close points on the curve.'

I paused to see how I was doing, but no one said anything. 'More precisely,' I continued, 'a straight line is said to be a tangent of a curve $y = f(x)$ at a point $x = c$ on the curve if the line passes through the point $(c, f(c))$ on the curve and has slope $f'(c)$ where f is the derivative of f.'

'I don't think I quite follow you,' said Burgess.

'I think I know where he is going with this,' said Blunt. 'Do go on, old man.'

'Thank you,' I said. 'You will see a purpose in this, even in that bridge, in a moment, Burgess.'

'You mean other than to walk from one side of Queen's to the other?' he said acerbically.

'Yes,' I said. 'Now listen.'

'Noah Webster in 1828 defined a tangent as a right line that touches a curve, but which when produced, does not cut it.'

'Meaning?' asked Straight.

'Meaning that a tangent only touches a curve at a single point,' I said. 'The Mathematical Bridge has only one curve but many tangents, which by careful placing actually create the curve.'

'So the beauty is in the touching,' said Blunt.

'Yes,' I said. 'The intuitive notion that a tangent line touches a curve can be made more explicit by considering the sequence of straight lines passing through two points, A and B, those that lie on the function curve, or in the case of the bridge, the bridge's structure and therefore purpose itself.'

'I still can't see the beauty in this,' said Burgess.

'You will,' I said. 'The principles that built the bridge, or rather those that maintain its structure, are the same as the forces that hold our bodies together.'

'But we aren't formed by lines,' said Burgess. 'Even if they create curves, surely we are made of as many circles.'

'Oh, you are listening after all,' I said. 'Well, you are right, of course, but let me explain. As it passes through the point where the tangent line and the curve meet, called the point of tangency, the tangent line is going in the same direction as the curve, and is therefore the best straight-line approximation to the curve at that point.'

'You've lost me again,' said Burgess.

'He means,' said Blunt, 'that we often denote the n-dimensional Euclidean space if we wish to emphasise its Euclidean nature. Euclidean spaces have finite dimension.'

'Oh, that's a great help,' said Burgess.

'What's Euclidean space?' asked Straight.

'It's three-dimensional, effectively,' I said, 'as with the bridge, and for a long time we understood that only that kind of space existed.'

'There are others?' asked Straight.

'Oh yes,' I said, 'many others, but the most important one most recently accepted is Einstein's general theory of relativity.'

'Why?' said Burgess.

'One way to think of the Euclidean plane,' I said, 'is as a set of points satisfying certain relationships, expressible in terms of distance and angle. For example, there are two fundamental operations on the plane. One is translation, which means a shifting of the plane so that every point is shifted in the same direction and by the same distance. The other is rotation about a fixed point in the plane, in which every point in the plane turns about that fixed point through the same angle.'

'I couldn't have put it more clearly myself,' said Blunt. 'Go on, Cyprian.'

'One of the basic tenets of Euclidean geometry,' I said, 'is that two figures of the plane should be considered equivalent if one can be transformed into the other by some sequence of translations, rotations and reflections.'

'I need another drink,' said Straight, and he got up to go back to the bar. I thought Burgess would take the opportunity to go with him, but instead he took his seat next to Blunt. Blunt didn't comment on this but instead asked me to continue.

'I don't know that there's a great deal more to say,' I said.

'Are you sure?' asked Blunt. 'You mentioned relativity?'

'Oh, I think that might be a bit complicated for the pub,' I said.

'*That* might be!' said Burgess. 'And what was the rest of it, child's play?'

'Well,' I said, 'to be honest, yes, Euclidean geometry is fairly standard stuff.'

'Maybe to you it is,' said Burgess, 'but wait a moment, didn't you say something about beauty?'

Straight had returned with the drinks and cast Burgess a look for sitting in his seat. Burgess barely noticed and didn't move in any case.

'Well, it means coming back to tangents,' I said. 'The forces that hold the bridge up are Newtonian...'

'At last,' said Burgess, 'you mean the falling apple at the college?'

'Allegedly that did happen at Trinity, yes,' I said, and continued, 'The force of gravity and the rest of it, but these are different from space, where time and distance are now known to operate outside of these rules, thanks to the work of Professor Einstein.'

'So what?' said Burgess.

'Well,' I said, 'this means that the Euclidean laws of space are different from those that fundamentally form space itself and by default time. However, the role of tangents only applies to the former.'

'He means,' said Blunt, 'that straight lines enable us to create the known world, but different worlds exist at the same time.'

'Quite,' I said. 'Everything we see is geometry but what is happening around it redefines even the idea of time.'

'Or existence,' said Blunt.

'Yes,' I said. 'If Euclid and Einstein can both be right, then what occurs beyond us may also occur within us.'

'A soul,' said Burgess, quietly.

'Yes,' I said, 'a soul; and not only that but, as with the Mathematical Bridge existing in a universe constructed of contradictory rules, the idea of tangents becomes even more powerful.'

'Why?' asked Straight.

'The clue is in the name,' I said. 'Tangent comes from the Latin verb, *tangere*, which can mean to touch, or in the second-person singular present passive imperative, also means to be moved or to elicit an emotional response.'

'Well, even I can follow that,' said Burgess. 'You mean love, don't you?'

'I do indeed,' I said. 'The Mathematical Bridge and its tangents are geometrical proof that when you, who are made of the same forms but exist in differential space, touch the person you love you are also touching one another's soul.'

I have had so many similar conversations in Cambridge over the years that I suppose I have grown to thinking that they are ordinary occurrences. It has never crossed my mind that we, even as young men, were spending our time on the profound. The philosophical to us was as prized as politics. It was a battle to be fought and a problem to be understood.

As many then were drawing lines between worldviews, we were using our time and education to build theories of whole worlds, so placing our own worldviews in perspective, or so we thought. I cannot think now that this was the most constructive way to come to conclusions about things we did not really understand. Certainly, it entertained us to play verbal games and to leap from love to bridges, from souls to black holes, from geometry to fascism, but perhaps that was the problem. The lightness of our intensity betrayed us from the start. We were never in a position to make the judgements we made.

In the whirlwind of such conversations, no one could hear the alarms.

*

When we went back into the room the sun was streaming through the window. I will admit to feeling cleaner, more comfortable following the bath. Michael said that as a reward he would attempt to raid the kitchen for a more interesting selection of biscuits than I would normally be offered over mid-morning tea. While he was gone, I sat in the armchair and looked beyond this place to the Cambridgeshire countryside. I thought about horizons.

Einstein had established the basis of the idea of the event horizon, the point beyond which events are unable to affect the outside observer, in other words, the point of no return. I considered the role of observer I had so carefully designed for myself during those early years at Cambridge.

'What are you thinking about?' asked Michael as he came back into the room.

'Oh, just mathematics,' I said.

'Aren't you going to tell me about it?' he asked. 'I'd love to know; it might give me a head start when I go up.'

'It might indeed,' I said, 'but you need to understand that mathematics is not in itself a pursuit; it is always a description, or a recorded example of real things, true events.'

'True events?' said Michael. 'Surely there is no other kind of event? By implication, they have to have happened to be an event.'

'Oh no,' I said. 'For example, hardly any stories are entirely made of true events alone; exaggeration is a kind of truth.'

'I'm not sure,' he said.

'You will be,' I said. 'I will show you some time.'

'OK,' he said, 'but tell me what you were thinking about just then.'

'I was thinking about horizons; well, to be more specific, event horizons,' I said.

'You mean relativity?' he asked.

'Very good,' I said. 'Yes, relativity; you have been studying hard.'

'I told you I had, with Christian,' he said.

'Indeed,' I said. 'Well, you'll know then that if you move towards a black hole there is a point, the point of no return, before which you can remain an observer of the darkness.'

'Yes,' he said.

'And beyond that,' I continued, 'if you cross that line all the rules change in terms of space and time. You cease to be an observer and become implicated. Moving into the black hole becomes as inevitable as moving forwards in time.'

'I didn't know that,' said Michael, 'but why were you thinking about black holes just after we've talked about ataraxia? One seems filled with fear and the other contentment.'

'You must always be aware of both, Michael,' I said. 'It is not enough to simply ignore fear in the hope that it will go away.'

'Out of sight, out of mind,' said Michael.

'That has never made any sense,' I said. 'Dangers can exist beyond sight and mind.'

'The event horizon,' he said.

'Yes,' I said, 'we can see it and can imagine it, but it is there always whether we are doing so or not. It is the point at which an observer becomes part of the darkness.'

'How would you know when you have crossed the line?' asked Michael.

'It is impossible to know,' I said. 'You wouldn't feel anything but your world would have changed. You would be out of time.'

'So the danger is in not observing?' he said.

'Yes,' I said, 'but there might be one benefit to crossing the event horizon.'

'Really?' said Michael. 'Surely you would be lost?'

Michael stood and considered this and then poured the tea. He brought it across to me and as he put the cup down on the table his arm brushed mine, two tangent planes meeting at only one point. *Tangere.*

'Being lost is only another way of seeing where you are,' I said. 'Beyond the event horizon anything can happen at any time, in any order.'

I have seen this happen. I have been an observer of those who fell beyond the horizon. They were so determined to be right, to be saved, to be together, that they didn't even notice the darkness.

I watched them but they were beyond me.

In darkness there is no light.

*

Angel
Easter

Seven – Icarus

The Easter term at Cambridge is no less intense than the other two, but as summer is almost visible it gives a sense that one should begin to look beyond the city. We had been planning a trip to London and another, an invitation from Straight to Devon, before the break. I could not have known that Blunt intended to connect them.

'Cyprian,' said Blunt, 'it is time I showed you that painting I mentioned earlier in the year.'

'Oh, by Poussin?' I asked, '*Dance…*' I started to say before he interrupted me.

'*Dance to the Music of Time*,' said Blunt, with a theatrical wave of his arm up towards the ceiling, 'the greatest painting I know by the finest artist I know.'

'I'd like to see it,' I said, 'and, for that matter, I'd like to go to London too.'

'And you shall, dear boy,' he said. 'There's someone I'd be keen for you to meet, a very interesting man indeed.'

'Oh?' I said. 'Who would that be?'

'Oh, his name is Otto, but all in good time,' said Blunt, 'all in good time.'

'Will we see some of the marches too?' I asked him.

'Oh, you've not forgotten Mosley,' he said.

'Not at all,' I said. 'I was very struck by what you told me last term.'

'Indeed,' said Blunt, 'all is not good on this sceptred isle...' and he deliberately exaggerated a slouching motion in his chair.

Straight came into the room and sat down with us, pouring tea almost in the same motion.

'Hello, you two,' he said, 'making plans?'

'Yes,' I said, 'Blunt is going to take me to London to see a Poussin he admires.'

'Oh, I expect he'll be showing you more than that,' said Straight, with a small smile.

'Really?' I asked, 'and what might that be?' I said, trying to appear innocent.

'Don't worry, Cyprian,' said Blunt, 'Straight is fully aware of who I want you to meet.'

'Oh,' I said, 'sounds like a conspiracy,' and I laughed. Neither of them followed, but instead looked at me quite seriously.

'I think you should prepare yourself for a grilling,' said Straight. 'Otto does not take to frivolity.'

'Oh, doesn't he?' I said. 'And what if I don't take to people who don't take to frivolity?'

'Now, now,' said Blunt, 'we must all be perfectly civil. Otto is an important man though, Cyprian. You must treat him with respect.'

'Why?' I asked.

'Well,' said Blunt, 'from what he has told me, he seems to be very well connected for one thing.'

'To whom?' I asked.

'To be perfectly honest,' said Blunt, 'I am not entirely sure, but it seems a lot more exciting than Cambridge dons; well, with one exception.'

'Wittgenstein?' I said.

'All right, two exceptions,' said Blunt.

'Well, who then?' I asked.

'Maurice Dobb,' said Blunt. 'He might not be exceptional, but he is an exception to my rule about having interesting connections; in fact, it was Dobb who put me in touch with Otto.'

'I was going to ask you something about Dobb last term, in actual fact,' I said.

'Mmm?' mumbled Blunt, not appearing to be particularly interested.

'I found a letter from you; well, he found it with me… in the JCR,' I said.

Blunt suddenly became more animated. 'What were you doing reading my letters?' he asked in an aggressive tone.

'I didn't read it,' I said, 'I just handed it to Dobb. I just thought it odd that he should have come looking for it in the JCR, that's all.'

'Leave him alone,' said Straight.

'Well, OK,' said Blunt, 'as long as you can assure me that you did not read that letter.'

'I didn't,' I said. 'I would never do something like that. I only saw your handwriting on the envelope.'

'No,' said Blunt, slightly more kindly, 'I genuinely believe that you wouldn't. Fine, we'll leave it like that. I still want to take you to London though.'

'Of course,' I said, 'and I still want to go.'

'Well, I'll make the arrangements then,' said Blunt. 'We needn't stay; we'll go there and back on the train.'

'And am I invited this time?' asked Straight.

'No, darling,' said Blunt, 'I want to take Cyprian by myself.'

'Oh well, just make sure he behaves himself,' said Straight to me whilst gesturing to Blunt.

'I'm sure I can't guarantee that,' I said.

'You most certainly cannot,' said Blunt.

We sat for a few moments in silence, something that only happened when Burgess was not around. It was a pleasant morning. The trees were already beginning to open to the sun and this seemed to be encouraging the birds, which sang almost incessantly across the college court. I could hear a clock ticking in the hallway beyond the room in which we were sitting. As we three sat and thought, a member of college staff came in to reset the fire from the previous evening. It was bright but still not warm outside so the warming routine of the fires continued.

The clock was not only emitting a ticking sound but also, I suspect, its pendulum action was in some way slightly moving the whole device against the wood-panelled wall against which it was stood. This created a slight thudding sound in time with the tick that had a mildly soporific effect on the mind. Cambridge can produce an equal sense of great movement and inertia at the same time. I have always been fascinated by this tension, as though time were passing but also static. In terms of physics, the whole city might be regarded as an event horizon, judged neither to be in stasis or making progress.

I looked across at Blunt and Straight who were both now reading the morning papers, which had been brought in by another member of staff. Straight was flicking quickly through the pages, but Blunt turned them slowly, reading each one intently. I sat and thought of Maclean and Philby, neither of whom I was seeing a great deal of during that time.

After initial introductions, and a very memorable time earlier in the year at Grantchester, I felt I was in some way being kept separate from Philby. He hadn't seemed to mix in quite the same way as the others in any case. Maclean was at a different college and his own manner seemed less amenable to those of Burgess and Blunt. Indeed, had Straight not come onto the scene I wondered if I would be meeting many others, and then the answer suddenly came to me: Blunt and Burgess had always seen me as Apostle material. They saw Straight in the same light. Philby had not been invited to become a member and Maclean could not be one. I happened to know there were others, but had not yet met them.

Blunt stirred from his paper. 'Cyprian, when we go to London I want you to promise me something.'

'Of course,' I said.

'I don't want you talking to anyone about who we meet,' he said.

'Fine by me,' I said. 'Who would I talk to anyway?'

'That young Turing of yours,' he said. 'I've seen the way he looks at you.'

'I can't think what you mean,' I said, genuinely taken aback at his perception.

'I think you know precisely what I mean,' he said.

'Oh, leave him alone,' said Straight, 'he'll be fine. Just show him your precious painting.'

They returned to their papers and I to my thoughts. Blunt did have an uncanny ability to know what I was doing. It was almost as though he was following me, but I could not see how this would be possible. The only real link between us was Burgess, and although he and I shared rooms, I didn't think that amongst all the tomfoolery and the drinking that Burgess would make a very good reconnoiterer.

*

I looked across my desk. It was now almost covered in notes for my last book and in formulae I was using whimsically to provide something different for my mind to do. The papers were not scattered so much as overlapping in low piles. I worked from paper to the computer much as I had done for the last few years. I brought together ideas about what I should say, or what I could remember by drawing them into shapes onto the paper. I could see, by this process, that my memory was a pleasing multi-layered form of expression. It did not matter to me that my friends would not have corroborated some of the chronology.

Indeed, it was beginning to feel as though this in itself was becoming a kind of testimony to them. They were already out of time. The world's cameras and newspapers had captured their later, more famous acts. Their downfalls and deceptions repeated so as to be cast in the stone of the public record, but they had all lied so often that diligence in recording events is unachievable.

It is not possible to write history from what are already fictions.

I remembered them differently, almost as ghosts in the changing light of youth and of Cambridge. They had all now died and I was left, custodian to their laughter and serious intent. They lived in my mind now not as infamous liars or unjustly maligned heroes, but simply as young men in a dangerous time, considering their individual responses to a terrible threat in a city of prepositions.

Cambridge allowed this to happen. It encouraged us to dream beyond our own country and perhaps even to be dismayed by it. They all departed but I stayed. Even as an Apostle I knew, once I left the society and became an Angel, I would not leave the city that gave me all I required.

My few possessions now, spread across this desk, are testament to that decision: this resolution to lead my life in the college where I met those remarkable men. I was comfortable with what the others regarded as a shelter. When I watched their lives unfold, as we all grew older, I could only wish for them that protection, but it was all too late. They had made their choices and I mine. I am now left to write, to remember and to recast events in any way I see fit.

I often felt subjugated by their brilliance or by their flamboyance. Now, it is I who holds the stage, the quiet professor whose comparatively dull life gave me the chance to rewrite their histories, their loves and their shared, mistaken youth.

I turned to see that Michael was standing in the doorway. 'How long have you been there?' I asked him.

'Not long,' he said. 'I was just watching you work. You don't mind do you?'

'I suppose not,' I said. 'I was just thinking about the past.'

'I could see that,' said Michael. 'I didn't want to disturb you, that's all.'

'Very thoughtful,' I said, and then quickly added, 'It's good to see you, though. I do tend to drift off somewhat when I'm by myself.'

'I know,' he said. 'It's not the first time I've watched you.'

'Oh?' I asked. 'Is it a hobby of yours?'

'Oh, I wouldn't say hobby,' he laughed, 'more of a vocation.'

'Like a guardian angel?' I said, in a jovial manner.

'If you like,' said Michael. 'Are you still working on your book?' he asked.

'Yes,' I said.

He seemed awkward that morning. 'And how's it going?' he asked.

'I think I've come to a decision,' I said. 'My memory is all I have, but even that seems to be playing tricks on me.'

'What do you mean?' asked Michael.

'It's all getting mixed up,' I said. 'Things are moving around as if in a fluid.'

'Does that matter?' he said. 'I mean you are writing about a long time ago.'

'I don't think it does matter, Michael, no,' I said. 'I'm not writing a history book, or a biography.'

'What are you writing then?' he asked.

'The truth,' I said.

'And doesn't the truth have to be accurate?' Michael said. 'I mean, you can't just make things up, surely?'

'I'm not making anything up,' I said. 'It all happened, just not necessarily in the order, or even in the way I am telling it.'

'And what about the truth?' he asked again.

'Oh the truth doesn't have to be precise,' I said. 'It can be found in stories, in contradictions. I have found a way to show the truth even with a bit of exaggeration.'

'Are you sure?' said Michael.

'Oh yes,' I said, 'quite, quite sure. Now, what did you come in for?'

Michael came further into the room and sat down by the window, before saying, 'I feel quite sad this morning.'

'Oh,' I said, 'why?'

'It would have been my friend Christian's birthday today, but as he's gone, of course, it can't be. I feel I miss him.'

'That's natural,' I said. 'You should allow yourself to feel like that, and even though it might sadden you, you should remember him as alive.'

'When I do that it makes me feel worse,' said Michael.

'Well that is wrong,' I said. 'Remembering someone should always make you feel better. They are still alive in your memories, remember.'

'Yes,' said Michael, 'OK.'

'Would talking about something else help at all?' I asked him.

'It depends,' he said, and then, without warning, put his hand on my leg. 'How are you feeling today?' he asked.

'I sense my own passing,' I said.

'Now,' said Michael, 'there's no need to talk like that.'

'There's every need,' I said, 'and I am not afraid. Did you ever hear of the story of Icarus?'

'Of course,' said Michael, 'everyone knows that story.'

'Do they?' I asked. 'Or do they only think they know it? What do you know?'

'Icarus tried to escape Crete by flying on wings made by his father,' said Michael, 'but he ignored his father's advice and flew too close to the sun, his wings melted and he fell into the sea.'

'Well, that's certainly part of it,' I said.

'What do you mean?' asked Michael.

'Well,' I said, 'that is *what* happened, but have you ever wondered *why* it happened?'

Michael thought for a moment and then said, 'To be honest, no, I haven't thought about it like that.'

'I thought so,' I said. 'So the real story is much more tragic, in my opinion anyway.'

'Go on,' said Michael.

'I believe that Icarus deliberately killed himself,' I said. 'I think he was trying to reach the gods, his god, and when he realised he could see them but not reach them, he carried on flying upwards in despair, even though he knew it would end in his death.'

'That's not recorded in history, is it?' said Michael.

'Many things that are not recorded are true,' I said.

'And I suppose you think many stories that are recorded are not true?' said Michael.

'Ah,' I said, 'now you are beginning to understand me.'

'But why would someone want to die after discovering that god, or their gods, really did exist?' he asked.

'Isn't it obvious?' I said. 'The discovery of beauty overwhelmed him.'

'Who did he discover?' asked Michael.

'Apollo, of course,' I said, 'the sun god.'

*

As Blunt and Straight finished their papers I was astonished to see Philby walk into the room, having only a few minutes previously wondered why I so rarely saw him.

'Ah,' said Blunt, 'when I said I wanted to take you to London alone, I must confess to being not entirely truthful.'

'Morning all,' said Philby cheerily.

'Philby,' said Blunt, 'you remember young Cyprian here?'

'Yes, of course,' said Philby, 'the mathematician.'

'Surely I'm more interesting than that?' I said.

'Oh, you certainly are,' said Philby. 'I understand you are coming to London with us.'

'Er, yes,' I said, 'to see a painting…'

'And to meet Otto,' said Straight.

'Oh, Straight,' said Philby, 'good to see you… keeping well?'

'Indeed I am,' said Straight, 'but I must say I'm a bit put out that I am not invited on this jaunt.'

'Listen, old man,' said Philby, 'Otto doesn't want to see you again,' and then added quite sharply, 'Sorry about that.'

'Why not?' said Straight.

'Ah, ah,' corrected Blunt, 'we do not question Otto, we listen to him, remember?'

'Well, I'm damned,' said Straight.

'You will be if you don't follow Blunt's advice,' said Philby.

Straight left the room. Philby took his seat and sat confidently. I had forgotten that he could appear quite elegant, not in the generally effete manner of Blunt, but in a masculine, slightly threatening way. I think Blunt always wished to charm his company into a sense of false security, whilst Philby chose to overpower those close to him. I was becoming a little more confident than earlier in the year.

'I've not seen much of you recently, Philby,' I said.

'No, you won't have done,' he said, 'Blunt is looking after you.'

'I'm not sure I need to be molly-coddled,' I said.

'Of course not, old man,' he said. 'I just meant that I am sure Blunt is keeping you entertained.'

'Oh well,' I said, 'he is certainly doing that.'

'I can but try,' said Blunt dryly, 'although it's not always easy being at the centre of attention.'

'You enjoy it,' I said cheekily. 'Anyway, I would have said Burgess held that particular position.'

'He would certainly say so,' said Philby.

'I didn't think you saw much of Burgess either,' I said.

'You don't see everything, you know, Cyprian,' said Philby, entirely without humour.

'I never suggested I did,' I said, 'it was merely an observation.'

'Fine,' said Philby, 'but don't make too many assumptions, old man; you're not always in your rooms to see what Burgess gets up to.'

'I see enough,' I said.

'I'm glad you think so,' said Philby.

'Now, now, gentlemen,' said Blunt, 'I think we've all said sufficient for now.'

Kim Philby never overly impressed me. I found him too knowingly arrogant, and perhaps not quite as clever as he thought, although he had a reputation for intelligence and he was certainly far from slow. His eyes were quick and his habit of keeping a distance from other men meant that he was not as involved with our group as the rest of us. I had heard that he didn't keep the same distance from women, but we would not have known much about that. We lived in a world of men, save a few women at college and more silent individuals in the kitchens and on the staff.

Philby was one of those for whom there is a great difference between being clever and acting intelligently. He was a master at the latter, but as for pure cleverness he was not in Blunt's league, or Burgess's for that matter. I could not compare him either to Turing, who I suspect was above us all in terms of purity of thought. Philby enjoyed men's company, whilst the rest of us delighted in the company of men.

We parted company and agreed to meet the following morning for our long-awaited trip to London. I walked part of the way back to my rooms with Blunt, who seemed very preoccupied.

'Blunt,' I said, 'if you don't mind me asking, what was in that letter that Dr Dobb was so keen to get hold of?'

'That's very unlike you,' he said, turning to look at me, 'the Cyprian I knew would not have asked such impertinent questions at the beginning of the year.'

'I'm sorry,' I said, 'I didn't mean to pry as such.'

'Not at all,' he said, 'I'm pleased you are coming out of your shell at last. What is the origin of this change? Is it becoming an Apostle?'

'It might be,' I said.

'Or might it be something else?' he continued. 'Have you found love?'

'Now you're being impertinent,' I said.

'Oh, so you have,' said Blunt. 'I knew it, I'm too late again,' and he raised his hand theatrically to his brow.

'Don't tell me you have feelings for me?' I asked.

'Oh, darling,' said Blunt, 'I don't have feelings for anyone, but I do like to get close to people that I… appreciate.' He said the last word as if discussing a work of art.

'I had no idea,' I said.

'Are you sure?' Blunt asked. 'You do appear to be very observant, always watching people.'

'I enjoy doing so,' I said, 'it's an antidote to mathematics.'

'Oh, I wouldn't go as far as that,' said Blunt, 'there are too many similarities between the ways in which numbers and people behave.'

'Do you think so?' I asked. 'I'm not so sure. People are far more unpredictable, don't you think?'

'Well, I can see you're still in your first year,' said Blunt, 'still a great deal to learn about both.'

He was right, of course. When one is young, one genuinely believes it possible to possess knowledge, but this is not true. One can experience things very thinly to the point where their intensity gives the impression of learning, but this is false. Such experiences only build into knowledge cumulatively.

'You still haven't told me,' I said.

'I haven't told you what?' asked Blunt.

'You haven't told me what was in the letter,' I said.

'No,' he said, before walking away, 'I haven't.'

*

Michael had not quite understood what I was saying about Icarus.

'I don't think I have an idea of what beauty is,' he said.

'I think you know precisely what beauty is,' and I smiled after I said it. 'It would have been his birthday today, wouldn't it?'

'Oh, well perhaps you know me better than myself,' said Michael quickly.

'Of course I do,' I said. 'I can see a lot further than you, it's the one benefit of being so close to death.'

*

Philby, Blunt and myself met at Cambridge railway station. It was raining and a strong wind sent people running into the shelter of the main foyer.

'Nice day to see London,' I said.

'Well, yes indeed,' said Blunt.

'Never mind the weather,' Philby said, 'we'll be inside for much of the day in any case.'

'Yes, I suppose so,' I said. 'I am looking forward to seeing this painting of yours, Blunt.'

'Oh dear,' Blunt said, 'if only it were mine.'

'Don't you own a Poussin?' I said, teasingly.

'Well, yes, just a little one,' said Blunt. 'That darling man, Victor Rothschild, lent me the money to buy *Eliza and Rebecca at the Well.*'

'I wondered how you had afforded it,' I said, 'and now I know.'

'Indeed you do, dear boy,' said Blunt, 'but don't let it be known more widely; all rather distasteful to have to borrow money.'

'I don't see why?' I said.

'No,' said Blunt, 'you probably don't. Now look,' he said, pointing through the gates, 'there's the London train.'

Despite his protestations over money, and indeed his frequent comments on class boundaries, Blunt had insisted that we travel in First Class. I believe Blunt resolved such a contradiction more generally in his life by accepting that even communism required leaders. He certainly never disregarded his love of an elite, within which he included himself.

The carriage was opulently decorated. Large burnt-orange cushions complemented deep upholstered seats in a strong pattern. On the headrests lay soft covers in pure starched white and this was matched in the tablecloths. The heavy curtains were of the same material as the cushions, which filtered what little light there was on such a wet morning into gold, mixing with that thrown out by small lamps on each table, covered by tasselled lampshades. The walls of the carriage were a highly polished walnut wood, which again, in addition to the ornate mirrors along its length, served to create an intimate ambience.

The tables were laid to breakfast. Silver cutlery rested on white serviettes and sparkling glasses dripped condensation attractively from the cold of just-served orange juice.

'This is how to travel,' said Blunt, happily.

'I must confess,' I said, 'that I have never travelled in First before.'

'Good god, man, why ever not?' asked Philby.

'My family are not wealthy enough,' I said, simply, 'although I wish you'd told me when you were booking the seats, Blunt. Wherever did you get the money for this?'

'Eliza's well is deep, indeed,' he said.

'You mean…' I started to say.

'I told you,' said Blunt, 'I don't like to discuss it. Let's just say that every great artist deserves a patron.'

'But you are not an artist,' I said.

'How dare you,' said Blunt, with a smile. 'To interpret the intentions of artists is in itself an art form.'

'I suppose that could be considered the case,' I said.

'It is the case,' Blunt said, definitively. 'Now, let's order breakfast from this delightful young man.'

The waiter appeared beside my shoulder and took our orders. Philby chose a full cooked breakfast and Blunt, poached eggs with salmon. I selected the same eggs but with bacon. The line to London from Cambridge took long enough for a leisurely breakfast. The eggs were perfectly cooked and with a little salt were delicious. We poured tea into fine china cups with the train company's crest on their sides, accompanied by gold rims.

'When was the last time you were in London?' I asked Blunt.

'Oh, a while ago,' he said. 'I try and get down to the National whenever I can, or indeed to the Wallace, where we will go this morning.'

'I've not been for a long time,' I said.

'I'm not surprised if you can't travel in First Class,' said Blunt.

'Don't be cruel, Blunt,' said Philby. 'You wouldn't be able to either without your benefactor.'

'There's no need to be facetious,' said Blunt. 'I think we are in for an interesting day.'

'This man, Otto,' I said, 'what does he want to see you about?'

'I'll tell you that if he wants to see you again,' said Blunt.

'There's nothing to worry about, though, Cyprian,' said Philby, 'just think of it as a kind of interview.'

'Yes, an interview,' said Blunt.

'An interview for what?' I asked.

'If you're successful you'll discover the answer to that soon enough,' said Blunt.

'In which case,' I said, 'might I ask a question?'

'Of course,' said Blunt.

'Why does he wish to speak to me?' I asked.

'It's on my recommendation,' said Blunt. 'Now get your things together, we're pulling into Liverpool Street.'

London has always astonished me. It is a city-state, another country. Even such a comparatively short journey as that between Cambridge and London serves to confirm that the capital is made of something different to the rest of England. Immediately upon stepping from the train I was taken aback by the pace and energy of the city. The platform was filled with steam from our train opening its boilers. From within the steam, boys in once-smart uniforms came running towards us outside the First Class carriages to offer assistance with our bags. We accepted and walked through the station to the waiting ranks of Austin High-Lot taxis, all in different colours associated with their respective fleets.

As we drove away from Liverpool Street station to our destination in Manchester Square, I read on the many newsstands of protests against Mosley. I then noticed that many of the people on the pavement were not only walking purposefully in the same direction but were also, many of them, wearing similar clothes. I recognised them immediately as Blackshirts. The men were dressed all in black with tight belts clasped in a large silver buckle. The women wore long grey skirts and black blouses.

'Just as I hoped,' said Blunt, 'it's not just paintings I want you to see in London, Cyprian.'

'Where are they all going?' I asked.

'I expect they are attending one of Mosley's rallies,' said Blunt.

I looked across at Philby, who was sitting silently and staring out of the window, his chin resting on a clenched fist.

'Surely we aren't going to follow them?' I said.

'Oh, I think not,' said Blunt, 'but let's keep our eyes open.'

I opened my eyes.

I could hardly believe what I was seeing on the streets of London. We moved slowly through the crowds and I caught a glimpse down one particular street of lines of men and women saluting, as Nazis did. I could just make out the figure of Mosley, dressed in military fashion with a cap and jackboots. I was aware that we had all talked about the threat of fascism in our quiet rooms in Cambridge. It was an entirely different thing to see it en masse in London.

'Should we go and take a look?' Philby asked suddenly.

'No, old man,' said Blunt, 'I think we might rather stick out, better to drive on.'

'I agree,' I said.

'You're just scared, Cyprian' said Philby.'

'No,' I said honestly, 'I'm not scared, but I am shocked.'

'Excellent,' said Blunt.

We drove on past the crowds and into central London. The atmosphere both inside and beyond the taxi changed for the better. Blunt seemed pleased to have seen the spectacle, but was now focused on our next experience. We rounded the corner into Manchester Square and drove through the gates of Hertford House.

'Follow me,' said Blunt.

We both did so and entered the great house, trying to keep pace with Blunt as he moved quickly through the drawing room and the great gallery of the Wallace to where hung the Poussin. Blunt stopped in front of it.

'Well,' he said, 'here it is, the greatest painting I know.'

I wasn't sure for a while what to say and Philby seemed relatively uninterested. Then I said, 'Do the figures seem to you to be unable to control the dance?'

'Very perceptive,' said Blunt, 'precisely right. They are moving through the seasons without being able to cease. You see Poverty, Labour, Riches and Pleasure holding hands, but in a circle, so that the dance always comes back to Poverty.'

'And the music?' I asked.

'That is Time, on the right, playing a lyre,' said Blunt.

'And in the chariot in the sky?' I asked, a little ashamed for not being more informed.

'That is Apollo, the sun-god,' said Blunt. 'He is pulling the Hours. It's a morning scene, you see,' he continued. 'The dancers represent the stages of life and Apollo shows the movement of the earth, but all are controlled by Time.'

'It is wonderful,' I said.

Blunt seemed genuinely pleased. 'Yes,' he said, 'this picture proves why Mosley is wrong.'

'In what sense?' I said.

'He is no more in control than any of us,' said Blunt, 'even Apollo will be consumed at some point.'

'The sunburst,' I said.

'Quite,' said Blunt, 'and for the rest of us there is nothing more we can do other than dance,' he paused, 'apart from try to make the dance last as long as possible.'

'How can we do that?' I asked.

'By fighting for what is right,' said Blunt. 'Now come on, I want you to meet Otto.'

*

I do not think there was ever a moment again when it was so clear to me that Blunt's views were fundamentally driven by his love of art. Through art he filtered all else. Michael had obviously been considering what I had said about Apollo.

'So Icarus was killed by Apollo?' he asked.

'You could take that view, I suppose,' I said, 'although it was not Apollo's fault that Icarus flew too close to him.'

'No,' said Michael, 'then it was Daedalus' fault for not taking enough care over his son?'

'I think that's a little unfair,' I said. 'Youth took over in Icarus because he was free.'

'I can understand that,' said Michael.

'Yes, I'm sure you can,' I replied. 'After all isn't that what youth is all about?'

'Well, yes,' said Michael, 'but at least Icarus died happy; after all, he had seen beauty.'

'No, no,' I said, 'quite the opposite. He had seen an unobtainable happiness, which is worse than never being elated.'

'Are you sure?' asked Michael.

'I am certain,' I said, 'and I think you know I am right. Seeing Apollo for Icarus was similar to you and Christian, wasn't it?'

'I'm not sure,' said Michael.

'It was, Michael,' I said. 'Losing happiness is the same as not being able to reach it.'

Michael sat quietly for a while in the chair. I let him do so, understanding that he would need some time to consider what we had discussed. The sounds of the home seemed very distant. It was as though we were in the tower built by King Minos for Daedalus and Icarus. Trapped together, we had to construct a means of escape.

I am an old man now and tired of living. I have seen a great deal in my life and been told many lies. My one task now is to come out of the shade, where even there it is too warm. I remember how I once linked two paintings to become one life. Blunt had shown me *Dance to the Music of Time*, in which Apollo drew the Hours across the sky along with the sun. I had seen my own life beginning in *94 Degrees in the Shade* on a visit to the Fitzwilliam Museum in Cambridge. I saw my future in both paintings: the first a vision of the circle of life, the second how that life would be lived in a shade, which gave no protection from what I knew. I had been lied to so many times that nothing could stop me from continuing the deception.

In our tower I could see Michael Gabriel, named for two angels, as someone who needed my help to fly. He had lost the ability to do so because he had lost so much.

'Are you feeling all right?' I asked him.

'I think so, thank you, Dr Cyprian,' he said. 'I just feel a little lost today without Christian.'

'I know,' I said. 'We have all lost someone like that, and it doesn't get any easier the older you become either.'

'Really?' he asked. 'I would have hoped that pain passes.'

'Everyone hopes for that,' I said, 'but it doesn't, and it shouldn't either, if you want my opinion.'

'I know,' said Michael, 'remembering means they are always with you.'

'It's true, Michael,' I said. 'Even Apollo himself will one day implode, but there will still be time, just as there was before Apollo.'

'Meaning?' asked Michael.

'Very simple,' I said. 'If time is existence, then there must be life beyond our physical lives because time cannot cease.'

'But don't some physicists say that time did not exist before the Big Bang?' said Michael.

'They do,' I said, 'but I do not agree with them. Effect always follows cause. People and things age – nothing stays the same or gets younger. Planets move, the universe expands.

These things don't happen in isolation – every time the Earth goes round the sun you get older, the trees grow a little taller and so on.'

'I see,' said Michael.

'The way we measure and think about time may be human concepts, but it exists independently of the human mind,' I continued. 'There was cause and effect before we came along and will be after we're gone.'

'If we ever really do disappear,' Michael said.

'Precisely,' I said. 'If no time passed before we could conceive it, how did we move from a state of non-existence to one of existence? Something had to change and, for things to change, time must pass.'

'And we can do nothing about this, I suppose,' said Michael.

'Someone once told me the only thing we can do is to try and make the dance as long as possible,' I said.

'How can we do that?' Michael asked.

'We need to fight for what is right,' I said.

Michael turned to look at me. I suddenly did not feel in his care, but rather he in mine.

'I'm not sure what is right.'

'That is because you have not yet learned how to fly.'

*

We were collected by another taxi outside the Wallace Museum and driven out into Manchester Square.

'Where are we going?' I asked Blunt.

'We will have an early dinner at Kettner's in Soho,' he said.

'Is it a Cabaret night?' said Philby.

'You'll be pleased to know that it is,' said Blunt, 'although we must be careful with young Cyprian here.'

'Why?' I said. 'I'm perfectly capable of looking after myself.'

'Of course you are, darling,' said Blunt, 'but I doubt in your, shall we say, sheltered little Cambridge life that you will have ever seen anything like this before.'

The rain had eased and the clouds cleared to produce a dim but not unpleasant evening. London always looks beautiful after rainfall and the streets in Soho were full of people looking for other people. We drew up outside Kettner's on Romilly Street and after Philby had paid the driver we went inside. The rooms were a great deal darker than might have been expected for that time of the day and my eyes took some time to adjust to the light.

It was a handsome place. Soft furnishings were placed carefully around the foyer and as we went into dinner I noticed that everyone was in black tie.

'Will we be allowed to dine without being dressed?' I asked.

'Yes,' said Blunt, 'it's not required here; everyone has just come like that for the party.'

'What party?' I asked.

'Good god,' said Philby, 'you've got a lot to learn.'

'Just keep close to me and only speak to Otto if he asks you a question,' said Blunt.

We found our table and sat down. Candles, both on the tables and all round the walls, lighted the dining room. The glasses glinted in the flickering light and in the corner a jazz band was warming up. I looked through the menu and found a number of items that I would like to choose.

'Drinks!' exclaimed Blunt, and a waiter came up quickly to the table. 'Given that we are bereft of Burgess for once,' said Blunt, 'we can bypass the usual surly determination to drink beer.'

'Agreed,' said Philby.

'Wine it is then,' said Blunt, and ordered two bottles of what turned out to be very good Chablis.

'Ah,' said Blunt, 'here he comes.'

I looked up and saw a square-faced man approaching our table. He was not smiling. His ears were a notable feature being almost horizontal to the side of his head. He was wearing a suit that looked as though he had purchased it before putting on a little too much weight.

'Otto,' said Blunt, shaking our guest by the hand, 'come and join us.'

The band struck up a fast tune, but they were used to playing in a dining room setting and so were not too loud for the moment.

'How are you?' said Otto to Blunt. 'And how are you, Philby?' he continued.

'We're well,' they said together.

Still no one had smiled.

'And is this our young Apostle?' said Otto, reaching his hand out to mine.

'Yes,' said Blunt. 'Otto, this is Daniel Cyprian.'

'Have you had a memorable day in London, Cyprian?' he asked me.

'Yes,' I said, 'Blunt and Philby have been most kind.'

'I'm sure they have,' said Otto. 'I suppose you've been taken to an art gallery?'

'Of course he has,' said Blunt. 'You should come with me some time, Otto,' said Blunt, in an attempt to bring some warmth to the table.

'I'll give the orders, if you don't mind,' said Otto.

'I only meant to say…' started Blunt.

'Never mind,' said Otto sharply, 'now pour me a glass of wine.'

'I received the letter you wrote to Dobb about our young Apostle,' said Otto, 'very interesting assessment.'

Blunt avoided my gaze.

The only aspects of the rest of the evening that I can remember are that the wine continued to be poured, the music became much louder and a number of scantily clad girls danced between the tables. The room filled with cigarette smoke and I was asked only a few questions by Otto, mainly about politics, but it became difficult to hear him and I found it disconcerting that, although there was so much jollity in the room, at our table the mood remained serious. Otto regularly whispered into either Blunt's or Philby's ear or occasionally shot glances across to me.

I do not recall the journey back to Cambridge, although from that evening on, perhaps because of the atmosphere in London or the mood around our table, I felt I had opened my eyes into a kind of darkness.

*

Eight – A Handful of Dust

I walked through Cambridge one late spring morning on my way to a lecture. Rather than taking my usual route along King's Parade, I walked through Trinity Lane down to the river and crossed at the bridge between Trinity and Trinity Hall. I looked back at my college. The Wren Library was glowing in the morning sun. The library served to remind us of our reason for coming here, our need to absorb, even though many of us, like most people our age, thought our views fully formed. I walked down to Queen's Road and turned left, then again at the Backs into King's College, where I had arranged to meet Turing in order to go with him to the lecture.

I waited for him outside the main doors to King's Chapel. I looked up at the great building and saw it as a jagged cliff face threaded with glass. The sun was driving into the whale-like interior of the church through countless windows. I could not resist a momentary glimpse inside, so I pushed the door open and stepped inside. The cold hit me immediately, almost catching my breath and sending my gaze upwards to the inconceivably long vaulted ceiling, as though only a giant spider casting webs in stone could have achieved it.

An organ scholar was practising Purcell. It was the anthem *Thou knowest Lord the secrets of our hearts*. The music was gentle and the building's acoustic gradually allowed it to touch all parts of its structure. It struck me what a perfect combination of sound and architecture this was intended to be, and indeed had become. Although I knew I had to meet Turing, I took a seat in the Choir, alone amongst the dark wood. The seats were resounding imperceptively to the music, but I could feel the bass notes in my body. In this building it was as if the music contained another, more physical dimension. There was no one else apart from the scholar in the church.

I closed my eyes.

It no longer seemed cold. The music grew in complexity but not in volume and it enveloped me as though silk was being spun round my head. My father's image came into my mind. I could see him standing in his pulpit declaiming certainties where most would merely accept possibilities at the very least. He raised his hands in the air as he spoke and then his image looked directly at me. His eyes were full of fire and he pointed, his voice unheard, although his image was speaking. I could only hear the music, feel it growing in my body as it reverberated like distant horses on hard ground.

I opened my eyes.

I looked up at the vaulted stone, appearing to be suspended by a greater force than any I knew in mathematics. I knew my father was using the name of the piece to warn me. It was a sense of knowing I have only ever had in King's Chapel. The building has a unique capacity to induce tears through authority. I understood things present and past as I waited for the feeling of being watched and cared for to pass. I suddenly remembered Blunt's hand-written envelope I had seen in the JCR, and the discussion with Otto in the restaurant – 'the fifth man?'

I got up from the stalls and walked through the Choir, directly beneath the organ and out into the body of the chapel. My shoes were loud on the stone but I needed to get to the door. I decided that I would have to lie to my friends. I realised that they too were all liars.

All but one.

I went out into the sunlight and Turing was standing there waiting for me. He was smiling. I could not lie to him. No one can lie to angels.

We walked across to the lecture theatre together and for once I was relieved that Wittgenstein would not be giving the lecture. His antagonism with Turing would have been too difficult on a morning when I had realised where I truly belonged.

During the lecture Turing was surreptitiously affectionate. He stroked my hand, then held it for the duration. I felt a sense of happiness that was new. My experience in the chapel resonated. I knew my father's warning was correct, but remained unsure of whether the pulpit was the appropriate means to deliver it as the portentous building itself drew from me a feeling of humility.

I had become so used to the confident statements of my group of friends, on almost every topic one could imagine, that being provided with an understanding of my own relative unimportance was a relief. I was sitting beside a great man, but even he was full of faults.

I knew that the shade would provide no cover. Blunt and Burgess believed they could hide there, that no one would realise their deceit. They were wrong. I had been scared by Otto. He said so little to me and yet appeared to be a threat. I knew that Burgess's comment about not being part of all that Cambridge represents, or at least not wanting to be part of it, was only the tip of their true views. But it was a glimpse into the abyss.

I resolved to write a record of lies, so being because what I observed were deceptions from one man to another and to each himself. I had been accepted as an Apostle, but I could not fully acknowledge the consequences of joining. I, also, could not allow anyone to know this. I would have to wait before committing what I had seen to paper. I would also have to lie about certain parts, exaggerate and embellish. It would be for a greater cause. It would be a cleansing and a revenge.

All this would need to be secret. I had become my own double agent.

Turing and I left at the end of the lecture and because it was still a beautiful morning we visited a tea shop for late morning tea. There was the inevitable wait as lines of undergraduates all wanted refreshment. Finally seated, I turned to Turing. 'You know, I had a wonderful few moments in your chapel this morning.'

'Really?' he asked. 'I didn't think you went in for religion after all you've said about your father.'

'Well, perhaps in more usual circumstances I wouldn't do,' I said.

'What makes these unusual?' asked Turing.

'I'm not sure I can really say at the moment,' I said, 'it's all a bit complex.'

'Now,' said Turing, 'I can't imagine it will be too complex for me,' he said with a smile.

'This isn't an equation,' I said, perhaps a little sharply, 'this is real life.'

'What a ridiculous statement,' he said, 'equations *are* real life.'

Turing took a serviette from the table and a pen from the top pocket of his jacket. On the paper he drew the letter *i*.

'What does that signify?' he asked.

'Obviously an imaginary number in an equation,' I said.

'Very good,' said Turing. 'Now, you have used both the words "complex" and "real" in the last few minutes to distinguish between problems I could help with or otherwise, have you not?'

'Yes, I suppose so,' I said.

'And you would admit to being a Platonist?' asked Turing.

'In what sense?' I asked.

'In the sense that you have no problem in asserting both the truth and falsehood of statements independent of their probability,' said Turing, almost too quickly to follow.

'You mean like Gödel?' I asked.

'Precisely,' said Turing. 'So this means that you are aware that the analysis of real numbers is closely related to the analysis of complex numbers?'

'Of course I am,' I said, 'but I don't see how this would help me explain the fact that I find myself in very unusual circumstances.'

Turing made space on the table for the tea things to be placed there by the waitress who had just come to our table. He rearranged everything that was on the table into a small square of items: salt and pepper pots, cutlery and a small vase containing a yellow flower.

'Complex differentiability has much stronger consequences than real differentiability,' said Turing.

'Indeed,' I said, 'go on…'

'Complex analysis is particularly concerned with the analytic functions of complex variables, agreed?' said Turing.

'Agreed,' I said, pouring out the tea.

'And because the separate real and imaginary parts of any analytic function must satisfy Laplace's equation, complex analysis is widely applicable to two-dimensional problems,' he said, sitting back with a smile.

'Remind me, what is Laplace's equation?' I said.

'Good god, man,' said Turing, 'we were discussing it in the lecture this morning, didn't you hear us?'

'No,' I said, 'not really. My mind was elsewhere this morning.'

'The real and imaginary parts of a complex analytic function both satisfy the Laplace equation,' said Turing, and then he opened out the serviette further and drew an equation.

'There,' he said pointing at his equation, 'do you see what I mean?'

'Not entirely,' I said.

'What I am saying,' said Turing, clearly trying to be patient, 'is that solutions of Laplace's equation are all harmonic functions; they are all analytic within the domain where the equation is satisfied.'

'I'm beginning to see where you are going with this,' I said.

'Good,' said Turing. 'So if any two functions are solutions to Laplace's equation their sum is also a solution.'

'You mean that I should not differentiate between what I view is real and what is complex?' I said.

'Exactly,' said Turing, 'and that property, which is called the principle of superposition, is very useful.'

'In what way?' I asked.

'Well,' said Turing, 'solutions to complex problems can be constructed by bringing together simple solutions.'

'So I should tell you what the unusual circumstances are in which I find myself and by looking at them as complex equations in terms of real numbers, or in fact reality, I will find a solution?' I asked.

'What could be simpler?' said Turing. 'So what are these circumstances?'

'I will tell you one day, you've convinced me of that,' I said, 'but not here and not now.'

'It's your decision,' he said.

'Yes,' I said, 'I think it may well have to be.'

I left Turing at the gates of King's and walked back down Trinity Street for lunch at my own college. Before going into Hall I went up to our rooms. The door was locked, so I assumed that Burgess was not present and let myself in. I could hear sounds coming from his bedroom and, worried that he was in difficulty after drinking too much, walked in without knocking. Burgess was in bed with another student. He turned, saw it was me and with a smile said, 'Ah, Cyprian, meet Julian Bell.'

I was taken aback but Burgess and Bell seemed not to be so at all. They both sat up, and looked at me.

'Would you get us some wine, Cyprian?' asked Burgess.

'No, I most certainly will not,' I said. 'It's not done to drink in bed.'

The absurdity of what I'd said and the awkwardness of the situation meant that both Burgess and Bell burst out laughing. I just left the room. A few moments later, Burgess came into the sitting room where I was slumped in a chair, thinking.

'I do hope you're all right?' asked Burgess.

'I suppose so,' I said. 'You could have left a note not to be disturbed or something.'

'Oh, don't be such a prude,' he said. 'I wasn't to know you would be coming back.'

'I do live here,' I said.

'I know, dear boy, but I thought we'd be safe as you would only have thoughts of lunch.'

'So I'm greedy as well as a prude?' I said, indignantly.

'Frankly, I would say so, yes,' said Burgess with a grin, 'but I still like you.'

'I'm not all you like, by the looks of things,' I said, and at that moment Julian Bell came into the room. As was the case with Burgess, he wore his trousers and braces but was shirtless.

'Sorry about that, old man,' said Bell. 'Never an easy situation to explain.'

'Oh, I think it's pretty easy to explain,' I said.

'Come on,' said Burgess to Bell, 'let's take a bath and leave him alone.'

'Righto,' said Bell.

'I'll see you later,' Burgess said to me.

'Fine,' I said, probably sounding more annoyed than I in truth was. I went for lunch, hoping to be alone. The experience at King's was still very much on my mind and for some reason I had not found Turing quite as intoxicating as in the past. His mind worked at such a ferocious rate that it was not always possible to fully grasp what he was saying. Instead, I focused on the Purcell and on the feeling that I had been warned. It was typical of my father to have chosen King's College Chapel in which to do it, but of course it was my mind that conjured the image. It was me who responded to the building in that way.

Blunt called me over in the Dining Hall, 'you look as though you've seen a ghost, old man.'

'Not a ghost,' I said, 'Burgess in bed with someone called Julian Bell.'

'He is an Apostle too, you know,' said Blunt.

'Really?' I asked. 'I've not noticed him before.'

'You will see more of him now,' Blunt said, 'he's quite the dashing young poet.'

'I thought all the poets were at Oxford,' I said provocatively.

'You know that's not true,' said Blunt. 'Not least, John Cornford is here too.'

'Yes,' I said, 'I've seen him, but he seems to spend a great deal of time in London.'

'With good reason,' said Blunt. 'As we have seen ourselves, London is where things are happening.'

'Oh,' I said, 'I think a great deal is happening in Cambridge too.'

'Yes,' said Blunt, 'hard to disagree with that. Will you be coming back to my rooms after dinner this evening?'

'Yes, of course,' I said.

I spent that afternoon considering what Turing had suggested as a way to deal with the contradictions in my life at that point. There was no question that this period in Cambridge was the most intellectually dynamic I would ever experience. I knew that to be an Apostle meant to be in the company of the greatest thinkers of my generation, or so we all thought anyway. This was guaranteed to induce as much fear as excitement. The times in which we lived were fraught with danger, and even Turing, who naturally analysed all this by reducing it to codes, was aware that a reality existed beyond real numbers. There had been something mesmeric about Julian Bell too, a depth beneath the rather sordid situation in which I had met him.

*

I turned in my bed and reached for the clock. It was only five in the morning and yet I was wide-awake. I had always arisen early and this had not changed in my old age. My ability to do something about it had, though. In the past I would get up in a sprightly fashion and go for an early morning walk before breakfasting in college and then, if not lecturing, would return to my study to work. I always enjoyed the aspects of being an academic that echoed those of our monastic forebears. Now, in the last days of my life, I was kept still by my weakening body.

There is a bell on the wall that I can press if I need someone to come to me. I never do so because eventually someone will in any case, usually Michael. He is very attentive but I must respect the fact that he cannot be here all of the time. He has his own life to lead.

I lay waiting. There is an odd sensation in places like this that the event we have all come here to experience could happen at any moment. The processes are all in place to deal with the moments that follow the last heartbeat.

Eventually he came. Michael entered the room carrying coffee and toast, as it said on my notes. This morning he had remembered my newspaper. I read *The Guardian* now as it has a perfect blend of politics and art. It reminds me of my early days in Cambridge and of all those discussions.

'Thank you, Michael,' I said. 'How are you this morning?'

'Better than previously,' he said. 'I appreciated talking to you.'

'I'll pour the coffee myself in a few minutes,' I said. 'Can you help me out to the chair?'

'Of course,' he said. There was, again, great kindness in his voice and in his hands as he lifted me up from the bed and steadied me, before walking me to the chair and easing me into it.

'What are you working on today?' he asked. 'More on the book?'

'Of course,' I said. 'I need to keep at it to make sure it is finished before I am.'

'Now, don't talk like that,' said Michael.

'Why not?' I said, gently. 'We both know that is why I am here.'

'I just don't think you should be dwelling on it,' he said.

'I don't see why not,' I said, 'and in any case, I wouldn't say I was dwelling on it as such, but rather that I am being realistic.'

Michael moved round the room in a purposeless way. He was usually a very efficient person when in my company, only clearing things that had been used and making almost no redundant gestures.

'Are you looking for something?' I asked him.

'No,' he said, 'just stalling.'

'Why?' I said.

'I need to ask you a question,' he said. 'It's about your own life, though, so I am nervous about asking you.'

'Well, I reserve the right not to answer it,' I said with a smile. 'After all, it will be in my book when I've completed it, but I'll be safe by then.'

'You're safe now,' Michael said.

'Oh, I wish I were,' I said, 'I wish I were; but in some ways this comfortable respite home is the most dangerous place I have ever been to.'

'That's just being melodramatic,' said Michael.

'All melodrama is one step away from actual drama,' I said. 'Now, what is your question?'

Michael paused and then said, 'I looked at the first page of your notes after you had fallen asleep last night.'

'You're not off to a good start,' I said. 'You know I don't want anyone reading my notes, that's not what notes are for.'

'I'm sorry,' he said, 'it's just that you seem to be working so intensely that I wanted to see a little of it.'

'You do see it,' I said. 'I talk to you all the time.'

'Well,' he said, 'you see, that is my question really.'

'Go on,' I said.

'I looked at the subtitle,' he said, 'it mentioned the word lies.'

'Indeed,' I said quickly, 'lies are only a different way of looking at the truth.'

'I don't understand,' said Michael, 'and it upset me to think that you might be lying to me.'

'I can assure you that I am not,' I said. 'I never would.'

'So all those things you have said about love and remembrance are true?' he asked.

'There is a difference between truth and honesty,' I said. 'An old friend once said that to me a long time ago and it's only now, when I am looking at him from a great distance, that I can see that he was almost right.'

'Who was that?' asked Michael.

'Ah,' I said, 'if I told you that now the cat really would be out of the bag. What I will say is that it is possible to discover truths by chance, even through the act of lying.'

'Give me an example,' said Michael.

'I've already given you two examples,' I said, 'Nimrod and Icarus.'

'Those are just stories,' said Michael.

'And so are lies,' I said, 'but they are also truths, are they not?'

'Only if they actually happened,' said Michael.

'And can you prove they did not?' I asked.

'Of course not!' Michael said.

'Then you are going to have to trust me, aren't you?' I said.

'Yes,' said Michael, 'and I do. I just get worried when I think someone is lying to me.'

'That's perfectly natural,' I said, 'but I must ask something of you in return.'

'What is it?' he asked.

'That you do not mistake my lies for dishonesty,' I said.

*

Dinner was served as always in the dining hall. It was a semi-formal occasion as we had a foreign ambassador visiting the college. It made little difference to those of us not at high table, except that we were required to be in white tie as well as black gowns.

'Burgess, are you going to Blunt's rooms after dinner?' I asked.

'Yes, of course,' he said. 'Bell is going to be there.'

'Oh,' I said, 'that explains it then.'

'Listen, Cyprian, I'm sorry again about earlier, it's just that you didn't knock.'

'I didn't realise there was reason to,' I said, 'but I will in the future.'

'Well, no harm done,' said Burgess. 'What do you think of him, anyway?'

'Of whom?' I asked.

'Bell, of course, you fool,' he said.

'I haven't had much of a chance to find out,' I said, 'although I've already seen more of him than some of my longer-established friends.'

'And,' said Burgess, cheekily, 'you must admit he is a bit of a dish.'

'I will admit no such thing,' I said.

'Well, I think he's wonderful,' said Burgess, 'very passionate.'

'I'm quite sure he is,' I said.

The dinner was very good. We began with a serving of mock turtle soup, which was a relief to some as not everyone wished to eat turtle. I would have done so, but this version was good, using very high-quality offal. It was a heavy soup, though, and the college had the presence of mind to leave a longer than usual gap between this and the fish course, which was fillet of sole with a 'remoulade' sauce and cucumbers. This was a much lighter dish, which cleansed after the rich soup. The main course was lamb cutlets a la Pondicherry, which were served very pink with onions and rosemary. Finally, the dessert course was a croquembouche, a tall pile of choux pastries served at precise intervals along the tables and dripping with threads of caramel and chocolate.

There was an unrushed atmosphere in the room as the Master was clearly enjoying his hosting role at high table. We were often required to eat quickly at the end of a meal if it were obvious that the Master had a post-dinner engagement, but not that evening. Eventually, though, the high table left and the staff began clearing the tables.

'Come on,' said Blunt, 'it's time for a party in my new rooms.'

'Which new rooms?' I asked.

'Oh,' he said, 'did I neglect to tell you? I've moved to Nevile's Court.'

'Very nice,' said Burgess, clearly a little jealous. 'How did you manage to secure rooms in Trinity's most beautiful court?'

'I'm sure you'd rather not know,' said Blunt.

'I'm sure you're wrong,' said Burgess, gently punching Blunt on the arm, before putting his own into Blunt's and almost skipping from the dining hall.

I followed, of course, and when we entered Blunt's rooms I must confess to being impressed. The sitting room seemed coquettishly chaste and was lined with white panelling and Annunciation lilies. The shelves were full of enormous seventeenth- and eighteenth-century tomes on architecture and art history. This was a place for parties and I could see that Blunt was already enjoying himself.

'Come in, come in,' he called from across the room, even though I could only have been a few steps behind him. I noticed that Burgess was no longer on his arm, but remarkably Julian Bell had now taken Burgess's place. He was not dressed as we were: King's clearly had not had quite such a formal dinner. Instead, he looked rather dishevelled, not least because the buttons on his jacket were fastened through the holes intended for the one above. Bell's hair too was unkempt. He looked as though he should be returning victorious from a fistfight, rather than on the arm of the distinctly aloof Blunt.

'What can I get you to drink?' Burgess asked me.

'We're all having gin and tonic this evening,' said Blunt.

'No choice?' asked Burgess.

'None whatsoever,' said Blunt.

'I'll have a gin and tonic then,' I said.

'Good choice,' said Burgess, and he mixed the drinks. A number of other people came in and I kept hoping that if Bell was here then he might have mentioned the party at King's and Turing might have thought to come.

'Tell me, Cyprian,' said Bell, 'what do you think of soldiers?'

'I haven't given it a great deal of thought,' I said, honestly.

'Cyprian thinks only of mathematics,' said Burgess, 'don't you, Cyprian? If it doesn't add up... well then, it doesn't add up,' he said laughing.

'Not at all true,' I said, 'and in any case, you imply that mathematics is purely theoretical, when you know as well as I do that it has practical uses.'

'Oh dear,' said Burgess, 'are you about to make a speech?'

'Certainly not,' I said.

'Then how about answering my question,' said Bell, in a friendly tone.

'Well, I suppose it depends on the context,' I said.

'What if the context, as you rather coldly put it,' said Bell, 'is Spain?'

'Well,' I said, 'in that context I suppose people on both sides are fighting for what they believe to be right.'

'But surely only one side can be right,' said Blunt.

'For once, and in that instance, yes, I accept that,' I said.

'And which side is it?' asked Bell.

'Oh, don't be so churlish,' said Burgess. 'No one in this country could consider supporting the Fascists.'

'Well, that means supporting communists,' said Bell.

'Naturally,' said Blunt, 'and that is the right answer, is it not Cyprian?'

'Yes, of course,' I said.

'And would you go to Spain to fight?' asked Bell.

'I don't know,' I said, again honestly, 'would you?'

'Without question,' said Bell. 'I have always wanted to take part in a war.'

'Then you must be certain of your convictions,' I said, 'especially as it involves someone else's war.'

'There is no such thing as someone else's war nowadays,' said Bell.

'I agree,' said Blunt. 'All wars against fascism are the wars of all men.'

Blunt, Burgess and Bell fell into a deep conversation about the fate of the world. They were enjoying one another's company and I felt a little outside of their discussion. I began to wonder whether it was right that I should have accepted the invitation to the party, or perhaps even more seriously, the solicitation for the Apostles. I put such thoughts out of my mind, though, and tried to get on with the evening.

Michael Straight appeared later looking very flustered. He went directly over to Blunt and whispered in his ear. Blunt looked visibly shaken and they both went over to pour themselves more drinks. I was intrigued and went over to join them.

'Is anything wrong?' I asked.

'Yes,' said Straight, 'Victor Rothschild has just killed someone.'

'Get Burgess,' said Blunt.

'Of course,' I said.

I went over to where Burgess was sitting with Bell, quite overtly fondling his knee. 'Burgess, go over and talk to Blunt, there's been an accident,' I said. My face must have appeared shocked, because Burgess dropped his usual flippancy and immediately went over to Blunt. I followed.

'What has happened?' asked Burgess.

'It would appear,' said Straight, 'that Rothschild has knocked over a cyclist and killed him whilst driving his Bugatti.'

'Good god,' said Burgess, 'where is Rothschild now?'

'He's being interviewed by the police,' said Straight, 'but he wants to see Blunt.'

'Of course. I'll go to him,' said Blunt.

'Shall I go too?' asked Straight.

'Yes,' said Blunt, 'perhaps you can think how to explain it.'

'I don't see how I could do that,' said Straight.

'Well, you're always driving sports cars, aren't you?' said Blunt. 'Only you and Rothschild can afford them.'

'Oh I see,' Straight said. 'I'll try and think of something.'

'The rest of you stay here and wait for us,' said Blunt.

'Shouldn't we return to our rooms?' I asked.

'Certainly not,' said Burgess, sounding more like himself.

*

Michael had been gone for a couple of hours and I spent the morning working. I had grown used to the sound of the commuter trains leaving Cambridge for London. When I first arrived at the home it disturbed me because I felt the world was moving on regardless of my own fate. Now, in a state of acceptance, it had the opposite effect of providing solace that others would have the chance to build lives for themselves just as I had done.

My early years in Cambridge seemed so far away to me as I wrote about them. I knew that the purpose of my diary was deeply driven by being retrospective, or perhaps even founded on hindsight. I knew that in some cases I was deliberately rewriting what had happened to suit my view of the main characters, my friends. I had decided in my closing years to think again of all that happened in those times and to build a story from what I had seen. The narrative of the writer is different from that of the historian. At the very least, and because so much had been kept secret, I knew that the only opportunity I had to tell the truth was to invent it.

This is important. I once looked at a painting and imagined a whole life for the person inside it. He was dressed in white to repel some of the heat. He was glad he had found some shade. He pulled his hat down his forehead and closed his eyes. He could not have known that the shade could not give enough protection from the heat.

Truth can be found in the unlikeliest places, even in lies, even in fictions. It can often be discovered by mistake and through invention. One man's act of creation is another man's lie.

I looked out of my window and beyond into the flatness of Cambridgeshire. This is the place I have chosen to spend my entire life. I have no regrets, but it is now time to make clear what I saw in those remarkable men when they were all at their most extraordinary. They had to be. They lived lives of significance in a notable place during exceptional times. They were destined to make errors of judgement but also to dream.

I thought of them now. Sepia young. Cambridge entering summer and the world entering darkness. I began to write again. I chose to invent coincidences, chance meetings, to measure fact against fiction because that is what they all did. Their final testimony would be incomplete without inaccuracy. Such is the life of the spy.

'Dr Cyprian?' said Michael. 'Dr Cyprian, are you asleep?'

'No, no, just thinking,' I said.

'I'm sorry,' he said, 'did I disturb you?'

'No not at all,' I said. 'Do come in. Am I supposed to be doing something?'

'No,' he laughed, 'I just wondered if you would like to have some lunch.'

'I don't think so,' I said. 'I'm really not hungry, but a cup of tea would be nice.'

'No problem,' said Michael 'I'll just go and get you one.'

'Thank you,' I said, 'I appreciate that.'

Michael came back a few moments later with tea and his now familiar smuggled biscuits. There were two cups. 'Do you mind if I join you?' he asked.

'Of course not,' I said, 'you're always welcome.'

'I wanted to ask you more about dishonesty,' he said.

'Really?' I asked. 'I thought we had got past that.'

'I have,' he started. 'I mean, I'm not sure I understand the difference between lying and being dishonest.'

'There is a big difference,' I said.

'Well, I can't see it,' said Michael.

'The difference is that it is not possible to be honest and dishonest at the same time,' I said.

'Yes,' said Michael.

'But,' I continued, 'it is possible to find truth by telling lies.'

'You mean when lies are called stories?' he asked.

'Exactly,' I said. 'All stories contain truths hidden by lies; that is why they are called fiction.'

'But what about true stories?' said Michael. 'Surely they do not contain lies.'

'There is no such thing as a true story,' I said, 'that is called history.'

'And if someone rewrites history as something that did not happen?' he asked.

'Then that becomes fiction, and ceases to be history,' I said.

'So when you say at the beginning of your book that you are writing a diary of lies, you are telling stories, not writing history?' he asked.

'Indeed,' I said. 'My book is about liars, so telling their truth would be dishonest.'

*

I could feel myself getting drunker as the evening grew late. Burgess was in the best of moods, apparently uninterested in the fate of our fellow Apostle. I had not yet met Rothschild, but knew him to be the man who had paid for Blunt's painting.

'I think you have become obsessed by war,' said Burgess to Bell. 'It's all too disturbing.'

'Don't be a hypocrite, Burgess,' said Bell. 'You know as well as I do that war is brewing all over Europe.'

'All over?' said Burgess.

'Yes,' said Bell, 'and the first chance I get I want to be a part of it.'

'You mean you intend to go to Germany all by yourself?' asked Burgess.

'No, not Germany,' said Bell. 'Spain is more likely to erupt first.'

'How do you know?' I asked.

'Their King is gone and their churches are on fire,' said Bell, 'and in any case, I have my sources.'

'How enigmatic,' said Burgess, 'how brave.'

'You don't have to be brave to enter a war,' said Bell, 'just fascinated.'

'By death?' said Burgess.

'Of course not,' said Bell, 'that would be madness; by passion.'

'Oh, I am already fascinated by passion, dear boy,' said Burgess, stroking Bell's leg.

'Not in that way, you fool,' said Bell, suddenly more intense. 'By the passion of political thought becoming political action.'

'Well,' I said, 'I find that interesting.'

'You would,' said Burgess. 'So tell me, Bell, this passion of yours, how is it different from all that has gone before?'

'You mean the last war?' asked Bell.

'Precisely,' said Burgess. 'That surely was driven by politics too.'

'Absolutely not,' said Bell. 'The last war was, if anything, driven by the egos of madmen. It had nothing whatsoever to do with political thought.'

'Indeed?' said Burgess.

'Yes,' said Bell. 'This, more than anything else, marks the difference between our elders and us. Being socialist for us means being rationalist, common-sense, empirical; means a very firm extrovert, practical, commonplace sense of exterior reality...'

'Well, I can see that is true,' said Burgess.

'We think of the world, first and foremost,' continued Bell, 'as the place where other people live, as the scene of crisis and poverty, the probable scene of revolution and war.'

'Well argued,' I said, 'worthy of an Apostolic paper.'

'Thank you, Cyprian,' Bell said. 'I'm getting rather obsessed about war, with a very ambivalent attitude. All my instincts make me want to be a soldier; all my intelligence is against it.'

'So which will it be?' asked Burgess, 'the head or the heart?'

'I have nightmares,' said Bell in a quieter voice, 'of "the masses" trying a rising or a civil war and getting beaten – being wasted on impossible attacks by civilian enthusiasts, or crowds being machine-gunned by aeroplanes in the streets...'

'Good god,' I said.

'No doubt it's better for one's soul to fight than surrender, but otherwise...' said Bell, 'one feels that a battlefield's a nicer place to die than a torture chamber, but probably there's not really so much difference, and at least fewer people suffer from the terror than would in a war.'

'What an extraordinary thesis,' said Burgess.

'Oh, I don't know,' said Bell. 'Personally I'd be for war every time, however hopeless. But that's only a personal feeling.'

'So it's the heart then?' I asked.

'Yes,' said Bell, 'I suppose it would be if it came to it. Things have changed in Cambridge, you know,' said Bell. 'In the Cambridge that I first knew, the central subject of ordinary intelligent conversation was poetry.'

'And quite right too,' I said.

'Yes,' said Bell, 'as far as I can remember we hardly ever talked or thought about politics. For one thing, we almost all of us had implicit confidence in Maynard Keynes's rosy prophecies of continually increasing capitalist prosperity.'

'Well, that hasn't exactly gone to plan, has it?' said Burgess.

'No, not yet at any rate,' said Bell, 'but back then only the secondary problems, such as birth control, seemed to need the intervention of the intellectuals.'

'Well, that is hardly an intervention required from an Apostle,' said Burgess, 'at least in practical terms.'

The party had grown in size as more people arrived. Some were talking about the rumour concerning Rothschild. Blunt and Straight still had not returned. There remained only gin and tonic, perhaps being one of Blunt's whims when hosting. However, there was what appeared to be a limitless supply of it, so we just continued drinking. Here was a room full of the most intelligent men in the country, or so we were ourselves convinced, drinking until the light changed over Cambridge and engaged with the future of the world. It felt, even following my epiphany at King's that being accepted by these Apostles was the greatest achievement of my life. But that is what youth is for, the conviction that one is at the centre of the universe.

'And how would you describe us now?' I asked Bell.

Bell sat up in his chair and said, 'We have arrived at a situation in which almost the only subject of discussion is contemporary politics, and in which a very large majority of the more intelligent undergraduates are communists, or almost communists.'

'Really?' asked Burgess. 'I didn't know there were so many.'

'Of course you do,' I said, 'and what about literature?' I asked Bell, knowing this to be his particular chosen topic of discussion.

'As far as an interest in literature continues,' said Bell, 'it has very largely changed its character, and become an ally of communism under the influence of Mr Auden's Oxford group.'

'Ah, yes,' said Burgess, 'there's always Auden.'

'Indeed, it might, with some plausibility,' Bell continued, 'be argued that communism in England is at present very largely a literary phenomenon, indeed an attempt of our second "post-war generation" to escape from *The Waste Land.*'

'You mean Eliot's *Waste Land*?' I asked.

'Of course,' said Bell.

'I will show you fear in a handful of dust,' said Burgess, theatrically.

'I didn't expect you to quote Eliot,' I said.

'I often do things people do not expect,' said Burgess.

'Even so, and accepting that a handful of dust could be our own bodies on a deserted battlefield one day soon,' said Bell, 'it would be a mistake to take it too seriously, or to neglect the very large element of rather neurotic personal salvationism in our brand of communism.'

'That seems to contradict your idea of passionate action,' I said.

'The world is full of contradictions,' said Bell. 'Our generation seems to be repeating the experience of Rupert Brooke's, the appearance of a need for "the moral equivalent of war" among a large number of the members of the leisured and educated classes. And communism provides the activity, the sense of common effort, and something of the hysteria of war.'

'And presumably you would include us in the leisured and educated classes?' asked Burgess.

'Well,' said Bell with a smile, 'in your case certainly leisured, but yes.'

'How rude,' said Burgess. 'But what is the key question in your great analysis then?'

'The burning questions for us are questions of tactics and method, and of our own place in a socialist state and a socialist revolution,' said Bell. 'It would be difficult to find anyone of any intellectual pretensions who would not accept the general Marxist analysis of the present crises.'

'Well, I do have some hesitation...' I started to say.

'All right then,' said Bell, 'there is a *general* feeling, which perhaps has something to do with the prevalent hysterical enthusiasm, that we are personally and individually involved in the crisis, and that our business is rather to find the least evil course of action that will solve our immediate problems than to argue about rival utopias.'

And so the argument continued. Bell was compelling and although he detested war it did not make him afraid. His destiny, like so many of my friends, was to meet a head-on collision with violence.

*

Nine – Castles in Sand

I opened my eyes.

I could hear college life outside my rooms. There was the sound of undergraduates running around the Great Court, avoiding the grass, their shoes echoing on the ancient stones. I had missed breakfast but could smell coffee beyond my bedroom door, which meant that Burgess also had. I pulled the curtains open at the window nearest my pillows and a bright sunlight came into the room. I would not be disturbed by bedders at this time of year as the early task of lighting fires was no longer needed. Cambridge was in summer.

There is no more beautiful place in the world.

I got out of bed and put on a dressing gown, which I had unusually flung on the floor. I was fastidious about order and for a moment could not think why I had done such an untidy thing. Then I remembered.

'Are you going to get some coffee?' said Turing from within the bedclothes.

'Yes,' I said, slightly startled.

'Would you be a dear and get one for me too?' he asked.

'Of course,' I said, 'and then we've got to think how to get you out of Trinity without the porters noticing.'

*

'It's all about confidence,' I said to Michael.

'That's just what the teachers say,' he said, 'but exams still scare me a little.'

'Well,' I said, 'I don't know how many exams I've done, and they've always been all right in the end.'

'Yes,' he said, 'but that's you; this is me and I haven't done as many as you.'

'Inevitably,' I said, 'but the point is the same, whether you've done one or one hundred.'

'Christian was always good at exams,' said Michael.

'Yes, I know,' I said. 'I knew someone like that once: nothing seemed to scare him in terms of exams.'

'Who was that?' asked Michael.

'Oh that doesn't matter now,' I said. 'Let's just say it was someone important.'

'Notable or close to you?' asked Michael.

'Both,' I said. 'Now which have you got first?'

'Advanced mathematics,' said Michael.

'Well, that's your strongest subject, isn't it?' I said.

'Yes, when I'm not under pressure,' he said. 'I just find it difficult going into a room and seeing that closed paper on the desk.'

'I used to be just the same,' I said, 'but there are ways round it.'

'What are they?' he asked.

'Rather than thinking of the next three hours and the paper, think about the next three years and where that paper will take you,' I said.

'I don't know where it will take me,' said Michael.

'Precisely, I said. 'The world is full of possibilities and the only thing you have to do to realise them is solve some equations.'

'And it's as simple as that?' asked Michael.

'As simple as that,' I said.

*

It was the morning of my first mathematical Tripos and although I felt prepared it remained a daunting prospect. I had got Turing out of the college, having taken coffee, and Burgess was still unroused. I thought it might help if I went to see Blunt, as the examination was not until mid-morning. He was usually in his rooms in Nevile Court until lunch.

I knocked on the door and Blunt answered. 'Ah, dear boy,' he said, 'do come in, but don't you have an examination this morning?'

'Not until later,' I said. 'I just thought that I should come and see you for some moral support.'

'Well,' said Blunt, 'I'm not sure I can offer anything as elevated as *moral* support, but I am happy to be an encouraging ear.'

'Thank you,' I said. 'To be honest, I am comfortable about the examination really. I was given some good advice last night.'

'I'm sure you were,' said Blunt conspiratorially.

I blushed slightly.

'Ah, so it was advice from the best?' asked Blunt.

'Yes. Well, I think so anyway,' I said.

'Always good to reach for the top,' he said. 'So if you don't want to discuss mathematics what is on your mind?'

'Oh, I was wondering if you'd heard anything further about Rothschild since the night he ran over that cyclist?'

'Oh dear,' said Blunt, 'a very sorry affair, but you know what these rich boys are like with their sports cars.'

'Not really,' I said. 'Is he going to be prosecuted?'

'Apparently not,' said Blunt, 'there's not enough evidence, the lucky bugger.'

'Is that the only reason?' I asked.

'Of course not,' said Blunt. 'He's a very well connected young man.'

'And the cyclist wasn't?' I asked.

'Not any more,' laughed Blunt, appearing not to feel that this was in some way inappropriate.

'Why do you ask, anyway?' he said.

'Well, he's friends with Straight, isn't he?' I asked.

'I'm not sure I would use that word,' said Blunt. 'They are both far too competitive for friendship. It's more like affectionate rivalry. But I ask again, why?'

'Oh, sorry,' I said. 'Straight has invited me down to Dartington after our exams and I just wondered if Rothschild was going.'

'Yes, he's invited myself and Burgess too, although he didn't mention he said anything to you,' said Blunt.

'And Rothschild?' I asked.

'No, not Rothschild. I think he is concerned that Rothschild may antagonise his mother.'

'Oh really?' I said.

'Yes,' he said. 'Dorothy Elmhirst is one of the wealthiest women in the world, you know, and I don't think Straight wishes to stir things up too much.'

'But he's invited you and Burgess,' I said.

'Well, quite,' said Blunt, 'we'll be the perfect guests. Burgess can be charming when he wants to be, you know.'

'Oh, I know that,' I said.

'And I am apparently to discuss art,' said Blunt with a flourish.

'So why do you think Straight wishes me to visit?' I asked.

'I expect he wants you to add to the air of normality,' said Blunt.

'Well, there's a compliment hidden in their somewhere,' I said.

'Indeed there is,' said Blunt. 'You see, I think Straight's mother is concerned that he has fallen in with a bunch of fanatics.'

'I'm not a fanatic,' I said indignantly.

'Precisely,' said Blunt.

'And neither are you and Burgess, surely?' I asked.

'Of course not, dear boy, and that is why we will be perfect guests at the great woman's house. Now, off you go to your examination.'

*

Michael came to see me and brought lunch. It was only tomato soup with a bread roll but I did not want it.

'One of your eyes is looking a bit odd,' he said. 'I'm going to get the nurse to come and take a look.'

'There's no need to do that,' I said.

'Just let me ask her,' he said, 'to be on the safe side.'

'The safe side of what?' I asked.

'Of life,' he said.

'There's no need for melodrama,' I said. 'I just feel a little tired.'

'I'm just following procedure,' said Michael, 'I have to.'

'I didn't realise there was a procedure for double vision,' I said.

'You have double vision?' said Michael.

'Yes, but I'm sure I've been writing too much, that's all,' I said.

'Let me feel your arms,' he said, and then, after he had done so, said, 'One of them is quite cold; can you lift it?'

I tried but it was too difficult. 'You see,' I said, 'I'm just tired.'

'I'm going to get the nurse,' said Michael, and he quickly left the room.

I, of course, knew that this was not tiredness. My left arm was not moving and I felt very strange. Also, the double vision was worsening. When the nurse arrived she asked me to move my feet and fingers. I did so, except in my left hand. She tested my reflexes and found they were absent. She asked Michael to stay with me.

'How are you feeling?' he asked after a while had passed.

'I'm fine,' I said, 'just feeling a bit strange.'

'Would you like a cup of tea?' asked Michael.

'I thought she asked you to stay with me,' I said.

'It'll only take a couple of minutes,' he said. 'Would you like one?'

'Yes,' I said, 'I think I would, but before you go could you pass me my notebooks?'

'You're supposed to be resting,' he said.

'And you're supposed to stay with me,' I replied.

*

Blunt had arranged to meet Burgess and myself outside Trinity at eight o'clock in the morning. Straight would be driving us to Devon. There were four of us, so we were travelling in his Bugatti saloon rather than one of his sports cars; but when he pulled up outside the college in it, people still stopped to look. It was a beautiful machine, very large and black. This was the kind of car both my father and mother were afraid of and I could see why.

'Jump in,' said Straight.

'There's plenty of room for your bags to be with you on the back seat,' said Blunt, looking very pleased with himself in the front passenger's seat.

'Righto,' said Burgess. 'I must say, I've been looking forward to this for an age.'

We got into the car and drove away from Trinity. It was very comfortable but still quite noisy in the back, which wasn't helped by Blunt's insistence on keeping the windows open.

'How did your Tripos go, Cyprian?' he said.

'It was fine,' I said. 'I just imagined where it was going to take me.'

'Oh?' said Burgess, 'and where is that precisely?'

'Probably nowhere else,' I said, happily, as I had decided even then that Trinity would be the aim of my ambition as well as the means to reach it.

'How unadventurous,' said Burgess.

'We all have different dreams,' I said.

'Indeed,' said Blunt, 'and one of mine is happening right now,' he said, turning to smile at Straight.

Straight drove very quickly and although the journey took many hours it was extremely pleasurable. I had not often been in a motorcar as my own family did not own one and only a few other people I knew at college, apart from Straight and Rothschild, could afford one. Indeed, only those two owned cars as expensive as this one. It was interesting to consider, after all the discussions we had proposed at Apostles' meetings about the need for equality and the proper dispersion of wealth, that so many of my friends were comfortable with their own comparative economic security.

Blunt's views on this were at least consistent, in that he never fully suggested the removal of an elite in society. Burgess was far more radical in that respect. From the first day I had met him and he had dismissed Cambridge from the bow of a punt, he had regularly talked about how things needed to change. I did not grasp what Straight's views on this were. He seemed both in love with his family's money and self-conscious about it.

As we drove through the countryside I could see that Cambridge was in some way an island. There was more poverty than we were ever led to understand in our own country. Blunt and a few others had been to Russia for a while, to experience for themselves the economic miracle of communism. They did not refer to what they had seen on that visit very often; indeed, the few comments I had heard made me wonder what they had been able to draw from it as inspiration. I knew that Blunt had been more interested in going to the Hermitage and other galleries than in viewing the Russian worker, but for such an important trip it was strange that they did not all return with tales of how the great Soviet State operated.

Beyond the windows of the Bugatti lay some pretty villages and towns, but they were interspersed with shabbily dressed people and there were very few other cars. England looked like a country unsure of its direction. It had suffered a recent depression and although we knew that most of the residual problems lay in the north, even driving through the south of England showed that there were still problems.

'Don't you think Cambridge is rather unique?' I said to Burgess.

'In some ways, yes,' he said, 'but why do you ask now?'

'It seems so wealthy; well, our experience of it does at any rate,' I said.

'I suppose so,' said Burgess, 'but why should that worry us?'

'I think it is a worry,' I said. 'Unless things take a turn for the better, I can see Mosley exploiting this situation.'

'That's precisely what he is doing,' said Blunt, almost shouting from the front. 'Why do you think I wanted to make sure you had seen that march in London?'

'I thought that was just a coincidence,' I said.

'Oh, dear boy,' said Blunt, 'it most certainly was not. I arranged to arrive in Liverpool Street at that time.'

'Why?' I said.

'To see what your reaction would be, of course,' he said.

As we moved into the West Country the scenery altered and crossing into Devon, the hills became deeper. We had to make an unscheduled stop for petrol in Exeter and although I would have liked to have seen the cathedral, Straight was determined to get to Dartington for drinks. We drove into the South Hams and I could see the vast ridge of Dartmoor rise up in the distance. We were now on much smaller roads, which Straight navigated with great skill.

Just before reaching Totnes, Straight turned into the Dartington Hall estate and welcomed us to his new family home. We drove up a long road, which was surrounded by fields, which Straight explained were the sites of his stepfather Leonard's agricultural experiments. Then, turning a corner, I saw Dartington Hall itself, almost as though we had been thrown back in history to medieval England. We pulled up outside the gatehouse to the Great Courtyard and, thankful of finally being out of the car, walked under the archway into the vast rectangular space reminiscent of some of the Cambridge courts. The principal difference was there were many unkempt parts of the building. However, this did not lessen the overall effect of seeing Dartington for the first time.

It was early evening and a pale yellow light was cast across the lawns. At the entrance a huge tree stood as though a gatekeeper to a magical kingdom. At the other end of the courtyard the clock tower and Great Hall appeared both homely and grand. From out of the main doors of the tower came Dorothy and Leonard Elmhirst. Leonard sauntered towards us, while Dorothy, focused only on Straight, seemed to almost float across the grass. She was a supremely elegant woman and warmly welcomed us after flinging her arms around her son.

'Welcome to Dartington, boys,' she said. 'You must be in need of refreshment after such a long journey? Did Michael drive safely?'

'Immaculately,' said Blunt, 'we couldn't have been in safer hands.'

'Excellent,' said Elmhirst, joining us beside his wife. 'Well, you'll all be wanting a drink.'

'Rather,' said Burgess.

'Very well,' said Elmhirst, 'just take your things into the hall and we'll meet on the rear terrace for some refreshment.'

'How delightful,' said Blunt.

We were all given separate rooms in one of the wings of the courtyard. Mine was simple but very comfortable. A bed was in one corner and there were two armchairs placed under a window in the eaves. A wireless had been placed on a small side table and I switched it on, astonished to find a good reception despite the surrounding South Devon hills. There was some jazz playing and I turned the volume up a little whilst I unpacked. I was travelling light, as requested by Straight who, unlike Blunt, did not think there was a great deal of room in the back of the Bugatti. Blunt had brought enough for a week's stay.

A small bathroom had been made through a natural archway in the building and inside there was a well-positioned shelf with a tall glass. I placed my toothbrush in the glass and returned to the bedroom to change. Elmhirst had said that we should not dress for dinner, so I chose a pair of green corduroy trousers, a dark yellow waistcoat I had found in an outfitter in

Cambridge and a dark brown tweed jacket in a light summer material. I finished with a yellow handkerchief in the top pocket and went down and across the courtyard to the door in the clock tower.

Passing under a medieval boss of a white hart on the ceiling, I pushed open the door into the screen corridor, which I assumed had originally been needed to keep the kitchen separate from the Great Hall. I walked along the corridor and out onto the rear lawn. The gardens stretched out and up a steep hill, which appeared to include terraces.

'Dorothy has been working hard on the gardens,' said Elmhirst, who was pouring drinks at a small table covered in a white cloth. 'What do you think?'

'I think they're beautiful,' I said, 'and what of those terraces?'

'Oh, they are original to the estate,' said Elmhirst.

Blunt and Burgess joined us.

'Are all your rooms to your liking?' asked Elmhirst.

'Very acceptable,' said Blunt.

'Yes,' said Burgess.

'I wouldn't have thought one could receive the wireless down here,' I said.

'Yes, it's quite a relief,' said Dorothy, appearing from the doorway. She was wearing a beautiful green dress and a stunning set of pearls that glinted in the evening sunlight.

'Good evening, darling,' said Elmhirst, 'have you had sight of your rakish son? I'm just pouring drinks.'

'No, not yet,' said Dorothy, 'but he'll be here soon enough, or at least when he hears the champagne being opened.'

'I'm not as bad as all that,' said Straight, coming out onto the lawns.

'No, I can vouch for that,' said Blunt. 'Michael is the epitome of elegance at the university.'

'I am glad to hear it,' said Dorothy. 'Now, how about a toast.'

'To the security of friendship,' said Burgess, raising his glass.

'To the security of friendship,' we all repeated, although I noticed Blunt did not, only raising his glass.

Following drinks, we went in for dinner in the Elmhirst's private rooms. We had all been on strict instructions from Straight to allay his mother's concerns that he had fallen in with a set of committed communists. Burgess was impeccable, even after a considerable amount of wine; when his constant chatter did turn towards politics he professed support for fascism without sounding too anti-liberal.

Blunt, on the other hand, hid in the shade of his knowledge of art.

'Of course,' he said to Dorothy at dinner, 'Raphael, in his painting *The School of Athens*, reflected the classical influence upon Renaissance art.'

'Really?' said Dorothy. 'I think I have seen that painting.'

'Oh, yes,' said Blunt, 'I am sure you have. You see, he also paid tribute to the men who inspired him by using the faces of da Vinci, Bramante and Michelangelo as philosophers participating in the debate between Plato and Aristotle.'

'Fascinating,' said Dorothy.

'Indeed,' said Blunt, 'and have you been to the Brancacci Chapel in Santa Maria del Carmine in Florence?'

'Why yes I have,' Dorothy said. 'You mean to see the Masaccio?'

'Naturally,' said Blunt, clearly impressed by Dorothy's understanding. 'You see, it was Masaccio who really began the style.'

'Oh,' said Dorothy, 'in what way?'

Blunt continued, 'In his all-to-brief twenty-seven years on earth, he developed a style that used perspective in a way that created an illusion of three-dimensions, a significant change from the flat style of painting that typifies medieval art.'

'I see,' said Dorothy, 'and tell me, Anthony, what do you know of our art collections here at Dartington?'

'I am sure I could learn more from you,' said Blunt, verging on the sycophantic.

'Well, perhaps we could discuss it tomorrow in the garden,' she said, 'so we do not have to bore all the others,' and she cast a glance at Straight.

'I'm sure that would be perfectly delightful,' said Blunt.

We finished dinner and, having had such a long journey decided the day should come to an end. I watched while all the others went back to their respective rooms and then took a walk round the courtyard.

Although it was dark, the temperature was still warm and I sat on the steps beside the archway for a while. Looking across at the Great Hall, its candles still burning behind the tall windows, and out to the left at the hills of Totnes, I had a feeling that one day this place might become home. Even though I would spend a lifetime in love with Cambridge, as I looked up at the black Devon sky and the countless stars I felt complete as I had never felt in any other place. It is the one regret of my life that I never returned.

There was something about Dartington that welcomed me as a close family might, upon discovering that *you* are the place's long-lost brother. I had a sense of totality there, of belonging and of peace.

In the morning, after breakfast, Burgess agreed to play cricket with Dorothy and Leonard's son Bill. I went for a walk with Blunt and Dorothy in the gardens she said she had been creating with her friend, Beatrix Farrand.

'I've just acquired one or two new works, Anthony, which I'm sure you have seen in the private part of the house,' said Dorothy.

'Which are they?' asked Blunt.

'The first is by a young English painter who is the real thing, his name is Ben Nicholson,' said Dorothy, 'he has entitled his work, *Charbon*.'

'Ah yes,' said Blunt, 'the picture containing a pack of cards?'

'That's the one,' said Dorothy. 'What do you think of it?'

'I think it's perfectly wonderful, Dorothy,' said Blunt, 'and if you don't mind my saying, how clever of you to purchase it.'

'Oh my,' said Dorothy.

'It's very confident yet pared back in style, is it not?' said Blunt. 'It has the air of a climax in an artist's period.'

'That is precisely what I believe to be the case,' said Dorothy, 'and did you see the Christopher Wood?'

'Yes,' said Blunt, 'a terrible loss in one so young.'

'Indeed,' said Dorothy. 'Leonard and I hope to rescue Mr Wood's name for posterity by collecting enough of his pictures to give a real conception of the breadth of his work.'

'What a marvellous plan,' said Blunt. 'I am sure we will all be indebted to you; the *Pony and Trap* is a very fine picture. The distorted perspective and exaggerated proportions are infused with uninhibited feeling and expression.'

'How wonderfully perceptive,' said Dorothy, 'that is precisely why we like his work. It so suits Dartington, don't you think?'

'Yes,' said Blunt, 'Wood's pictures are at home here.'

Following lunch, we departed in Straight's Bugatti. He had said little on the visit but seemed satisfied that Burgess and Blunt had convinced his mother that there was nothing to be alarmed about. I could see that Dorothy thought Burgess, with his cherubic appearance, to have sensible, middle-struck views and that Blunt's knowledge of art led her to an impression of him as a Christian aesthete. Each had performed exactly as Straight had intended. I had no idea how she regarded me.

*

'You were a long time,' I said to Michael.

'I had to make some calls,' he said. 'You have friends at the college who wanted me to let them know what is happening.'

'Oh,' I said, 'and what is happening?'

'I think you know,' he said.

'Yes,' I said, 'I suppose I should.'

'The doctor is coming in a minute,' said Michael, 'he will tell us more.'

'I've just seen the nurse,' I said.

'It was her who called him,' said Michael. 'Now, are you relatively comfortable?'

'Relative to what?' I asked.

'To being uncomfortable,' he said, trying not to sound frustrated.

'In that case, yes, thank you,' I replied.

The doctor came into my room and examined my eyes and performed all the same tests that the nurse had previously. He said that I should prepare for a second stroke, and then added that at least my family was with me. I thought this cruel, as I have not seen my family for years.

'I'm not sure you should be writing any more,' said Michael.

'Don't be silly,' I said, 'I've never written with my left hand in all my life.'

'I didn't really mean that,' he said.

'I am nearly finished.'

'I know.'

*

The journey back was uneventful and when we returned to Cambridge I suddenly wished to see Turing.

'Straight, could you leave me outside King's, old man?' I asked.

'Yes, of course,' he said.

'Why do you want to go to King's?' asked Blunt. 'Ah, don't tell me… to discuss mathematics,' which he said with a glint in his eye.

'Never you mind,' I said. 'I'll see you all later.'

The car drove away down King's Parade and I talked my way past the King's porters by saying I needed to speak to a friend from my supervisory group about something I was worried I'd put in my Tripos. I walked into the court and again was left almost breathless by the sight of the chapel. In the late evening it had a new personality, one of knowledge and omniscience.

The choir was practising and I was drawn to look inside. They were singing the Purcell piece being rehearsed by the organ scholar previously, *Thou knowest Lord the secrets of our hearts*. It had been transformed by the addition of voices. I stood transfixed in the central aisle of the great church, until a verger gently tapped me on the shoulder and asked if I was feeling quite right. I did not realise I had been crying.

I left quickly, embarrassed and confused. Why should this one place speak to me so directly? All of the rest of my time at Cambridge was comfortable with the decline and fall that constituted our discussions at the Apostles. I had become immune to the deceit, the lies, the entertainment of my friends and forgotten that only one man I had met seemed to me to be in some way above all of that.

I knocked on the door to Turing's rooms. He called me to come inside. I ran to him and felt his thin body against mine, a runner's body. He smelled of soap, clean and unblemished. His desk was covered in paperwork and the room was in disarray.

'What are you doing in here?' I asked him.

'Oh,' he said, 'just working.'

'On what?' I asked, a little annoyed at the apparent lack of warmth in Turing's welcome.

'I've been reading some of G. H. Hardy's papers,' said Turing. 'He seems to be making an almost moral point in some of his narrative.'

'Interesting,' I said.

'Implicitly,' said Turing. 'It's like reading a mathematical interpretation of Wilde, in that utility is irrelevant to value.'

'I think I could accept that too,' I said.

'Really?' said Turing, 'but it plainly isn't true. I mean, utility is a motivation for real mathematical thought, wouldn't you say?'

'I'm not entirely sure I would say so, no,' I said. 'Mathematics can be pure and without purpose beyond the discovery of truth.'

'Ah,' said Turing, 'but what truth then provides a purpose?'

'I'm not sure I follow,' I said.

'No,' said Turing, 'I can see that you don't and that is why we can no longer see one another.'

I took a step backwards in surprise. 'What?' I said quietly. 'Just because I do not agree with you on something?'

'But this is not something,' said Turing, 'this is everything. Don't you see that within the gamut of mathematics lies its strange special harmony with the physical world?'

'Not necessarily,' I said.

'And hence,' continued Turing, 'follows the prophetic role of mathematics as the precursor to useful science.'

'I think I can see that,' I said, suddenly not thinking clearly.

'For example,' said Turing, 'differential geometry had to come before relativity.'

'Yes,' I said.

'Well, that is what I am working on,' said Turing. 'I want to do something useful, not lie about in Cambridge making patterns.'

'Is that how you see my work?' I said.

'That is how I see you, Cyprian, not only your work,' said Turing with a new harshness in his voice. 'You will be happy in Cambridge for the rest of your life.'

'So would you be,' I said.

'No,' he said, 'I need more. You can and will lie, I cannot.'

'I most certainly will not,' I said.

'Oh you will,' said Turing, 'you already are, being seen with that set of communists. It'll only be a matter of time before you are hiding in the shade of marriage.'

'I don't see how you can know that,' I said, now genuinely angry.

'It's obvious,' he said. 'They all lie and you will lie with them. Of course there will be the call of a higher purpose, saving the country or the pursuit of mathematics, but all you will ever do is save yourselves.'

'I don't accept that,' I said.

'Of course you don't,' said Turing, 'you lost your *liberum arbitrium* on the day you met Burgess.'

I left him without looking back. It was the last time I held a conversation with him. I saw Turing a few times over the years in Cambridge, but he never spoke to me again. I believe he knew that for his mathematics to have purpose he needed war, and war means loss.

I never knew a man like him. His life was a series of chess games. His most famous would be that against the German encryptor and logician, Gisbert Hasenjaeger, on either side of an Enigma machine. He won that game but ultimately lost against those with no interest in men playing games with one another.

I did not know where to turn, so I went to the only place I thought I would not be alone.

I had planned to warn them. I wish I could have shown them my painting and told them that it would still be too warm hiding in the shade, unsafe, they would be found. They would not hear the horses until it was too late.

Burgess was sitting on Blunt's settee in his white-panelled rooms. They were drinking pink gins, 'to recover from the motorcar journey', according to Blunt. The evening was still light and warm and Blunt had opened all the windows in his rooms.

'Back so soon?' asked Burgess.

'We've parted company,' I said.

'Oh, my dear boy,' said Blunt. 'Well, these things will happen.'

'You don't care about anyone as I do,' I said to him.

'No,' said Blunt, 'I'm quite sure I do not: that is why I am happy and you are not.'

'And are you happy?' I asked him.

'Of course I am,' said Blunt. 'I have friends, the finest rooms in Trinity, an impressive brain and a belief that the world will eventually deal with its present woes.'

'I wish I had your confidence,' I said.

'Then join us,' said Burgess.

I closed my eyes.

*

To anyone who may read this diary, my name is Michael Gabriel. I am Dr Cyprian's grandson. I visited him almost every day in the last few months of his life, although he was unable to recognise me.

His disease separates people from the truth. I now see, having read this diary, that he thought I was his nurse.

My grandfather had no recollection of his family, and in particular of the car crash that killed my father, and mother – his daughter.

But these are not ramblings.

Grandfather appears to have recorded all our conversations in this diary without realising that he was talking to me. I remember all that he said. I did not know that he had the life he claims to have had in Cambridge when he was younger.

I do not know if everything in this book is true, as my grandfather always had a difficult relationship with the truth.

If this diary is being used as a confession, please understand that my grandfather's mind was damaged. His version of events is likely to be unreliable.

He says he became a liar.

We all have made mistakes.

Give him peace.

He taught me how to fly.

*